'I just loved Oliva's voice and story, the whole world the novella manages to evoke. And then *The Velvet Gentleman*, in voice and style, was a complete volte-face but, as I recovered from being jolted out of Oliva's world so shockingly and unexpectedly, an equally intriguing and compelling story.' Lucy Caldwell, author of *All the Beggars Riding*

'I am usually suspicious of books that mingle fiction and non-fiction, but *The Velvet Gentleman* is an exception – the idea so ingenious and Skinner's style so translucently clear.' Michael Holroyd, author of *Lytton Strachey: A Critical Biography*, *Augustus John: A Biography* and *Bernard Shaw*

'Elegant, intricate and other-worldly . . . A richly provocative story of our faiths and choices.' Kerry Fowler, *Sainsbury's Magazine*

'Two extraordinary stories that resonate together, and stay in the mind long afterwards. Crescendo and limbo.' David Burnand, author of *Stolen Hours*

'I was so impressed with how the voices of Oliva and Satie achieved the thematic unity of the book . . . The stark simplicity of Oliva's sentences capture the stark simplicity of her surroundings, and her surroundings are what make her. Satie's mercurial intelligence and witty aphorisms contrast sharply with the bare stage-set of purgatory, and he bursts with life.' David Savill, author of *They Are Trying to Break Your Heart*

'The British writer Richard Skinner has found new inputs in Erik Satie's creation in his dual/double narrative *The Mirror*. From the mundane to the imaginary, without adding anything, you just follow the stream of impressions, the silences that occur and the freedom in the small and simple . . . Through the feat of dissolving the real contours, Skinner manages to get the dream architecture to emerge, not unlike Satie's cartoon fantasies of Gothic cathedrals and hidden schemes.' Magnus Haglund, *GöteborgsPosten*

The Mirror

RICHARD SKINNER

FABER & FABER

First published in 2014
by Faber & Faber Limited
Bloomsbury House, 74–77 Great Russell Street
London WC1B 3DA

This paperback edition published in 2015

Typeset by Faber & Faber Ltd
Printed in England by CPI Group (UK) Ltd, Croydon, CR0 4YY

The right of Richard Skinner to be identified as author of this work has
been asserted in accordance with Section 77 of the Copyright, Designs and
Patents Act 1988

A CIP record for this book
is available from the British Library

ISBN 978–0–571–30508–7

2 4 6 8 10 9 7 5 3 1

With thanks to Lee Brackstone

With thanks to Lee Brackstone

THE MIRROR

Every mirror is false because it repeats
something it has not witnessed.

Chazal

The Convent of Sant'Alvise,
Venice, 26th March 1511

The earth shook today. The bell woke me, and I lay for a moment not knowing if I was awake or still asleep. I imagined it was ringing for matins, and if it was, I could not understand why it was ringing so unevenly. I opened my eyes and saw that dawn was breaking through the window high up in the wall. I knew then that I had already missed matins. The Abbess was sure to punish me for missing it again. The bell continued to jangle, without rhyme or reason, and I realised that it wasn't just our bell ringing, but everywhere outside our walls, throughout the whole city. The earth trembled, great rumbles from somewhere deep below me. The candle on the altar spluttered, and I lay on my bed of straw, listening to the madness that was in the sound and wondering what was making the earth shake so. For a moment, time seemed not only to stop, but also to go backwards and I imagined that my feet were growing smaller and the uncles I never knew were coming back to life. The dormitory seemed to shrink and yet everything seemed very near. This strange impression brought me to my senses and it was only when I was fully awake that I realised I was in great danger. I rose from my bed, put on my clogs and quickly left the dormitory. In the cloisters, the chickens were running around everywhere, frantically beating their wings. The bells were still clanging. The convent was deserted and silent. The tree in our courtyard stood bare. It was usually adorned with sugared almonds, but all these had been shaken off and now lay on the ground like hailstones. The morning air was cold. I ran down the cloisters and when I got to the front door of the convent, it was wide open with dust billowing in. It looked like some great monster was blowing smoke into our convent. I ran towards the block of milky light in the doorway and jumped through it, coughing when I reached the other side. Through the clouds of dust wafting around, I could see the outlines of people huddled in small groups near me. Then someone approached me and I saw it was the Abbess. 'Thank the Lord,' she said and embraced me. 'I thought you were gone.' Her habit smelled of dust and sweat, but I felt secure in her arms. The bells were beginning to calm down, but I could still hear the clanging bell of the campanile in St Mark's. We were too far away to see it, but we could always hear it.

'Where is Signora Lucia?' I asked. The Abbess took me to where she was being held up by Signora Sordamor and Signora Lucretia. She was still dressed in her bed clothes. I could see in her sightless eyes that she was frightened, too frightened to speak. I could not imagine what must have been going through her mind. I held her hand and kissed it, but she didn't notice me. We stood like that for what seemed an eternity as we watched the dust settle and the world come back into view. The sky outside was so big, so blue, the rising sun a glowing ball of yellow, like a golden ghost. It was the first time I had stood outside the convent since I had arrived four years before and I marvelled at how pure were the sun and sky. I could hear many voices from across the canal. On the skyline, some bell towers were bent out of shape and leaning over at a horrible angle. I looked up to our small bell tower, but it was not affected. Then I noticed that some of the taller buildings just across the canal had lost their chimney pots and were afflicted with cracks and the walls had burst open. Dust rose from the long line of buildings, making them greyer and pinker in the morning sun. In the dust, I could see the blood-red marble of the palazzo of Aldramin. Venetia is neither land, nor water, nor sky. The Abbess has told me that our city is a myth but, to me, it will always be a celestial heart and it saddened me to think that it may be destroyed. Was the city destroyed? Some far-off bells were still occasionally clanging in the red air. I stood, not knowing what to do, waiting for the earth to shake again. I listened to the people on the other side of the canal calling to each other. Mothers to their children, husbands to their wives. Some long minutes passed and it slowly dawned on us that the earth had ceased trembling. We made our way back to the entrance of our convent, and passed through the front door. Signora Sordamor and I helped Signora Lucia. The chickens were clucking with annoyance and strutting about. The Abbess told Signora Pellegrina to see to them. The Signora was not pleased to be told to do such a lowly task, but she began shooing them back down the cloisters to their coop in the gardens.

'Is everyone here?' the Abbess said to us. We accounted for all eleven of the Signoras, but it soon became clear that Ottavia was missing. The Abbess ordered the front door to be closed and locked. She assigned a sister to each of the spaces in our convent to check for damage and told Signora Arcanzola to prepare some bread and hot soup. I watched the sisters walk along the cloisters and disappear through doorways.

'Oliva.'

I looked at the Abbess. Her countenance was one of calm and courage.

'Take Lucia back to the infirmary and put her to bed. Then go and find Ottavia,' she said. 'Check our cells first.'

I nodded and began walking with Signora Lucia along the cloisters. 'Oh, good heavens!' she said. 'You are walking too fast. I shall tumble and fall,' and so I slowed down. We passed into the kitchen and out into the gardens. Signora Pellegrina was still trying to get the chickens into their coop. She kept ducking and waving her arms, but this only made the chickens even more afraid. I guided Signora Lucia into the infirmary, to her bed in the corner. The air in the room was stale, the light dim as the candles had gone out, but I couldn't see any damage to the walls. She sat on the bed and I lifted her legs up. She was like a child ready to be put to bed. I pulled the sheets up to her chin and kissed her forehead, telling her that I would come back soon. Retracing my steps, I walked towards the first of the cells that ran along the main cloister. It belonged to Signora Gratiosa. I opened the door and looked around. The straw bedding was empty, the fine rugs were still attached to the walls. Even her cross and chalice were standing upright. I was puzzled that there was not more damage. Pulling the door to, I went to the next cell, which was also empty. I checked every cell of the Signoras and then went to the dormitory where Ottavia and I slept. The long dormitory is poorly lit at its entrance, it is only at the altar that there is any light. As I passed through the darkness something caught my eye. In the gloom, I saw two pinpricks of light, looking at me. It was difficult to know if they were near or far from me. It took me a few moments to make out a pair of eyes and a face and then a body – it was Ottavia and the look on her face was the purest look of fear I had ever seen. Then the figure disappeared into the shadows and I stood still, unsure that I had seen anything at all. Or perhaps what I had seen was the fear in my own eyes?

Some hours later, sunlight filled the courtyard as I made my way to the choir. The hours for lauds and prime had passed without our attendance because of the quake and the bell was ringing now for terce. I went through the door in the cloisters and climbed the steps to the choir. The Abbess was already there.

She handed me the psalters and watched as the sisters came in and took their places. When I had finished handing out the psalters, I crossed myself and knelt beside all the *suore*. We waited a few moments for the congregation below us to take their seats, then the priest said a prayer for the dead souls and we joined the congregation in chanting a mass. I did not need to look at my book as I knew the words by heart and, although I sang them for those who had been lost in the city that morning, I also sang with joy and thanks for the spared lives of Ottavia, Signora Lucia and the Abbess. I sneaked a glance at the Abbess – she was singing with her eyes closed. Ottavia was behind her with her head inclined. She always displayed a kind of agitation, but I could see the look on her face was still more than that. She must have been thinking of her family, if they were still alive. What damage had been done to the city and its inhabitants? We would only know when the priest came and brought news with him.

Just the day before, everything had been so different. It was the day of the Feast of the Annunciation and to celebrate the feast, the *suore* had brought some blue and white silk ribbons into the chapter and we hung them on the walls. The colours looked beautiful. Then we gathered in the courtyard and

9

the *suore* gave each other little gifts. We sang some hymns, practising our polyphony, the courtyard alive with the sound of sparrows. Their noise is incessant, but I must not be unkind for, like me, they are God's creatures, but they do chatter so. It was a beautiful morning and a happy way to start the New Year.

The day of the quake was also washday and so Ottavia and I were excused from prayer until the lighting of the lamps. On leaving the choir, we walked along the cloisters to the kitchen and I asked if her family were safe. 'I don't know,' she said, wringing her hands in agony. I tried to reassure her, but my words sounded hollow, even to me. I did not believe that Ottavia was really in agony, but she was always in the most melancholy humour. In the kitchen, I tried to distract her by giving her jobs to do, jobs that I hoped would occupy her mind. I told her to fetch water from the well while I lifted the vats into the fireplace. After filling the vats, I put wood under them and lit the fires. It takes a whole hour for the water to heat, so I told Ottavia to collect the dirty linen from the infirmary and from the cells of the Signoras. But all this activity and hard work could not stop Ottavia from talking about the quake. As we put in and stirred the cloths and sheets from the infirmary, she constantly splashed me with water and said, 'Were you frightened?' I explained that I had been asleep in the dormitory. 'Oh it was terrible,' she said, 'I did not know where to go or what to do.' As she spoke, she was reliving it all again in her mind. I did not mention her apparition – I did not think it wise, for Ottavia has a delicate mind and I did not want to throw her further into the pit of agony. I assured her again that I thought her family were safe and asked if any of them would be visiting this week.

'Yes, my brother will be coming on Friday.'

'Will he bring any food?'

She nodded and smiled. 'Some fishes. He said he would catch the fish himself, so let's see. My brother is so handsome – you would like him, I know you would.'

I took no notice of her remark. I never said a word to her about what was going on in my soul.

'Oh, Oliva, don't look so surprised! Don't you ever think about men?'

I continued to stir the sheets. With her temperament, fear made Ottavia shrink back, but any mention of love made her rush forward. 'Do you?' I said.

Ottavia laughed, showing her small, fine teeth. 'Yes, all the time. If the Abbess only knew what passed through my mind all day, she would have the Doge lock me up!'

Despite Ottavia's sinful words, I could not reproach her. She is no younger than me, but she is like a new, fresh doe trying to find its feet. Her soul is still so green and unused. Words and feelings come gushing out without her knowing what she is saying and I fear for her so. I looked at her face, a radiant expression of joy and hope looking back at me, and thought that a little bitterness in her heart would be better than all that sweetness.

'Come on, help me get these out,' I said. 'They have to be dry by evening.'

It rained all the next day, and I was told that it was a good sign because it would help put out any fires in the city. After compline, I crossed myself, kissed the hand of the Abbess and walked to the dormitory along the gloomy cloisters. The rain fell in huge drops onto the gravel of the courtyard. The lamps were barely bright enough to light the halls and passageways. There were only a few of the *suore* there that evening. Most stayed in their cells for the last office of the day, passing the time with their sisters, cousins and aunts. Sometimes, when they deem me fit enough, they invite me in and I sit in a corner and have a nibble at the bread and cheese offered to me, or a sip of their wine. I sit perfectly still and listen to them talk about their families and the husbands they never had. I never knew my mother, or my father, and I know I shall never have a husband. I do not know what it would be like to be tied to a man, to a single person above all others. Men are such strange beings, but I have never been familiar with a man, so I cannot know for sure. Neither have the sisters, but they would like to know. They do not seem to think it wrong to talk about it. They seem to miss it, but how can you miss something you never had? I cannot think about it. The world the *suore* talk about has no meaning for me. Like the sparrows, they chatter on about nothing in particular. I am curious to hear their tales, but the world they talk about is as far away from me as the sun. I have no one to talk about and, although I am among the *suore* day and night, I am very alone. The *suore* do not understand what it is like to be alone in the world.

As I passed through the deep shadows of the corridors that evening, it felt as though all below me was dark water, swirling soundlessly, waiting with certainty for the moment I would fall in and drop to its depths. Was there pure love in my heart? Could I, like Ottavia, let temptation into my mind? I entered the dark dormitory; Ottavia was nowhere to be seen. Two candles had been lit on the altar. I crossed

myself and dropped to my knees. With head bowed,
I exalted to the stars the sanctity of my vocation.
Will I make a good bride for Christ? Do I have the
strength to endure the sufferings that will surely in-
crease whenever I grow weary of the surrounding
darkness and I try to find peace and strength by contemplating eternal life? Is there love enough in my
heart for that struggle? I picture my soul as a patch
of bare ground, on which Christ is building a grand
pavilion. I am only happy if no one takes any notice
of me, except You, of course. You are my radiant sun,
shining on my upturned face. I will be the patch of
ground for Your pavilion, a lovely edifice built with
tears and draped in my veils. Until then, there is no
veil and no pavilion, only a white wall which rises
to the sky and hides the stars. In my ecstasy, I heard
His first call, like a nearby murmur which heralded
His joyful arrival. Then, behind me, I heard footsteps and the rustle of fabric, but I did not want to
stop my prayer. Far off, I heard whispers and bells,
as though something was trying to attract my attention. I have seen so many ghosts and apparitions
in the corners and alcoves of these rooms. You can
tell they are here for the flames of the candles turn
blue when they go by, but I have learned that I must
remain calm and still, for they will pass. Yet I fear

them. I fear the appearance of temptation. I know it is cowardly to fight a duel, so if the devil arrives, I will turn my back on him and never look at him face to face. I got up from the altar and turned to face whoever had entered the dormitory, but there was no one there. I wondered where Ottavia could be. With that thought in mind, I lay down on my bed of straw, pulled a blanket over my head and tried immediately to fall asleep. She would come of her own accord.

The next day, it had stopped raining. After the reading at breakfast, the Abbess stood up and announced that the Bishop was visiting our convent that very morning. What a commotion her declaration made. The elder *suore* started fussing so, at a loss as to how to receive such an esteemed visitor at such short notice. Ottavia and I looked on in bewilderment, for we had never seen the Bishop in the flesh. The Abbess raised her arms.

'Hush, hush, my sisters. Calm yourselves. It is not an inspection, he will only be here for a moment, so there is no need to tidy your cells.'

The *suore* seemed relieved to hear this.

'Congregate in the chapter in one hour,' the Abbess said.

At the appointed hour, we were all gathered in the chapter, the Signoras sitting on benches either side of the high chair and Ottavia and I sitting on the ground. I like the chapter because it is the brightest room in our convent. There are two big windows overlooking the orchard. They are so enormous that they fill the room all day with sunshine. My eyes are always drawn to the altar beneath the great windows and the silver altarpiece adorned with pearls that catch the sun. Footsteps and low voices outside the door to the chapter heralded the arrival of the Bishop and the *suore* covered themselves with their veils. When the doors opened, the Bishop entered and we all stood up. The Bishop was wearing a white mitre and a robe of white ermine that trailed along the ground, and he held a crozier. I had never seen such a luxurious costume before and I stared at him as he walked past. Ottavia whispered in my ear, 'Doesn't he look splendid in his white raiment?' and I looked at her to be quiet. The Abbess entered after him and took her position next to the Bishop. He offered his hand to the Abbess and she kissed it, whereupon he sat in the high chair.

'Greetings from the Pope, the Doge and the Diocese,' the Bishop said. 'All greet you warmly. News of the quake is bad. In St Mark's, the marble statues of the four kings fell. We had already engaged the architect Giorgio Spavento to initiate a renovation, and now his plans are to be executed under the direction of Bartolomeo Bon of Bergamo. We will add a new belfry, in marble, and the sculpture of the lion of St Mark and Venetia will be placed on a new attic. Lastly, we will add a new spire, in gold leaf. The tall houses in the ghetto have been much damaged and many lives were lost, but the Lord showed mercy and Sant'Alvise, being such a small convent, was thankfully spared. The Abbess has told me that the damage is limited to a few cracks in the walls. If your convent had been bigger, there would surely have been lives lost, so thanks be to God.' The *suore* said, 'Amen,' and crossed themselves. Ottavia and I did likewise.

'Your convent may be small but it is highly valued by the church, as all our convents are, but this earthquake is nothing but a sign from God. Misfortunes occur on account of sins and the State of Venetia is full of these. I have heard from my confessors that fathers are interfering with daughters, brothers with sisters, and so forth. The city is becoming irreligious. In other years, the confessors would have heard the New Year confessions of half of Venetia by this time, but they have so far heard no one but the female tertiaries and a tiny number of others. There is disorder in the city and this has incurred the wrath of God. In order to appease Him, I have ordered processions at St Mark's for three days, and processions in the evenings, and three days' fasting on bread and water for all the citizens of the city.'

The sisters again said, 'Amen,' and crossed themselves. Ottavia and I followed their lead.

'As you know,' the Bishop said, 'the family of the Abbess has kindly offered to engage higher officials to make a Book of Hours of the Passion of Christ for your convent. Our Christian devotion will be expressed in it by means of illumination and decoration. It will be the most beautiful Book of Hours in all Venetia.'

There was a murmur of approval, which the Abbess acknowledged.

'But that is not all, my sisters.' Gesturing to a man standing next to him, a man whom I had not noticed until then, the Bishop said, 'This man is Signor Avílo, a renowned painter. Last year, the Diocese engaged Signor Avílo to paint eight episodes from the good book. Even though Signor Avílo does not usually make paintings for devotional, allegorical or historical purposes, he agreed and we are privileged. He has at last finished and they will soon adorn the convent walls.'

There was another murmur of approval. The man nodded in acknowledgement to the sisters. He was bearded and wore a tunic with enormous blue sleeves.

'For a further fee of fifty ducats, Signor Avílo has been newly commissioned by the Abbess to paint her portrait.' The Bishop turned to the painter and said, 'Sir, your portrait should conform to pious decorum and sacred beauty and should avoid using scandalously rich colours and profane ornaments. Some outsiders think this convent is a place of vice and indiscipline, but that is not the case. It is rather a bastion of chastity and prayer that serves the Lord and compensates for the corruption of the laity. The purity of the nuns atones for the sins of the city – that is what I want to show them.'

The painter bowed slightly, but he didn't speak.

'The Abbess will not be able to sit often for your portrait, as she is exceedingly busy, so you will have to find another to model on. The suggestion of the Abbess is that you use the lay sister called Oliva. Where is she?'

All the *suore* and the Abbess turned and looked at me. I had never had so many eyes bearing down on me before. I burned with shame and discomfort at having so much attention paid to me.

'The Abbess tells me that it is common knowledge

how alike you are to her, and I see that it is true. Quite striking, in fact. If it were not for your humble beginnings, I would say you were two peas from the same pod.'

'We all look like those we love, Bishop,' the Abbess said.

The Bishop continued to regard me, so much so that I had to avert my eyes.

'Good luck with your portrait, Signor Avílo. I look forward to seeing it in due course.'

With that, the Bishop got up and left the room, giving us benediction as he went. His white robe trailed like a curtain. The doors closed behind him with a thud. No one spoke for several moments. It was as though he had never come. His visit seemed like a dream. The Abbess clapped her hands.

'Sisters, you may go about your business,' she said. 'Oliva, stay where you are.' The sisters got up and left the chapter. The Abbess turned to the painter and said, 'Welcome to Sant'Alvise, Signor Avílo.'

'Thank you, Abbess Querini,' the painter said.

'I wonder how we will accommodate you into our life here.'

'You will not notice my presence, I assure you.'

'The Bishop tells me that you were an assistant to Giorgione?'

'That is correct.'

'I am very sorry for your loss, Signor Avílo.'

'Thank you, Abbess.'

'We all have our masters, but sometimes our masters desert us.'

The painter didn't say anything.

'Well, let's see where we can put you. Oliva, come with me.' The Abbess walked out of the chapter, accompanied by the painter, and I followed. In the courtyard, near the main entrance to our convent, lay a small wooden box and a long case. The Abbess pointed to them.

'Pick those up, Oliva, and follow us.'

She turned to the painter. 'Where would you like to work, Signor Avílo?'

'Where there is most light, Abbess.' His voice was slow and sweet, like treacle.

'This way then,' she said.

We walked through the cloisters, past the tree and the well. There were a few chickens running loose in the courtyard.

'You are no longer an assistant to anyone?'

'No, Abbess. It is because of my master's passing that I now find myself striking out on my own. You could say I am a mendicant.'

The Abbess stopped walking and turned to him.

She then did something I have never seen her do before – she smiled.

'Have I said something to offend you, Abbess?'

'No, it is just that no one has talked to me in such a jocular fashion since I was a young girl.'

'My apologies, Abbess. I am a heathen *tedesco*.'

'It's quite all right, young man. In fact, it is rather pleasant.'

She carried on walking.

'How long have you been in our city, Signor Avílo?'

'These past few years, Abbess.'

'And do you like it here?'

'Oh yes, Abbess. Venetia is an extraordinary city; its blue is unlike any other I have seen. The light constantly shifts and the water reflects everything. All shapes here have soft edges and outlines. Everything is blurred and dark, whereas in Florentia, everything is hard and bright.'

'You have been to Florentia?'

'Yes, Abbess.'

The Abbess looked impressed. We came into the kitchen, which was empty, and crossed to the storeroom. The Abbess stood still.

'Tell me, on your way here, did you see any men wearing yellow hats?'

'I did, Abbess.'

'Do you know who they are?'

'No, Abbess.'

'They are Jews,' the Abbess said. 'The city has made the ghetto their new home. We are on the edge of the lagoon here and there is nowhere else for them to go. They are rounded up like sheep every night and forced to stay in their homes. I have a lot of sympathy for them, for their plight is much the same as ours. The lay sisters here cannot leave the convent, of course, but for a hundred years, we nuns from noble families have been allowed to come and go when it suits us. But no longer. The Magistrate also wishes to keep us, like the Jews, *in clausura*. Because the blood of Venetia is to be kept clear of foreign bodies, the Magistrate tells us that we at Sant'Alvise are no longer allowed to accept into our order any non-Venetians, women without a surname, or Jews. Vice is to be contained and virtue safeguarded, Signor Avílo. The Magistrate tells us it is for our benefit. He calls the Jews "vile and perfidious", but he treats us just like them, so what does that make us?'

The Abbess pursed her lips, which she always did when she was displeased. The painter remained silent. The Abbess told me to put the boxes down.

'This is our storeroom,' she said. 'What you lack in light you make up for in space.'

He looked about the small space where we kept the loom. There was only one small window, high up.

'This corner will do very nicely, Abbess. Thank you.'

'The place of salvation is very small, Signor Avílo, maybe just a window.' She looked the painter in the eye. 'Good day,' she said and led me out.

Ottavia and I spent the following morning cleaning out the chicken coop and preparing the vegetable garden for planting. Because it was Lent, we could not eat meat and so relied solely on eggs and vegetables. We put the old straw in the kitchen fires and spread new straw for the chickens. Signora Arcanzola is in charge of the kitchen and she is the one who knows the most about the herbs and vegetables we grow in the garden and the fruit we grow in the orchard. Signora Lucia used to work in the gardens, until she became too old. She still knows the name of every herb in the garden. Signora Arcanzola is difficult to please, so we worked hard weeding and turning over the beds. The sun shone and the air was warm and we were both soon quite hot. I have no feeling for living things, but I love the trees in the orchard. There are so few trees in our city. The pomegranates, figs and peaches are beautiful creations, but the Abbess has told us that we are not allowed to pick or eat them. They are grown as gifts solely for the Bishop and Magistrate, and for those men who give money when they come to visit.

As if reading my mind, Ottavia said, 'The *tedesco* looked very fine yesterday, didn't he?'

'He did,' I said and carried on digging.

'I know he is very old, but he still looks handsome.'

I said nothing.

'Oh how wearing it is to find oneself always sitting at the same table with the same food! What a torment to retire every night to the same bed, always to breathe the same air, always to conduct the same conversations and to see the same faces! I am bored, Oliva!'

Ottavia spent a lot of her time crying and complaining. I felt sorry for her but I had learned to ignore these remarks.

'Seeing the Bishop in his fine costume made me think about what it would be like to be with a man,' she whispered.

'Ottavia!' I said. 'What a wicked thing to say. Have you forgotten your vow of chastity?'

'We make a great many vows that we never keep,' she replied.

'Hurry up,' I said, 'it will be lunch soon.'

We worked in silence for another long while until it was time for her to leave. I watched as she crossed the grass and disappeared through the entrance to the cloisters. She was gone in a flash. My sisterly affection for her was more like a mother's love. I was devoted to her and full of uneasiness about the state of her soul. He had united us with bonds much stronger than those of blood.

When it was time for me to finish, I returned the tools to the storeroom and, when I came out, Signora Arcanzola was in the kitchen. 'Quickly, child, you're late for lunch,' she said. I washed my hands and ran across the garden to the refectory. As I came in, Ottavia was already reading from the Bible and the sisters were eating their meal at the communal table. I was always jealous that Ottavia could read and write better than me. She came from a noble family with too many sisters for them all to be married, but at least her family taught her to read and write before they put her in the convent. I took my place at the end of the bench, next to Signora Gratiosa, and broke the bread on my plate. She pointed at the wall and there I saw four paintings hanging. She told me that all eight of the *tedesco*'s paintings had arrived early and she and Signora Agnesina had spent all morning fixing them to the walls of the refectory and the chapter. They were small and square. The colours were dark brown and dark green. Signora Gratiosa pointed to one of them and told me it was of the gold colossus of Nebuchadnezzar. The people in the painting were playing harps and flutes, and the three Jews were burning in the fiery furnace. Another was of Joshua taking Jericho. The towers were crumbling, just like the chimney pots in the earthquake, and the horses were frightened. Two men blew their trumpets and Joshua stood with open arms, dressed in long, bright red pantaloons.

'Sisters.'

The Abbess stood in the centre of the table, with the other noble nuns either side of her, like Christ with his disciples at the Last Supper.

'It was brought to my attention that Oliva missed matins on the night of the quake and, for that, there must be a punishment.'

She looked directly at me and I felt quashed under her gaze. 'Oliva, you will be given only bread and water to eat tomorrow. Miss matins again and you will eat only bread and water for a week. When you have finished your meal, you will spend the afternoon sweeping the cells and cleaning the wash-room.'

The sisters looked at me, some with expressions of pity, but the look on Signora Pellegrina's face was one of satisfaction. I guessed it was she who had made sure the Abbess knew of my absence. Why is she so bitter? What have I done to deserve her contempt? I do not know, but I know I must bend to the will of my superiors. The orders of the Abbess are my compass and I am certain she will guide me in the right direction. If I should stop following this compass for a moment, I am sure the dark waters will swallow me up, so I took my punishment without complaint.

After I had finished my meal, I fetched a broom and went to the cells of the Signoras, opening them one by one and sweeping them clean. It does not matter how often I sweep them for the dust always seems to collect in the corners straight away. By the bed in each of the cells the Signoras all had their own breviary, with gold letters and beautiful red covers. All the walls were decorated with tapestries. I opened a few of the *casse* – I wasn't supposed to, but I couldn't resist. Inside were linen robes, handkerchiefs, tablecloths and altar cloths. There were silk garments, too, and I knelt down to touch the material. They felt as smooth as water. There were crucifixes, too, encrusted with jewels, and there were many beautiful candleholders. The beauty of these things no doubt reminded the Signoras of the splendour of their homes. It took many hours to sweep all the cells. I was tired, my lack of sleep made me melancholic and nervous, but I tried to lose myself in my task and carried on working.

When I finished sweeping the last cell, Signora Pellegrina was standing outside. 'Have you finished?' she asked. I nodded and kept my head bowed. 'You are not worthy of anything more than this, Oliva, for you are a spoilt child lacking in manners. You place yourself more highly than your position warrants, but remember, all is vanity. You may go now.' I left, glad to be out of her way. How she enjoyed tormenting me. How her words pierced my soul. Was she right? Was I vain? I guessed she was almost certainly right, but I also knew that she had as much vanity in her soul and vexation in her spirit as I did.

When I had finished cleaning the washroom, I put away the tools and made my way to the infirmary to read to Signora Lucia. The lamps would be lit soon and I wanted to see her before the bell sounded for vespers. Her kindness is a pillar to me. When I arrived four years ago, she was already old and bed-ridden, but she treated me like a daughter and she is the closest thing I have to a mother. When I got to the infirmary, she was lying completely still in bed, as she had done for weeks. There was nothing more to be done for her except look after her and keep her in comfort. Her hands lay either side of her, like two dead leaves. I touched one of them and said, 'It is me, Signora. How are you feeling today?'

She looked in my direction but she could see nothing. Her eyes were milky. 'How nice of you to come, my child.'

'Shall I read to you?'

'That would be pleasant,' she said.

I picked up her breviary, which was also red and gold, opened it at random and read aloud. Some months before, the Magistrate had banned all books from our convent except the breviaries belonging to the Signoras, psalters and the writings of St Augustine. When the Magistrate's assistant announced this dictate, the Abbess became angry, more angry than I had ever seen, but it made no difference to me as the only books I had ever seen were the psalters and breviaries. Even with her failing eyesight, Signora Lucia had taught me to read when I first came to the convent. Signora Pellegrina didn't want me to learn to read at all because she said it would divert my attention away from my duties in the convent, but Signora Lucia taught me anyway. I struggled over some words, which Signora Lucia corrected from memory, and I continued to read to her until she put her hand on mine for me to cease. I closed her breviary and sat by her side for some moments.

'Is something the matter, child? What is it?'

I smiled. Signora Lucia is well known in our convent for her secrets, which she is always revealing. She cannot help herself. But, without moving from her bed, she also seems to know all that goes on in our convent.

'Signora Pellegrina wants to destroy me, Signora.'

'Nonsense,' she said. 'If you have anything to fear, it will not come from her.'

'But she hates me so,' I said.

'She does not hate you, Oliva, she fears you.'

'But I have done her no harm.'

'You do not need to have done her any harm for her to fear you. She is jealous of the purity of your soul.'

I tried to take in what the Signora was telling me, but as soon as I thought about myself in such a way, my thoughts disappeared.

'I have known Pellegrina Malatesta for a long time. We grew up together. You didn't know that, did you?'

'No, Signora,' I said.

'My family knew her family, we were practically sisters. I was better-looking than her, though, and she always resented it. I had a lot of admirers, but she had none. When she was sixteen, she was lured to this convent by her aunt, who promised her a life of luxury and comfort and pledged that she would receive frequent visits from her family, but those promises proved false. Her family abandoned her and she has been here ever since. And when you entered our convent, she began tormenting you because she saw herself in you, a younger, prettier version of herself. She is like a beast that attacks its own reflection in a looking glass.'

The bell sounded for vespers.

'Do not worry, my child. You cannot have much to say to your superiors because your soul is very simple, and when you are perfect, you will be more simple still. The nearer one gets to God, the simpler one becomes.' She squeezed my hand. 'Now go and come back soon.'

'Yes, Signora,' I said and kissed her forehead.

I left her and made my way to the choir. As I walked, I wondered what other secrets Signora Lucia had locked away in her heart. What made Signora Lucia so different from Signora Pellegrina? They had endured the same life, yet they had answered it in such contrary ways. Why?

Ottavia was handing out the graduals when I arrived. I had not seen her all afternoon and I smiled at her. She smiled back and I took a place by the grille. This was my favourite part of the day, for I love to sing. Below me, the Bishop was in front of the congregation, about to hold a special mass for those who died in the quake. Someone took her place behind me, but I didn't bother to look around. Then a voice said, 'After service, go directly to your bed, my child. You may miss compline and matins today. You are dead on your feet.' It was the Abbess, my compassionate Madonna. I nodded. The figures of the people below came in and out of my vision. I saw that the painter was amongst them. He was sitting with folded hands, looking directly at the crucifix and, when the mass started, I sang with all my heart, but it did not prevent me from being distracted and feeling sleepy. I closed my eyes and sang in harmony, as is my desire, for all the joy in the world.

A few days later, after prime, we were all congregated in the chapter, where the Abbess was setting out our tasks in the gardens. As it was spring, all the planting had to be done in the following few weeks. As the *suore* talked amongst themselves, there was a knock on the front door and Signora Gratiosa was told to attend to it. With no one watching me, I glanced again at the paintings on the wall. In the paintings, the human figures were very childlike, and the animals were drawn as if by a child. One of the people held a golden umbrella that had golden fringes and a big pompom on top. All the hats were very elaborate and the dresses very heavy and long. The shoes were fine and pointed. My eyes were attracted to Joshua in his red pantaloons. That spot of bright colour brought up a heat in me and provoked in me a shameful tug, but my daydream was broken when Signora Gratiosa returned to the chapter and said that the painter was waiting to speak to the Abbess.

'What does he want?' the Abbess asked.

'He says he wants to show us something.'

The Abbess sighed and said, 'Very well, bring him in.'

The sisters pulled their veils over their faces, and the painter stepped into the chapter carrying something large and rectangular that was covered in a sheet. He leaned it against the wall.

'Good day, Abbess Querini,' he bowed. He was wearing his smock with its huge blue sleeves.

'What is it you want, Signor Avílo? We are conducting our daily business here.'

'Forgive me, Abbess, but I need your permission to bring this into the convent.'

'What is it?'

The painter removed the sheet to reveal a rectangle that seemed to be a hole. As I looked into it, I could see a portion of our own chapter, but the portion wasn't right. Where there should have been part of a wall, there was a piece of the opposite wall. Looking into it caused my mind to slip up.

'It is a mirror, Abbess.'

'I can see that, Signor Avílo, but why have you brought it here?'

'I need it for my portrait. Now that the glassmaking furnaces have moved to Murano, I cannot collect a mirror each time I come here as I was able to from the Rialto, so I request that I leave this one here until I finish my work.'

Signora Pellegrina wasted no time in showing her displeasure. 'This is impossible, Abbess. Mirrors have no place in a convent. It will corrupt our cloistered seclusion.' Signora Lucretia and Signora Agnesina murmured in agreement.

'Abbess,' the painter said, 'I know it is unusual, but consider for a moment that the Virgin was the mirror of Christ, and God Himself is the mirror in which one sees oneself. In addition, you, and all the *suore*, are His mirror in which He contemplates His creations.'

Signora Agnesina was looking at the mirror. 'It's diabolical,' she said.

'It is not diabolical, Abbess, it only reflects back what it sees. It is not the surface of things that is important, only what lies inside. When we look into ourselves, isn't the soul merely a mirror in which we know God?'

But Signora Agnesina would not give up. 'What is our self-worth if we need to seek out a false truth?'

'I say again, Abbess, just as the soul contemplates itself in the mirror of Divinity, so this mirror will uncover only what He wills.'

The Abbess looked long and hard at the painter. 'You need this mirror to aid you?'

'Yes indeed, Abbess. I need it to put perspective in my picture.'

'And answer me this, has the Bishop already consented to its use?'

'He has.'

'Then, in reality, it matters little whether or not I give you my consent. Isn't that true?'

The painter nodded and I could see that the Abbess struggled to hide her anger. 'Very well, Signore, I have no choice but to agree to your request.'

'Thank you, Abbess. I wish to start straight away, if I may.'

'It seems you are to have everything you wish for, Signore.' The Abbess turned to me and said, 'Go with him, Oliva. You are excused from your duties for as long as Signor Avílo has need of you.'

The painter bowed and put the sheet over his mirror. I got up from the floor and followed him out to the courtyard.

'Show me the way,' the painter said.

I walked along the cloisters, conscious of the painter behind me. I had never seen a mirror before. I had seen reflections in water, but the reflections in this looking glass were so real. It was hard to tell what was real and what wasn't. We came to the kitchen and crossed to the storeroom. The painter's box and case were there in the corner. He leaned his mirror against the wall with great care and took off the sheet. I could see the ceiling in it. What should have been above me was now below. He spent the next few minutes unpacking, putting up a stand and placing paper on it. He fetched a stool and positioned it near the window.

'Sit,' he said.

I sat.

He took a position behind his stand.

'Sketches first,' he said and spent several minutes looking at me with a gaze I found unnerving. He took up a black stick and started making marks on the paper. The sounds of his scratching echoed in the small room, making the silence even more distinct.

'How long have you been in this convent, Oliva?'

'Four years, Signore.'

'Four years in the same place? How you must yearn to travel, to see the world?'

He carried on making his marks on the paper. I wondered how long I would have to stay sitting here. Ottavia and I had work to do.

'Ah, you are one of the quiet ones, are you? Then I shall talk, for talk fills the void. I cannot imagine spending four years in one tiny patch of ground. I have travelled far and wide in order to find a landscape as deep as my imagination, but, to my disappointment, the only thing that changes from place to place are the skies. I have been searching for the truest blue and the ultimate yellow. Blue is the colour of adornment, the colour of the Madonna's robe, but also the colour of the sky, space, emptiness, nothingness. It is the tint of the marvellous and inexplicable. When blue becomes bluest, it is black, and yet, a small amount of blue added to white paradoxically makes white appear whiter. Yellow, on the other hand, is always the sun, and the sun is God. It shines from one source and shines alike upon all. This light in its glory is as golden in its grace. The yellowest thing I have ever seen is saffron, which is a stain as well as a spice. Have you ever tasted saffron, Oliva?'

'No, Signore.'

'It tastes of blood.' He spoke with great passion, so much so that I became alarmed by his passion for something that was merely a spice. What was a passion for a spice compared to a passion for Christ?

'My master Giorgione taught me everything I know about colour. I used to buy his pigments from the apothecary and prepare the panels of egg tempera for his work. He would sit with me and discuss what he was about to do. After he had laid down his precious foundations, he turned the picture round to face the wall and left it there, sometimes for months, without looking at it, and when he wanted to reapply his brushes, he examined the picture with a rigorous scrutiny, as if it were his mortal enemy, in order to see if he could find fault with it. He did this again and again, and then covered the picture with layers and layers of living flesh, so that they only lacked breath. When he was satisfied, he would leave his picture to mature, like wine.'

'You loved your master, Signor Avílo.'

'She speaks!' He looked long and hard at me before saying, 'Of course you haven't seen my master's Venus. She is lying down, quite without clothes, but instead of being a huddled, defenceless body, it is balanced, prosperous and confident. Her hair is a flaming red. She lies with her closed eyes, turned toward me, offering no obstacle to my glances over her body. It is the most beautiful image a man could ever make.'

'But it is false worship to make images like this.'

'All works of art seek to elicit buried feelings. Some reach into us so deep that we may be afraid they will expose our most shameful instincts. There are people who dislike being revealed to themselves in this way, and who condemn the artworks in question.'

The painter was busy examining me, but at the same time it was as if he had almost forgotten I was there. 'How I wish you could see it,' he said.

'I am about to become a bride of Christ, Signor Avílo.'

'Yes, of course,' he said. 'If I wasn't in love with the body, I believe I would be a mystic too, but I try to keep myself open to extreme possibilities.' His hand moved over the paper in front of him and from time to time he glanced in the mirror. He remained quiet for many minutes while he did this and I began to feel my resistance to silence and stillness rise to the surface. Signor Avílo's words puzzled me, but I guessed he was unable to love, as though there were too many obstacles in his way, and I felt an urge to tell him that there was no purpose in suffering over obstacles to love. The final answer always comes from above, but it occurred to me that Signor Avílo thought it would come from below.

'How odd you look, Oliva. Whatever are you thinking?'

'Nothing, Signore.'

'You have a fine face. Hold it up to the light.'

I did what was asked of me.

'My portrait will be a frontal view in flat light against an uncluttered background. I don't want to tell a story, I want to paint my feelings. I want nothing more than to execute you,' he said, looking at me with an attention that made my ears and cheeks burn.

The bell for lauds woke me for the second time that night and so I rose and made my way to the choir. Ottavia had already risen. It seemed as though no time at all had passed since matins. Rising in the night ails me so, making me irritable, and the cold makes me shiver. The cloisters were dismal in the candlelight. A draught bit at my ankles and I wrapped my shawl around me. A few of the chickens had strayed out of the garden and they moved out of my way as I approached them. I had crossed the courtyard in darkness a thousand times but I could not shake off the murk inside me. Thankfully, I could see day breaking above. It was the time of day when a white thread could be black, and a black thread could be white. My heart had been troubled ever since I sat for Signor Avílo. He talked of suns and stains, but I wanted no stain on me. There is a divine light that illumines my soul, and which removes all stains. In my mind, I mark lucky days with a white stone and unfortunate ones with a black stone. Yesterday was marked with a black stone. I fear Signor Avílo, for he may catch me away, with an allure and a wickedness that could pervert my thoughts. My greatest fault is self-love, I know, and I am sure Signor Avílo has been sent to test me, as God sometimes appears veiled under signs and figures. Such witchery has come to tarnish my honour, but I have to remain pitying and gracious, patient and rich in mercy. All his praise heaped on me must not make me vain and the knowledge of my wretchedness must never leave me for a moment. I want to be ignored and regarded as nothing, so that I may find joy in contempt for myself. I need to heed this sign. Can I toss Signor Avílo's words out of my heart? Is my heart open enough to admit Him? His face is my radiant sun and I shall look at no other.

The choir was gloomy, too. Ottavia was handing out the psalters. I smiled at her and her face broke into one of her beautiful displays of joy. The other *suore* drifted in, as if still dreaming. I took my place in the back of the choir, out of everyone's way. The Abbess was at the front, as usual, standing still and straight. She is such a tower of strength. When everyone was present and in place, she kneeled, bowed her head and made every reverent gesture according to the correct procedure of the office. She then began the chanting of the psalms to our Lord Jesus, and we all followed her lead. While we were chanting Psalm 130, Signora Ursia was fidgeting with her rosary. My hearing is sharp and the loud noise irritated me. I wanted to turn and stare at her until she stopped, but deep down I knew it was better to endure it patiently, so I gave myself up to our glorious harmony. *'Bless the Lord, ye His angels, that excel in strength, that do His commandments, hearkening unto the voice of His word.'*

Then I heard a noise like a sack of potatoes being knocked over and I saw that Signora Ursia had fallen to the floor. The sisters around her dropped their psalters and attended to her and our singing stopped. There was a gasp from the few people gathered in the church below. What could have happened to her? Her eyes were tight shut, but she did not look in pain. Her hands were clenched tight. Signora Gratiosa tried to revive her, shaking her and calling her name, but Signora Ursia was as stiff as a board and didn't respond. They looked at each other for guidance, not knowing what to do, and the Abbess said to carry her to the infirmary. The rest of us were rooted to the spot as we watched four sisters take Signora Ursia's arms and legs and carry her off like a corpse. The Abbess ended the service and told us to go straight to the chapter. Then she left herself.

In the chapter, all the talk was of Signora Ursia's fall. Was she all right? What was the matter? The Abbess eventually arrived and calmed the sisters, telling us that Signora Ursia was 'perfectly all right'. She had just seen her and she was resting in her cell. 'She will be on her feet soon, my sisters, so do not worry.'

Signora Agnesina asked, 'But what is the matter with her, Abbess?'

'She says she had a vision of Christ,' the Abbess said.

'Heaven be praised,' Signora Lucretia said.

Signora Agnesina dropped to her knees, said, 'Hallelujah,' and crossed herself.

'Oh yes, it is a marvel, I know, but this presents a problem for us,' the Abbess said. 'The Magistrate is a sceptic and does not look kindly on such visions. If word of this gets out, I fear he will bring Signora Ursia before the Inquisition and charge her with feigned sanctity. He wishes to control us, sisters, not nurture us. We must close ranks and hold firm. Not a word of this to anyone, do you understand?'

The sisters looked at each other in confusion.

'Do you understand?' the Abbess said.

The sisters succumbed and murmured their assent.

'And now to our meeting,' the Abbess said. 'Is there any business?'

Signora Pellegrina immediately stood up. 'The chickens are running loose in the dormitories again, leaving their mess everywhere. It is Oliva's job to round them up but this child does absolutely nothing!'

A flame of indignation rose in my breast, but I remained silent. As usual, Signora Pellegrina spoke of me as if I were not in the room. She did not stand on ceremony and the freedom of her speech delighted her.

'Oliva.' The Abbess looked at me. 'Isn't it your duty to look after the chickens?'

'Yes, Abbess,' I said.

'Then do your duty and round them up into the coop. As today is a fast day, you are to collect their eggs as well.'

'Very well, Abbess.'

'You can go now.'

I got up and left the chapter, humiliated once again. I wandered in and out of the cells of the Signoras, but could only find one chicken astray. Signora Pellegrina is a liar as well as a wicked being. I drove it out of the cell. There were a few other chickens in the kitchen. They squawked and flapped their wings as I shooed them into their coop in the gardens. They fled to one end of the coop as I crawled in to collect the eggs. I counted the eggs as I put them into the basket. Fourteen. I took the basket with me into the infirmary. In the corner, Signora Lucia was dozing in her bed, her skullcap on and her shift undone. She looked very old today. I put down the basket of eggs and rubbed the back of her hand.

'Signora,' I said. 'It's me.'

At the sound of my voice, her eyes opened and remained open for several moments.

'It's me, Signora.'

She smiled. 'Ah, my dear Oliva. You are the sunshine in my life.'

I sat on a stool near her bed and told her the story of Signora Ursia's fall. The Signora liked stories, so I made sure to furnish it with as much detail as I could remember. I told her about the hushed crowd below, the astonished look on the faces of all the sisters, how stiff Signora Ursia was. When I had got to the end, Signora Lucia started to chuckle.

'That Ursia is a crafty one,' she said.

Of all her responses, I had not thought that Signora Lucia would laugh. 'What do you mean, Signora?'

'I have more faith in my little finger than Ursia has in her whole being,' she said. 'She has always been like that, making up stories, seeing things. She thinks it promotes her in the eyes of the Abbess.' She lay back on the pillow, laughing quietly to herself. 'She probably picked some salvia from the garden and put it in the bread, to flavour it.'

'What's salvia?'

'It is a herb that makes you have visions. *Salvia*

divinorum. It is an old trick. Go to the kitchen and see if there are any bits of green leaves in any bread she has baked herself.'

I picked up the basket of eggs. 'I will, Signora. How clever you are.'

'I am not clever, my dear Oliva, just old. Go now, child, and come to see me soon.'

I crossed the garden and went into the kitchen. Signora Arcanzola was there, busy preparing lunch.

'There you are, Oliva, you're late,' she said.

'Sorry, Signora, I was visiting Signora Lucia.'

'Hand me those eggs. Quickly!'

She took them from me and placed them all in a huge pan of boiling water. The oven was ablaze, sending heat out into the whole room, yet the corners were still dark and murky. Signora Ursia usually helped Signora Arcanzola in the kitchen, but now that she was resting in her cell, Signora Arcanzola was left on her own to cook. I went to the tables, where there was some bread lying around. I picked it up. There was a bitter smell to it and, when I broke it open, I saw tiny bits of green in it. I smiled. Signora Lucia can see nothing, yet she knows everything.

'What are you doing, child? Stop loitering and take this to the refectory.' Signora Arcanzola handed me a large bowl of vegetables. I did what I was told and left the Signora to her work.

In the afternoons, between none and vespers, the sisters usually gather in their cells to embroider and gossip. When the sisters congregate in the cell of Signora Pellegrina, she keeps me there to serve the sisters their wine and to fetch anything they need. Today as always there were fine delicacies – marzipan, sugared fruit, biscuits – and my mouth watered at the sight of them. Once the sisters had arrived and settled, I lit a platter of candles and the sisters started their needlework. There is a loom in the workrooms and, every Lent, the sisters spin and tie golden thread on it, which they use to make golden flowers on altar cloths – some of white or red damask, but the most beautiful one I have seen the *suore* make is one of mulberry velvet. It took Signora Gratiosa three years to make it. I saw her toil on it with my own eyes. These cloths are highly prized by people in the city and they can sell for a lot of ducats. They also use the golden thread to make fringes and borders for handkerchiefs to sell outside. Ottavia told me that one handkerchief had been ordered by Jacopo Negretti, a friend of her family, who would pay the convent handsomely. It was the only time I never saw any discord between the sisters. It was as if they were sewing themselves together.

'Oliva, read to us while we work,' Signora Pellegrina said. 'I suppose we must hear from our St Augustine again, as that is all she can read. Here,' she pointed to her bedside table.

I picked up the huge book and returned to my spot by the candles.

Signora Gratiosa looked up from her sewing. 'You drive that poor girl too hard. She will turn on you one day and bite you.'

'Nonsense,' Signora Pellegrina said, 'she doesn't have it in her. And, besides, she needs the discipline.'

'Sit down to read, my child,' Signora Gratiosa said. 'There's no need to stand.'

I did as Signora Gratiosa said and opened our saint's book, *City of God*, and began reading the words slowly. 'The demons have knowledge without charity, and are thereby so inflated or proud that they crave those divine honours and religious services which they know to be due to the true God, and still, as far as they can, exact these from all over whom they have influence . . .'

No sooner had I begun reading, though, than Signora Ursia came into the cell. She seemed to fill the doorway and the expression on her face was one of radiant happiness. Her entrance caused quite a stir and the sisters paid me no more attention. They ushered her in, sat her down and began throwing questions at her. Was the Blessed Virgin carrying the Child Jesus? Was there a great blaze of light? Signora Ursia nodded at all the questions and said, 'I'm in love with Jesus – He's courting me. What can I do but receive His grace?' The sisters were excited by this news. Jesus is their husband and child. The wooden baby Jesus they cradle every Christmas is the child they could have had. He is also their brother and father. He is their whole family. When women are shut away among themselves, what do they talk about? Just men.

Signora Ursia took a place among her sisters and told them the whole story again, from start to finish. The sisters were deeply satisfied by the turn of events. Signora Ursia embellished so, and I took satisfaction from knowing that it was all lies. I had knowledge that they did not, and it made me feel less lowly. If only they knew what I knew, but I kept my nose in the book and heard all that was said, though it sometimes might have been better if I hadn't. The talk turned to the *tedesco*. They spoke of his stature, his robes. Signora Arcanzola looked at me and said that she wouldn't mind having her portrait painted by him. Her face looked pale and drawn in the candlelight, but I could see envy in her eyes. She could take my place and I wouldn't mind a bit, but I said nothing. My position wouldn't allow me to.

'Portraiture is the devil's work,' Signora Pellegrina said. 'It steals souls.'

The Signora's words filled me with fear for the painter was coming for his weekly visit the following day and I had to sit for him again. The painter craved something from me that I did not want to give. His long hair, his beard, his blue robe all spoke of the devil to me. Signora Pellegrina looked at me and said, '*Corporis munditia conformis sit anime.*' She laughed, saying that, of course, I could not understand. She knew that the only things I know in Latin are the psalms and prayers of the divine office and I know those only by rote. I do not know what they mean. Signora Pellegrina ordered me to carry on reading, so I tilted the book towards the candles and recited the words for the pleasure of the sisters.

The cloisters were empty as I made my way toward the workrooms the next morning. The bell rang for terce, but I had been excused. As I walked, I struggled with what had been taught me, that suffering is important, but not an end in itself; that hope is the light that illuminates the living soul in the dark of the night; that the love of Jesus lights me up from the inside and cleanses me. I am filled with suffering and darkness, but my soul will climb to the summit through gentle hope. Despair is the mortal enemy of the soul. It does not come from Heaven, but is sent by an evil spirit. I must cling to my hope. This is what I have been told.

I turned the corner and entered the kitchen, where Signora Arcanzola was busy, as usual. She glanced at me as I walked by. In the adjoining workroom, the painter had already set up his stand in the corner, a weak light falling on it from the window. Paints and brushes were lying on the floor. The looking glass was uncovered and leaning against the wall.

'Ah, good day, Oliva,' he said. 'Please sit.'

I sat where he indicated, under the window. He opened his pad and looked at it for several moments. I did not know what I should do.

'You seem tired today, Oliva. What is troubling you?'

'Nothing, Signore.'

'Come, come, tell me, child.'

'It is just that we are few here and there is always so much to do.'

'They work you hard here, do they?'

'Yes, Signore,' I said.

'But there's something else, isn't there? Something you're not telling me.'

He had stopped what he was doing and was waiting. I was sick of the way Signora Pellegrina treated me. I could not complain but neither could I hold it inside. Before I knew it, I was telling him of Signora Pellegrina and of how she disliked me and, for no good reason, made me work even harder than before. As I spoke, he looked between his mirror and me, and worked on his drawing. He didn't say a word. When I had finished, he said, 'You seem helpless here, a victim of your cruel Signora. She is a tyrant.'

'She taunts me, it is true,' I said, 'but I have more here than I would on the outside.'

'You are mistaken. In the end, you will find the same things on the inside that you have left on the outside.' He came towards me and tilted my head toward the light, pulling my vestments straight. My skin burned where his fingers touched me, a sensation like the divine fire of Jesus that burns yet does not destroy. 'The only people who get involved in religion are the ones with something on their conscience,' he said. 'The Church is nothing but chicanery.'

I did not know what the word meant, but I felt a heat rise within me. It was an unfamiliar feeling, one I couldn't name.

'Many of the nuns are vain and undisciplined, but not you, Oliva. Indeed, it is precisely your virtue that separates you from them. Surely you know that?'

I shook my head. 'I am not virtuous, Signor Avílo. I have much to learn before I can become a bride of Christ.'

'Where is your mother? Didn't she teach you anything about becoming a bride?'

He carried on with his drawing, but I said nothing.

'My dear Oliva, why do you look so angry? All I meant by my question is that mothers often have a lot to answer for. If you feel without virtue, it is perhaps that a daughter's wrongs would be partly provoked by a mother's faults.'

'I did not know my mother, Signore.'

'Oh?' He stopped his painting and looked at me, expecting me to say more, but I didn't want to say any more. This man was pulling out of me things that I hardly knew about myself and which were precious to me. He demanded of me what I was least willing to give.

'Ah, I see,' the painter said, 'your mother was a prostitute. Yes, that is obvious now.'

My cheeks were aflame.

'The palaces of the prostitutes here in Venetia are famous. They are a paradise for the lovers of Venus, like me. Each glittering room is glorious to behold. The walls are adorned with tapestries, gilded leather and red velvet curtains. And the courtesans themselves wear chains of gold and oriental pearls and rings with diamonds and rubies, like a second Cleopatra. They wear gowns of beautiful damask, petticoats of red camlet edged with a golden fringe and stockings of carnation silk. And their chambers of recreation have milk-white canopies of needlework, silk quilts embroidered with golden thread, and, by their bedsides, there is even a picture of your Lady with Christ in her arms.'

I wanted him to stop, so I said, 'The Abbess says that, although these women are sinners, they are a necessary evil because they help to maintain the virtue of the city as a whole.'

'Well she would say that, wouldn't she?' he said. 'The trouble with courtesans, Oliva, is that they open their quivers to every arrow. In the case of your mother, she could not have been a good courtesan, for the best carpenters make the fewest chips. Maybe it was her beauty that was her undoing?'

Signor Avílo spoke in riddles, but his words made me think of my mother. I often wonder if my mother was beautiful. Every Candlemas, the prostitutes of Cannaregio gather in our church to seek guidance or to unburden themselves. I often peer down through the grille to see if I can see a likeness to me in any of their faces, but I never have. There is a house near St Mark's used for no other reason than to bring up the abandoned children of courtesans. In the walls of this house, next to the iron gate, there is a hole the size of an infant, in which courtesans place their unwanted offspring. When I was a baby, my mother placed me in that hole in the wall. When the women of the house found me, there was a bag of olives wrapped up with me, so the women called me Oliva. I grew up in this house, neither an orphan nor a child with parents. I never found out who my mother was. I started singing when I was young, and soon the women of the house realised that I could sing the harmonies, those notes that made the singing of others sound more beautiful than it was. When I was twelve years old, the women of this house considered *maritar ò monacar* for me. They said that, although I had a face that men would not turn away from, I had no dowry, and so would not find a husband. The women said to me, 'If you cannot have a husband to govern you, then you will need a wall to contain you,' and so I was to become a nun. They asked many convents to admit me, but as the women could not pay the dowry for that either, none would accept me. When the women approached Sant'Alvise, they begged the Abbess to take me, but the Abbess asked why she should take me when all the other convents had refused. When the women told her that I could sing like an angel, the Abbess agreed to hear me. The next day, the women took me to Sant'Alvise and when the Abbess heard my voice, she agreed to take me *gratis*. I had little choice but to say yes, for if I had said no, I would have been homeless.

The next day, I left the only house I had known and walked to a place I knew nothing about. I said goodbye to the women of the house, but they were not too sad to see me go, for they had their hands full with dozens of other foundlings. Their memories of the people that come and go in that place do not wound them. They are like a knotless thread drawn painless through their hearts. I walked northwards through the city to Cannaregio, crossing many bridges and turning many corners. It was the hottest day I can remember. The streets were like a furnace and the sun was like an executioner. As I walked, I passed by street vendors crying out to sell their fish, and spice markets selling cinnamon and ginger. I can smell the spices now. I turned every corner and walked along every edge, feeling the life of the city as if for the first time, for I would not see these things ever again. I soon reached the edge of the lagoon. There was nowhere else to go after that. It was the end of the world. I arrived at Sant'Alvise with nothing but memories of the halfway house and those sounds and smells. The Abbess welcomed me and showed me to the chapter, where I met the *madri di consiglio*, the noble Signoras who made all the decisions in the convent. I was nervous about meeting them, for they held my future in their hands. The Abbess told me not to expect to become a nun overnight; she said that my becoming a nun would happen over a long period. The first thing I was told to do was to cast off my lay garments. I had no other clothes, so the Abbess directed me behind a curtain to the communal *vestiario*, which was replenished with the clothes of the sisters that had died. I chose a plain habit and a white wimple. When I came out, the Abbess told me to remove the white wimple and replace it with a black one as I would not be allowed to wear a white wimple or veil until I had married Christ our Lord. Then Signora Lucretia produced a pair of shears and my hair was cut short. I watched with sadness and humiliation as the locks of my hair floated to the floor. It was all I had left of me and it was being taken away. Wearing my habit, and with my hair cut to the skull, I then had to take a vow of poverty, chastity and obedience in the church next to our convent. Some of the sisters were present at my vows. The others were watching from the choir above. The Abbess said that, by casting off our lay garments, we were casting off the vanities of the world, and by wearing the habit, we were enveloped in a cloak of virginity. I lay down on the ground, my lips touching the stone floor, as I had been instructed. A black cloth was thrown over me, and lighted candles were placed at my feet and my head. One by one, the sisters stepped over me. Up in the choir, the litanies were sung. I remained perfectly still, as though I were dead. I was to be the witness to my own funeral.

Soon after I had arrived, the Abbess called me to the chapter one morning after lauds. There we were quite alone, except for Signora Arcanzola, who was holding a small wooden box. The Abbess told me that all new entrants to the convent were allowed to see and touch the greatest possession the convent had in its keeping. She signalled to Signora Arcanzola, who stepped forward and opened the lid. I looked inside. There was nothing in it but a long rusty nail.

'Take it out,' the Abbess said. I did so. It was a nail, just like any other. 'This is one of the nails from Christ's cross,' she said.

I looked at it again.

'That's right, my child, you are holding one of the nails that was driven through the hand of our Lord Jesus Christ.'

I pictured an unnamed centurion putting the nail against the palm of the hand of our Lord and banging it in with a wooden hammer. I could not imagine how painful it must have been.

'You may kiss it,' the Abbess said. I did so and Signora Arcanzola put it back in its box.

'You must never speak of the nail in front of anyone except the sisters. If the Magistrate or any of his priests should find out, they will take it away from us. Do you understand?'

I nodded.

'Very well. You can go.'

In the following days, my faith became clear and vigorous. I saw no other way for me. I was ready to wait for four years before becoming a bride of Christ. Now those four years are nearly up and I am about to take the veil, I am not so sure. Every evening before I get into bed, I kneel at the altar in the dormitory and meditate upon the glories of my virginal state. Then I examine my conscience lest I have offended the Lord during the day. There is complete silence in the convent at this time of night. It is as quiet as a grave. Whilst praying, I watch the candlelight flickering against the wall. It is a sickly hue, a smouldering, unclean yellow, lacking in any goodness. We are not permitted to put out the candles and so they burn all night, giving off a hideous yellow smell, and sometimes when I wake up in the night, I can see a face in the wall as I lie there, and a faint figure seems to shake the pattern of the candlelight, as if it wanted to get out. But what am I to do? For me, the convent was once a haven, but now it seems to me more like a jail, an inferno and a tomb.

After breakfast the next morning, the Abbess called a special meeting in the chapter because one of the Magistrate's priests had come with an announcement. I cleared the breakfast things in a doze. I had slept badly and could not rise for matins again. I would receive my punishment eventually. The sisters filed through to the chapter next door and sat on their wooden chairs and benches. Ottavia and I sat on the floor. When the priest entered, they covered themselves with their veils. The priest did not smile. He was carrying a scroll. He bowed to the Abbess, who said, '*Prete*, what can we do for you?'

At such a lack of courtesy from the Abbess, the priest hesitated. 'Abbess, Magistrate Priuli has instructed me to read you a message.' He took up his scroll. '*Suore* and *signore*. By decree of the Diocese, I hereby forbid the employ and use of an organist during mass and the office. In addition, it is hereby forbidden for the *suore* to sing in polyphony. Such emotive singing is a lure for foreigners, who come to hear the nuns sing, and who would fall in love with the women and leave money to have their way with them. Singing the mass and office in polyphony may be edifying for you, nonetheless it displeases me. Singing is seductive and therefore Satanic, and leads straight to public prostitution. From now on, you are ordered to speak the litany, not sing it, but if you must sing, you will only sing plainchant.'

The priest rolled up his scroll and bowed again to the Abbess before taking his leave. When the door had closed behind him, the *suore* erupted. Never had I seen them so agitated. Ottavia turned to me and said, 'Oliva, this means you won't be able to sing any more.' I contemplated being robbed of singing to our Lord, of expressing my joy in that way, and I became agitated as well. Why was the Magistrate so strict with us? The Abbess, however, remained calm.

Signora Pellegrina was the first to appeal to the Abbess. 'This is an outrage. What is your response?' she asked.

63

The others waited for the Abbess to speak, but she seemed not to notice anyone.

'Abbess!' Signora Pellegrina said again. 'You must act quickly and decisively. Do not waver when you need to show strength.'

'Enough!' the Abbess said, making everyone stop their chattering instantly. She looked at Signora Pellegrina. 'Do not presume to tell me how to do my job. When you are Abbess, I will not tell you how to do yours, but you are not the Abbess, I am, and so you will do as I say until then. Do you understand, Pellegrina?'

It looked as though a thundercloud had crossed the face of Signora Pellegrina, but she remained silent. I could not help but smile inwardly. The other sisters kept their counsel, too. We all waited for the Abbess to speak.

'Sisters, you all know as well as I do that our sisterhood is rife with whispers, little conspiracies and jealousies, but we must try to put aside our petty squabbles and come together against the Magistrate. We all want the same thing. We all want our way of life to continue as it is, but for this to happen, we must unite and arrange ourselves as a phalanx against the Magistrate. He wants to reform us, but I say we oppose reformation.'

My spirit soared at her words. Her tongue is ever

poised to speak, gently but with much authority and dignity. How I wish I could be like her.

'This is what I propose we should do. We will seemingly abide by the Magistrate's orders, but unknown to him, I will hire the organist to come to our convent for our feast days. He will come in for Ascension Day, and again for the Assumption of the Virgin. I will also hire him to play on the day of our St Augustine. For this, as he will be acting directly against the orders of the Magistrate and thereby risking his livelihood, I will pay him a ducat each time he plays for us. Agreed?'

One by one, the *suore* agreed. Those who loved the Abbess as much as me looked at her with undisguised adoration, but Signoras Lucretia and Agnesina, who did not love the Abbess, agreed with reluctance. Signora Pellegrina said nothing. Signora Gratiosa, quill in hand, was about to record the payment in the book of accounts when the Abbess said, 'Do not mark it, Gratiosa, this payment shall be off the books.'

'You will be able to sing, after all,' Ottavia said to me. Her eyes were shining with delight.

'Yes,' I said.

The Abbess stood up to leave. 'That's settled then. You can all go about your daily tasks now.'

Two days later was Easter Sunday. In all my time in the convent, there wasn't a feast day that was more celebrated, apart from Christmas Day and the day of our St Augustine. Ottavia offered to be let out to buy the food for our meal, but the Abbess would not allow it, saying that none of us was permitted to leave the convent any more. The Signoras once again opened their *casse* and spent the morning putting up in the courtyard ribbons of silk in the colours of our Lady – yellow, white, blue. Usually, the sisters use ladders to pin up these ribbons between the arches of the cloisters, but the Magistrate had recently forbidden any decoration for festivities that needed a ladder. It had infuriated the sisters yet again, but the words of the Abbess had brought them together, and so we put up the ribbons at head height. The Magistrate would not spoil our day.

To celebrate the end of Lent, the Abbess had spent sixty ducats on a pair of fat pullets, two hundred eggs to make the cakes, and a barrel of good wine. In addition, she had ordered thirty large candles to illuminate every quarter of our convent. She instructed me to go to the vegetable garden with Signora Gratiosa and Signora Ursia and we spent an hour there plucking the last of the carrots and potatoes from the ground. Then Signora Arcanzola walked into the herb garden and picked tarragon and rosemary for the pullets. She was in a good mood. After a short service at none, we had our meal. The roasted pullets were served on platters. There were ten bowls of boiled vegetables, and jugs of red wine. The sisters always become a little red-faced when they drink wine, but I like seeing them smile so. It is better than the faces they usually pull. I looked again at the four paintings hanging over us, the golden umbrella and the red pantaloons, and I looked at the sisters laughing and talking and thought that this was how it must be on the outside when people sat down to eat with their families. Our meal took much longer than usual and then we congregated in the courtyard. The sun was low and dull like a plate. The sparrows chattered and pecked at the crumbs of bread that Signora Arcanzola threw for them. Ottavia and I watched as the sisters gave each other posies and linen handkerchiefs and necklaces. Sister Ursia approached us and gave us each a baby Jesus carved out of wood. The expression on His face was sweet and His hands were tiny. I pictured the rusty nail being hammered through one of his hands and tears pricked my eyes. Ottavia was delighted with her baby Jesus and hugged Signora Ursia, who then looked at us both and said, 'May the Lord be with you always.' I did not know what to say on being given such a lovely gift. I was not worthy of it and knew suddenly who should keep it. I left the courtyard and walked along the cloisters. I went through the kitchen and crossed the garden to the infirmary. Inside, I stopped and waited a few moments for my eyes to adjust to the darkness. The gloom came and went before my eyes, like a blanket being thrown up and down. Gradually, I saw that there was another person in the room, sitting beside Signora Lucia. It was the Abbess. I hadn't noticed her absence in the courtyard. She was sitting so still, holding the Signora's hand. I waited for a few moments and the Abbess looked around, clutching her throat.

'My child, you gave me a scare,' she said.

'I'm sorry, Abbess. I didn't want to intrude.'

'Never mind, come closer.'

I stood by her side, looking down at Signora Lucia. Her mouth was open slightly, her breathing shallow. A bell rang.

I held out the baby Jesus.

'That is very beautiful,' the Abbess said.

'Signora Ursia gave it to me, but I wanted to give it to Lucia.'

The Abbess smiled at me. 'You are very kind, Oliva, but she is fast asleep. Put it by her bed and she will find it when she wakes.'

I put the baby Jesus on the table next to the bed. There was a beautiful missal on it. It was covered in red silk and embroidered with golden thread.

'Is that your gift to the Signora?' I said.

'No, it is her gift to me,' the Abbess replied. She picked it up. 'Come, we must go to vespers.'

We walked together in silence to the choir, where the sisters had already congregated. They had each brought their own missals and sat in their chairs waiting for the Easter mass to begin. I stood by the grille and peeked down into the church. It was full of the laity. Men, women and children crowded into the pews, genuflecting and praying. The priest entered the church and the congregation kissed his hand while he passed down the aisle. At the altar, he turned and began the mass. The sisters rose as one and began to follow the prayers. For half an hour, the priest, congregation and we all recited the mass to our Lord. At the end of the mass, the priest covered the chalice with the pall, genuflected, rose, bowed towards the altar and said, '*Agnus Dei, qui tollis peccata mundi, miserere nobis.*' He repeated this prayer three times, each time striking himself on his chest with his right hand while his left hand held onto the altar. I closed my eyes. The words of the priest echoed in me. Jesus saw that I was ripe for His love and I felt the hand of God move inside me.

After the priest had ended the service, the congregation emptied out of the church. The Abbess made a signal for us to stay still and be quiet. She looked at me and gestured that I should keep watching below. It was a few minutes before the last of the people left. Then, one of the choirboys moved around the church, snuffing out all the candles. We stood silently in the choir while he did this. When all were put out except those three at the altar, he left. Eventually we heard a door close and everything was quiet. We all looked at the Abbess, who stayed still, listening. Before long, she seemed satisfied that the church was empty and nodded to Signora Gratiosa, who left the choir. We waited in silence for a few more minutes, then there was the sound of a door being opened and I saw light grow into the shape of a man carrying a candle. He walked to the organ, where he carefully placed the candle next to the music stand and sat down. He turned over some sheets of music and then, when he was ready, he looked directly up at me. It was a shock to see a man in church look up at the choir. Perhaps they did so all the time, to see if they could catch a glimpse of a nun, but we were instructed to stand away from the grille during service exactly for that reason and so we never knew if they did. But this man continued to look up and I felt his gaze on me like cold water being poured down my neck. The Abbess could tell from the way I glanced at her that the organist was ready. Then, in the darkness, the Abbess intoned the *Haec commixtio* and her words rang through the church, echoing off the walls and returning to us over and over. It was the most beautiful recital I ever heard her say. She nodded to me and I looked back at the man and nodded at him. He turned round and prepared himself to play. Soon he began the mass and we all sang to our Lord. I sang with all my heart, more than I had ever sung before and the other sisters did too, for we knew that we had been forbidden to do so and so it seemed sweeter.

'How much does an urn of ashes weigh?'

The painter had stopped painting and was looking at me, waiting for an answer. It was still morning, but I had been sitting for him since very early. I had arrived in the storeroom with nothing in my head other than our singing and the words of the Abbess from the night before echoing in me. After our service, Ottavia and I had walked back through the cloisters, the wind blowing bits of straw into the courtyard. The dormitory was draughty, the wind biting like teeth, but I didn't mind, as I was happier than I had been for many days. I lay on my bed and fell asleep immediately, and I was even able to get up in the night at the sound of the bell, full of the happy memories of all the sisters smiling to each other after our illicit singing. And now the painter was fixing me with his stare. How he frightens me.

'I don't know,' I said.

'As much as a dying breath,' he said and carried on painting. 'We are but shadows, my dear girl. Nothing but dust.' He kept on with his work, glancing at me from time to time and then in his looking glass. I remained as still as I could for I didn't want to provoke any outcry from him, as there had been before, that I was wriggling and moving out of position. I wanted to give him no cause for complaint. If the painter's canvas could speak, I wondered if it would complain at being constantly touched and retouched by his brush. Would it know that it owes all its beauty not to the brush but to the artist who guides its scratches and strokes? No, the brush cannot take any credit for the masterpiece it paints. I am the tiny brush with whom Jesus has chosen to paint. He has always used human beings to accomplish His work among souls.

The painter pointed to his looking glass. 'Take this mirror, for example. We may turn out not to be people, after all, but only their reflections,' he said. 'And it is not we who approach a mirror, but it is the reflection of someone unknown who approaches us from the other side.'

He had no idea that my thoughts were not at all on what he was saying. He thought I was hanging on to his every word. What did he want? What did he mean? His words made no sense. 'A devil has climbed into you, Signore, and has tied up your soul and you don't even know it.'

'I do not think I have a soul any more, my dear child. I see that you have, but your soul is trapped within your body.'

'I do not know what you speak of, Signore.'

'We should let ourselves go free, Oliva, not lock ourselves away. We were born yesterday and we shall die tomorrow – we belong only to today, so why have you locked yourself up?'

'Sir?'

'Why have you withdrawn from life?'

'To protect it.'

'Yes, I see that this place might very well be a sanctuary for the soul. Are you afraid of God?'

'No, I love him, Signore.'

'You're not afraid at all?'

'I am free and fear nothing.'

'Ah, perhaps love is something like that, like fear backwards. You are in pursuit of perfection, but, believe me, there is no such thing as perfection. It is a kind of death. We must embrace our faults, we must understand that it is better to be happy and imperfect. All that your struggle towards a perfect life means is that you will be smashed down sooner or later, for your idealism borders on lunacy.'

I closed my eyes and prayed. I begged for You to speak through me, since I could find nothing to say and had no idea how to carry out the opposition laid upon me by duty. But there was nothing, and in order that I did not fall prey to the dark waters swirling beneath me, I began to think of my soul as if it were a castle made of a single diamond, or a very clear crystal, in which there were many rooms, each filled with Your light and love. I imagined endless days forever filled with such light.

'Look at me, Oliva.'

I opened my eyes. The painter was standing before me, holding my chin up. My vision was filled with his blue sleeves and his long beard. His face was so near mine that I could see deep blue reflections in his beard. He stared into my eyes and I could feel his breath on my skin. I could not move. He had me within his grasp.

Ottavia threw her arms around her body. 'Oh, it is cold this evening! Are you not cold, Oliva? Why are you never cold?'

It was chilly, she was right, and the refectory was barely lit up, but I continued to sweep the floor to keep warm and urged her to do the same. We still had the chapter to clean and it would be vespers soon.

'Oliva, you always do what's right. Sometimes I wish you would do something wrong for a change,' she said.

I glanced up. 'Tell me about your brother's last visit.'

Ottavia picked up the brush and began sweeping again. 'He had lots of food with him: some sweet-meats, fruit and nuts. He is so kind and thoughtful.' The sound of the bristles on her brush rang through the chapter. 'But the Magistrate's priest was there, listening to everything we said. Why is there never any privacy in here?'

'Are your family well?'

'Father is poorly, but he always is at this time of year. The damp gets into his bones. He always says that we Venetians are born tired and live to sleep. If only I could sleep more!'

I remembered the many nights she rose from her bed and left the dormitory. I wondered where she got to on these nights, but I didn't follow her. I could sense she needed solitude. Ottavia is a restless soul, always jittery and nervous. She cannot stay in one place for more than two minutes.

'Look at that, Oliva.'

She had stopped sweeping yet again and was gazing up at one of the *tedesco*'s paintings on the wall. She picked up one of the candles and held it aloft. It was of the Finding of Joseph. He sat on a throne in a golden robe, holding a staff. The throne was in a beautiful garden, with cypress trees and a lake. All about him were men and women on their knees, praying and paying homage. Some of the people in front of Joseph were much smaller than him, even though they were nearer to me.

'What fine clothes they have on,' Ottavia said. 'That lovely golden shawl and those red jerkins. I wish I could wear clothes like that.'

'Ottavia!' I would much rather endure a thousand reproaches than utter one, but her words bothered me.

'Oh, don't be so shocked. I can see by the look

on your face that you wouldn't mind wearing nice clothes for a change!'

I thought about the painter's big blue sleeves, but I didn't say anything about what happened when I sat for him. His fingers still burned where they had touched my face. They seemed to penetrate through my body and the sensation sent a shiver through me.

'You are cold, after all,' Ottavia said and laughed. 'Oliva, look at me.'

I stopped sweeping and looked up.

'Can you keep a secret?' she said. Her eyes were focused on me with a seriousness I rarely see in her. When she speaks to me in this way, I ensure that I mortify myself and avoid asking her any questions to satisfy my curiosity.

'You are so pure, Oliva, so unmoved by all the petty squabbles in here. I can't speak to the Abbess, for, although she would understand, she would not be able to help me because of her position. And the other sisters – Gratiosa, Arcanzola – they would not understand. And you are a lay sister like me. You seem much older than me, but I know that you are the only one I can talk to because you are my age.'

In everything Ottavia and I say to each other, I must sacrifice my own feelings, and so for that reason, I heard myself say, 'Go on.'

Ottavia sighed. 'You know I have had all these visits from my brother?'

'Yes,' I said.

'Well, the man who visits me is not my brother.'

When she said that, I realised I knew all along that that was what she was going to say. 'Jacopo?'

Ottavia nodded. 'We are in love,' she said.

'How do you know you are in love?'

She shrugged and said, 'I just know.'

'But how did the priest not know it wasn't your brother?'

'The priest has never met my brothers. No one has, not even the Abbess. It was my father who brought me here. Jacopo just said he was my brother and no one knew any better.'

'Are you really in love with each other?' I asked.

Ottavia nodded again. 'Ever since we were children,' she said. 'His father and my father are cousins and we grew up together. He has promised to marry me if I leave the convent.' She seemed suddenly to grow in stature as she said this.

'Leave? Ottavia, how can you leave?'

'Why shouldn't I leave? I was brought here against my will and I have wanted to leave ever since. You have grown accustomed to your solitude, but I have not,' she said.

Her eyes shone in the darkness, as though light poured from them, not into them. I could not take in what she was telling me. The walls in the room seemed to close in and I felt crushed by their weight. My world was falling in on me and I could not bear it. I felt warmth and wetness rise in me.

'Don't cry, sweet Oliva.' She put her arms around me and we both fell to the floor. I put my hands to my face and wept. 'Please be happy for me,' she said. 'It is what I want.'

'When are you leaving?' I asked.

'Do you really want to know? You will be punished if you do.'

I realised she was right and I shook my head.

'Clever girl,' she said.

I looked at her. 'But how have you managed to arrange this?'

'The handkerchiefs. At night, I go to the chapter and write a note on them using Signora Gratiosa's quill. Then, when he comes to see me every month, I fold it and give it to him. The priest never suspects a thing.'

Despite what she was telling me, I smiled. 'No wonder you made so many. I thought it was just so that you could earn a few ducats.'

It was her turn to smile. 'We have been planning it

for a long time. It's all arranged,' she said.

I looked at my sister in a new light. Everything she was telling me crowded my mind and I was unable to take it all in, but I knew for certain that I had misjudged her entirely. All those moments I thought she wanted to be left alone were probably the very moments she needed company. I had got it all wrong and that realisation was the most shocking thing of all.

'There's more, Oliva.' There was a smile of victory on her face. 'We are lovers,' she said.

I stared at her.

'Jacopo comes to me at night. He climbs down the tree in the courtyard and we go to the storeroom. So, you see, I am not a virgin any more and cannot be a bride of Christ.'

Ottavia and I went to vespers together, without saying another word to each other. Along the cloisters, the sisters were lighting the lamps. I saw three of them in different corners of the cloisters, stretched against the wall, dressed in white, looking like moths. Up in the choir, it was empty. We took out the graduals from their cupboard and stood either side of the door to hand them out. One by one the sisters came in, like ghosts. I did not hear their footfalls or the rustling of their robes. I could not hear anything. I stood still, questioning myself whether or not Ottavia was a *monaca spiritata*, one of those spirits possessed by carnal lust that I had heard of. There were many apparitions that came to me in the dark places of the convent, but a *monaca spiritata* had never presented itself to me before.

The priest starting mass in the church below pierced the silence around me and I took up my place at the back of the choir. He recited passages from St Augustine about our vows of poverty, chastity and obedience that I had heard a thousand times before and that I know so well, but then he reached a passage about our chastity that invaded my thoughts. 'I in my great worthlessness – for it was greater thus early – had begged You for chastity, saying, "Grant me chastity and continence, but not yet." For I was afraid that You would hear my prayer too soon, and too soon would heal me from the disease of lust which I wanted satisfied rather than extinguished.' Away in the distance, I heard the music of a small orchestra and I pictured a richly furnished and decorated parlour, glowing with light and containing fashionably dressed young women exchanging compliments with young men. I saw that one of the women was Ottavia and one of the young men was Jacopo. Then I looked across at poor Ottavia, but instead of music, I heard her pitiful complaints; instead of elegant decoration, I saw the bare walls of our convent. Ottavia stood still with her head bowed, displaying nothing out of the ordinary, as though this mass was like any other. The Abbess had always told me that the priest used the words of our blessed saint to control the sisters rather than inspire them, and I could see at last what Ottavia felt. I could not understand her plight, but I could feel it. I am told that every soul cannot be alike, but I realised that with Ottavia's leaving, a part of my own self would also be leaving. She would roam free, sending out nervous threads into the city, letting it know her desires, feeling along its streets and into its shops and houses, but she would also be picking up signals from the world she left behind. I knew then that I had to use Ottavia's departure as a test of will and nerve. The words of the Holy Ghost filled me: 'A brother that is helped by his brother is like a strong city.' I had to become more devout now that Ottavia was leaving, for the more devout I am, the freer Ottavia will be to lead her new life.

After mass, I kissed the hand of the Abbess and made my way down to the chapter, where we were all to wait for the convent confessor, Father Brittonio, to give each of us our monthly communion and offer each of us confession. We waited until Father Britto-nio was comfortably seated on the other side of the grille and then Signora Arcanzola knelt before him to receive communion.

When it was my time, I knelt before him and crossed myself. He placed a small piece of flatbread on my tongue, which I swallowed, and then he passed a chalice of wine through the grille for me to sip. He told me what these represented and then gave the sign of the cross over my head.

'Child, do you want to confess?' he said.

'Forgive me, Father, for I have sinned.'

'What is your sin?'

'I have had improper thoughts, Father, impure thoughts,' I said.

'What is the nature of these thoughts?'

'I have contemplated being with a man, Father.'

The priest looked up. 'But you have not acted on it?'

'No, Father,' I said.

'How old are you?' he asked.

'Sixteen.'

'My child, I am more concerned with converting sinners than directing nuns. However, your innocent soul is like soft wax on which any imprint could be stamped and so, before God, the Blessed Virgin, the angels and all the saints, I declare that I hope you have never committed a single mortal sin.'

'No, Father.'

'Are you soon to marry Jesus Christ and take the veil?'

'Yes, Father,' I said.

'Then beware of your sexuality. Only last month, I witnessed a friar burned to death against a pillar in St Mark's Square. Do you know why, child?'

'No, Father.'

'Because he got a sixteen-year-old noble nun with child. He was her father confessor at Santa Lucia for five years and had watched this child grow and he saw her not as a noble nun, but as a woman. His body was aflame and fell into a heap of ashes before my very eyes. I have never seen such a horrific sight. And it was not just he who was punished. His monastery was razed to the ground, the nuns of Santa Lucia were made to bestow their monies upon poor families and their church was made into a hospital. Let that be a lesson to you should you contemplate such a thing again.'

'Yes, Father,' I said.

'Remain a virgin, as pure as Vesta herself. If human nature could allow such a strength, I would suggest that you should flee extreme Love. Because a soul disordered in its affections is an incurable disease from which derives oblivion from God, and from yourself, diminution of honour, infamy on your house, the indignation of your relatives, disregard for property, and ever arguments, fights, exiles, homicides, poisonings and finally death.'

'Yes, Father.'

'Pray for your soul, child, but your prayers must be spoken not only with the tongue, but also with the heart. Your faults do not distress God. I now stand in His place as far as you are concerned and I tell you, from Him, that He is very pleased with the state of your soul.'

'Yes, Father. Thank you.'

He made the sign of the cross again above my head. 'I absolve you of your sins. Love the Blessed Virgin and go in peace,' he said.

I got up from my knees and returned to the corner of the chapter, where I sat on the floor. I was glad to be sitting, for the words of Father Brittonio had shaken me to my core. I knew I had to show willing to be humiliated by confessing my struggles and defeats, but I never knew how close I had come to falling into the dark waters that lay swirling just beneath my feet. I was only glad that I had taken communion before giving confession, for I was sure Father Brittonio would not have given me absolution if he had heard my confession first.

I sat there, chastised and blessed, for another hour as Father Brittonio heard the confession of the other sisters. When the last had finished, Signora Arcanzola handed Father Brittonio through the bars of the grille a basket full of eggs, which he received with hardly a glance, and then he left.

In my bed that night, I lay on my side, wide awake, for I could not shut my thoughts away and close my eyes. Every time I tried to do so, they would bounce back open, like a box with a spring in it. Ottavia's bed was in the corner, near the altar, and there was a spare bed in between. Ottavia lay perfectly still, as she had done ever since we returned to our beds after matins. She had hardly put a glance my way ever since the morning. I didn't know whether this was because she felt ashamed or guilty or regretful. It was as though, in her mind, she had left the convent already. The altar candles flickered in the draught, casting shadows about the room. The light they threw into the corners was a dull orange in places, a poisonous sulphur in others. Soon, the walls would become bloated and alive with movement. I would lie awake and watch the curves swell and sink with the light, following the endless patterns until it seemed obvious to me that there was a woman trapped in the wall and the movement of the walls was because of her pushing and heaving against them, trying to get out. I used to lie awake, terrified that she would break out at any moment and wreak a terrible revenge. I would wait until the sun shot its first long ray of light through the high window, and then I watched it creep down the wall, slowly filling the dormitory with more and more light. Only when there was more light than dark would I know I was safe again.

Just as sleep was beginning to fill me, I saw a movement in the corner of the room and realised it was Ottavia. She got up quickly and looked in my direction. I looked at her. She stood still for a few moments, to find out whether or not I was asleep, but in the darkness she could not see that I was, and then began moving around the room, gathering her trinkets and putting them into a cloth bag. She picked up her small breviary, a gift from her father that she had brought here, and put it in the bag. When she had finished, she looked about the place. Satisfied she had everything, she took off her wimple and placed it carefully on the bed. She shook her hair free and smoothed it down with her hands. It was a jolt to my system to see her stroke her hair so. She picked up her bag and stepped lightly to the foot of my bed. She looked at me and I sat up. She said nothing, but looked at me intently for a long time and then she smiled. I smiled back at her. She stepped to the door and looked out, waiting for her moment. She stood still, listening, but there was no one awake. She disappeared in a flash of white. After a few moments, I too got up, placed a shawl around my shoulders and went barefoot to the door. There was no one in the cloisters, so I stepped out and crossed to the courtyard. I stood by the well. Looking up in the tree, I saw Ottavia climbing the last of the branches that led to the roof. The moon had risen in the night sky and was pouring its silvery light over the sleeping world. On the roof, I could see a silhouette, waiting for her. The white shape made a last step up to the roof and an outstretched arm pulled her up. There was a brief moment of hesitancy, and then the two figures vanished over the other side. For a few moments, I doubted that anything I had just seen was real, as though it was all a dream, but then I realised with absolute certainty that she was gone, on the wing over the city like a cuckoo that has flown its nest.

*

The bell rang for lauds. I got up off my bed and left the dormitory. I had not slept a wink. The court-yard and the tree looked the same. The sky was the colour of peaches. It would have been impossible to convince anyone of what had taken place here just an hour or so ago. It was the most unhappy walk to the choir because I knew that Ottavia's disappear-ance would be noticed sooner or later. It was not like her to miss lauds. She was always so sleepless and restless that she never found it difficult to get up in the night. When I got to the choir, most of the sisters were already there and had taken psalters for them-selves. I picked one out of the cupboard and stood in the corner, not wishing to be seen, but during the service the Abbess turned and looked at me ques-tioningly, and I just shrugged my shoulders.

The next few hours were a torment. I went about my daily tasks as normal, collecting the eggs for Signora Arcanzola and making sure the chickens had enough feed and water. I drew water from the well and filled the cooking pots, all the while knowing that the discovery would be made soon. I knew that Signora Pellegrina would hold me responsible.

When the time came, I crept into the chapter for

our daily meeting and stood at the back. The sisters hardly noticed me, so agitated were they, but soon they turned and looked at me one by one. The Abbess strode in and clapped her hands. The sisters fell silent.

'Well, as you all have surely gathered by now, it seems that Ottavia has disappeared.'

The sisters started mumbling to each other and my stomach sank.

'This puts me in the very difficult position of having to ask you all a question. I do not want, or like, to ask it, but I must. It is my duty.'

The sisters waited for her to speak.

'Bless our sacred house,' the Abbess said, 'but did any among us here today have a hand in her escape?'

There was a silence. Some of the sisters were searching for guilt in the faces of others, while the truly innocent kept their own counsel. I watched these thoughts pass around the room until, finally, the sisters began looking at me. Signora Pellegrina stood up.

'Oliva must surely have something to do with it,' she said.

There was a murmur of assent from many of the sisters. Signora Pellegrina was exultant and I shrank from her gaze. The Abbess clapped her hands again.

'Will all the sisters please leave the chapter,' she said.

The sisters filed out one by one. I thought I could see a look of sympathy on the face of Signora Gratiosa as she left. When they had all gone, the Abbess regarded me.

'Come here, child, and sit next to me,' she said.

I did what she asked and sat on the bench near her.

'Look at me, Oliva.'

I did so. Her expression was one of calmness. 'Is this true?' she asked.

I said nothing.

'Tell me the truth now. Don't be afraid. Did you help Ottavia to leave this convent?'

'No, Madonna Aurelia, but I knew she was going to leave,' I said.

The Abbess leaned back in her seat and stared at me. 'Did you now?' She remained silent and I knew she was deciding what level of punishment to give me. She sighed. 'I need to think how best to handle this situation. You may go now,' she said.

I left the chapter and, with reluctance, went to the storeroom where I was to sit again for the painter. The air in the courtyard was warm, the sky very blue. The sparrows chirped as they pecked at the breadcrumbs thrown for them. This is how God looks after me. He cannot always offer me the nourishing bread of humiliation, but from time to time, He lets me eat its crumbs. In the kitchen, Signora Arcanzola was preoccupied with her work. I walked quickly through to the storeroom, where the painter was waiting, his canvas and paints ready.

'Hello, Oliva,' he said when he saw me standing at the entrance.

'Good day, Signore,' I said.

'Please take your seat,' he pointed to the stool placed under the window. 'It is a fine day,' he said as I sat down. 'You look pale and drawn today – how are you?'

'I am well, Signore.'

'Ah, that is good, for I will need your attention and patience today. My portrait is at a critical stage.'

He uncovered his looking glass and leaned it against the wall. As he tilted it near me, I looked into it and saw a frightened child looking back. As I studied this unfamiliar person staring back at me, the surface of the mirror grew cloudy with a blood-coloured mist until I could only partially see myself.

The painter looked at me. 'You have your menses today, Oliva,' he said. My cheeks burned and I looked away.

'It is nothing to be ashamed of, child. It is perfectly natural.'

I did not know what to do with myself. I felt his scrutiny bearing down on me like a weight.

'Tell me, what is it like to have the menses? I cannot imagine it,' he said, but I could not speak for shame.

'Quiet as a mouse, as usual,' he said. There followed a period of silence as he went about dabbing paint onto his canvas. 'The Abbess has told me of the disappearance of the novice nun,' he said. 'You were close to her, weren't you?'

I would not be drawn into talking to him.

'Ah, loyal to the end. You know, I cannot blame her for leaving. Your city has a strange atmosphere. The mildness of the climate, which encourages sensuality, the frequent sirocco, the moist airs, all contribute to make the blood run languid in the veins, and loosen the muscles and render them unfit for daily strenuous toil.'

I sat in silence as he went about his work.

'I don't suppose there can be anything more charming than to see a young and pretty nun, dressed in white, with a bunch of pomegranate flowers in her hair, walking the streets of Venetia.'

He put down his brushes and reached inside his

smock. He held up a piece of fruit and broke it open.
It was a pomegranate.

'The Abbess gave me this delicious fruit from your
garden this morning,' he said. 'Have you ever tasted
pomegranate sherbet, or herbed raspberry kvass?'

'No,' I said.

'Would you like to?'

'No, Signor Avílo.'

He put the fruit to his mouth and sucked noisily.
When he had finished, he threw the peel on the floor
and wiped his hands on his smock.

'In Egypt, Cleopatra used to have her face painted
to make it look whiter. Did you know that?'

I sat still, averting my eyes to resist his gaze.

'Every morning, she ordered a mixture of egg
whites, powdered eggshells, alum, borax, poppy
seeds and mill water to be made. Then her minions
applied it to her face, turning it into a perfectly white
mask, made even whiter by her blue eyes. And here
in Venetia, the noblewomen take after her and are
well known for their extravagant way of dressing.
You nuns are forced to wear such modest and sombre
uniforms – flat shoes, long wimples, high-cut habits
and an abundance of veils – but there is so much
splendour out there, so many high-heeled clogs, fine
silks and coloured fabrics to adorn oneself with.'

'We dress only to keep warm, Signore,' I said.

'That is a shame, Oliva. You would look beautiful in such clothes.'

He picked up his palette and started to mix some paints with his fingers. He tasted it and seemed satisfied. He stepped out from behind his tripod and stood before me. He reached down and raised my face to his.

'Your lips are bloodless because of your menses. This cinnabar will make them look more lifelike,' he said and dabbed the red paint on my lips. He smeared it all over them with his thumb. At that moment, Signora Arcanzola came into the storeroom and said that I was to go straight to the chapter. When she saw the colour of my lips, she was horrified. She looked from me to the painter and I could see on her face an expression of unconcealed desire. I could not stand to be there for another second and so ran straight to the washroom next door and scrubbed off the red paint.

In the chapter, the sisters were sitting neatly on their benches. I came in and sat on the floor at the back, but I was not the last to arrive. When we were all present and correct, the Abbess raised her arms for silence.

'Clearly, the Magistrate must be told of Ottavia's flight. I have spoken with Oliva and she has admitted to me that she had foreknowledge of Ottavia's departure.' Signora Pellegrina cast a quick glance to me and smiled. 'However . . .' the Abbess said, raising her voice over the chatter, 'I have decided not to inform the Magistrate of this.'

The sisters protested. They all knew, as I did, that when the Magistrate learned of what had happened, he could shut the convent down and we would be scattered in the city like dust. What would become of me then? I had nowhere else to go. I dreaded the possibility of having no home.

'Sisters, be quiet,' the Abbess said. When the noise had died down, she spoke. 'We have one weapon against the Magistrate over this affair – his *ascoltatrico* should have heard something when Ottavia had her visits, but he didn't, and that is the key. It is partly the fault of the Magistrate's priest that Ottavia was allowed to leave. That is our position. If the Magistrate finds out about Oliva's foreknowledge, he will punish Oliva so severely that she would probably never recover. I will not let that happen.'

Signora Pellegrina stood up. 'That which is crooked cannot be made straight, and that which is wanting cannot be numbered,' she said.

Again, she spoke of me as if I was not there. A wave of approval rippled among the sisters who supported Signora Pellegrina, but there was silence from those who followed the Abbess. No matter how much they disliked me, each of the sisters feared the Magistrate much more. The Abbess stared at Signora Pellegrina, who looked back at her in defiance, but the Abbess kept up her severe gaze and the Signora reluctantly sat down.

The Abbess said, 'I was once free to walk in the city if I so wished, but the Magistrate has put a stop to that. He has turned us into prisoners. It is for that reason that I wish Ottavia good luck rather than wanting to punish her. It is something I myself should have done years ago.'

We all stared at the Abbess. Like me, they simply could not believe that she had uttered something so sacrilegious. She stood in front of us with a firm expression on her face, an expression that showed she had finally unearthed a deeply buried truth.

The Abbess did not yield and, eventually, there was nothing else for the sisters to do except leave the chapter and get on with their daily business. I stayed in the corner, watching them go. I knew that Signora Pellegrina would not let this pass. My sense of relief was mixed with a fear of reprisal. She would wait for her moment. I did not know when it would come, but it would come.

When the chapter was empty, I got up and walked to the Abbess, who had sat down in her chair. She looked spent, like a fire that had gone out. I sat down next to her. We sat in silence for a few minutes, then I said: 'Thank you, Madonna.'

She smiled at me and patted my hand.

'I fear this is the end of us, child. I have stalled the inevitable, but when it comes, I will not be able to withstand the fury of the Magistrate. He will crush me like a fly.'

'He will see sense, Abbess.'

She smiled again at me. 'It is not long now till your blessed wedding day. Let us last till then, at least.'

'Abbess,' I said, 'I am worried.'

'Do not worry, it is natural for any bride to be anxious about her wedding day.'

'No, Abbess, that's not what I mean.'

'What is it then?'

'I mean that I don't know if I am suited to life as a *suora*. I don't know if I have it in me.'

'You do not feel worthy?' she said.

'No, Abbess.'

'But He does not call those who are worthy, but those He chooses.'

'But I have sinned against Him, Abbess.'

'My dear Oliva, we have all sinned against Him. Our St Augustine sinned against Him most of all, but it is precisely this sin that makes Augustine so holy in the end. He showered extraordinary favours on those saints who sinned against Him, like St Paul and our St Augustine. A pure soul does not love with the same passion as one who has sinned and repented. Becoming a bride of Jesus will make you realise that you should please Him by unquestioning obedience. Perfection of your soul consists in doing His will.'

How well she knew the secrets of my heart, yet I was so short-sighted. I could not help thinking that God cared more for the Abbess because she had deeper spiritual insight than me. I tried to embrace what she said but, oh, how contrary her divine teachings were to what I felt inside. Without the Abbess's grace, it would be impossible, not only to follow them, but even to understand them. Even my simplest thoughts and acts became a source of worry. I found peace unburdening my soul to the Abbess but the peace only lasted a moment. It went in a flash and my torment began all over again.

Sensing my lingering doubt, the Abbess said, 'Let me ask you a question, child. Do you have faith or belief in our Lord?'

Richard Skinner

I thought about her question. 'I am not sure, Abbess.'

'Does the person who says "I know" differ from the person who says "I believe"? What is the difference? Is faith a belief about things we cannot know?'

'I do not know the difference,' I said.

'The difference, child, is that you must learn to trust in what you cannot see. You must learn to have faith, because with faith you let go, you trust. But with belief you cling on, because you are full of fear and doubt. Our St Augustine said that he wanted to be certain of things unseen, such as that seven and three make ten. He says that he had not reached that point of madness which denies that even this can be known, but he wanted to know other things as clearly as this, spiritual things that he did not know how to conceive of except corporeally. But he says that he was like a man who went to a bad doctor and then did not trust a good one. So it was with the health of his soul, which could not be healed except by faith, but refused to be healed that way for fear of believing falsehoods. But he was resisting the hands of the Lord, who had prepared the medicine of faith and applied it to the diseases of the world.'

The Abbess laughed and looked at me kindly.

100

'To become a nun one must suffer a great deal, always seek what is best, and forget oneself. You, my dear child, have been doing that ever since you joined us here. Have no fear, your wedding day will be a glorious occasion and you will make a good bride for Christ.'

I tried to follow her thoughts, but I couldn't. Even so, the words of the Abbess soothed me because what she said had, as if by magic, driven off the devil in my mind. Her words had given me wings and I could avoid becoming entangled in the net he had set for me. Instead, by voicing my fears, I knew I had entrapped the devil. 'Thank you,' I said. I kissed the hand of the Abbess and left the chapter.

The storm that the Abbess predicted arrived two days later. I had returned to the dormitory after lauds and was sleeping lightly in my bed when I heard voices and footsteps out in the cloisters. I rolled over and listened. There was shouting and a lot of movement outside, and then a man – a priest – came bursting into the dormitory.

'Get on your feet and leave the dormitory immediately!' he shouted. I sat up in astonishment and looked at him. His expression was one of cold anger. 'Get up!' he said.

I rose and put a shawl around me. Some of the sisters were already in the cloisters, standing outside their cells in their nightdresses. Two priests were running about, opening doors and shouting, then another confused sister would emerge clutching her clothes. Signora Gratiosa looked the most afraid, but the priests ignored the terror they were causing the sisters. These men acted more like soldiers than priests.

A man, who I had not noticed before, stepped forward and told them to stop. He wore a black cloak and his shoes were shiny. He announced that this was a *visita oculare*. The Abbess said with as much composure as she could muster:

'Magistrate Priuli, you have no right to come here and disturb us like this.'

'Be quiet!' he said. 'As you well know, Abbess, I have every right to do as I please. The Senate has been informed of the absconding of the lay sister, Ottavia di Vannucci, and is launching an investigation. You will not speak again, Abbess, unless you are spoken to. Is that understood?'

I had never heard anyone talk to the Abbess in this way, not even the Bishop, and I could see how enraged she was.

The Magistrate addressed his priests. 'Search the cells,' he said.

The priests raced into the cells and there was a terrible noise as they rummaged about. One of the priests emerged from the cell of Signora Gratiosa and dumped at the feet of the Magistrate a Persian rug, a tapestry and her fine altar cloth of mulberry velvet and golden flowers. The other priest came out of the cell of Signora Ursia and threw down a pile of coloured fabrics and a wooden box of jewellery. The box flew open and the gold earrings and necklaces skidded across the ground. We all stood helpless as the priests searched every cell and came out with long dresses, handkerchiefs, woven carpets and silk underwear. I had not seen most of these things before. They had remained hidden in their *casse* and not been shown to the likes of me. When the priests had finished searching all the cells, there was a pile of the most beautiful and valuable dresses, shifts, gloves, jewellery, rugs, tapestries and altar cloths at the Magistrate's feet. He picked up a pair of stockings.

'Silks? Your clothes are fit for nymphs, not nuns! How I abhor the nunneries in this city and this convent is no exception. It is a bordello, not a convent, and you are all nothing but public whores!'

The sisters looked at the Magistrate in complete fear. Some couldn't look him in the eye at all. They knew their whole existence was hanging by the slenderest thread. It would take only a snip and the Magistrate could send our world crashing down around our ears.

'All of you, get into the chapter now!' he said.

We huddled together like cattle and were herded into the chapter, where the sisters sat on their benches and I sat on the floor. The Magistrate took up a position in the Abbess's seat. In his cloak and shiny shoes, he looked like a crow. He looked in turn at each of the sisters, who could not return his gaze.

'The reform of 1509 forbids the possession of clothes, carpets or other vain and superfluous things improper to the status of a nun. It has come to my attention that you make altar cloths and handkerchiefs to be sold outside the convent. I am confiscating everything we have unearthed in your cells and all the money I raise through its sale will go directly into the pockets of the Senate. It has also come to my attention that you sell the fruit that you grow in your orchard. I will take that too, and what I don't eat I will give away.'

He pointed to the priests. 'Go and pick all the fruit you can find!' The priests hurried out of the chapter.

'Abbess,' he said, 'step forward.'

The Abbess stood up and stepped forward. She

was like a woman walking to her own execution.

'I have been informed that on summer evenings very few of your nuns attend compline because it is now customary for them to eat in groups in their cells. Your laxity as abbess is to blame for the ruin of the Venetian state!'

The Abbess could barely stand still for the anger passing through her body.

'By the law of the Senate, I order all of you to render your spirit more ready for devotion by mortifying your flesh! From now on, you will confess your sins during chapter meetings and fast and whip yourselves as punishment! Is that clear?'

No one spoke. The Abbess stood before him, but with her gaze averted.

'Is that clear, Abbess!?'

'Yes, Magistrate Priuli, perfectly clear,' she said.

'How dare you let one of your own escape! You will all suffer until I am satisfied that it will not happen again.' He stood up and made the sign of the cross above the head of the Abbess.

'*In nomine Patris, et Filii, et Spiritus Sancti.* Amen,' he said. 'I will leave you now, Abbess, and expect greater governance from you in future. If not, I will shut you down for ever.' With that, he walked calmly out of our chapter.

No one spoke for several minutes. It was as though we had all been beaten around our heads so much that we were without our senses. Signora Arcanzola put her head in her hands, Signora Gratiosa began crying.

'The Magistrate has a vendetta against me!' the Abbess said. Her face was red with rage.

That night, the Abbess fell ill. In direct disobedience of the Magistrate, she had told everyone not to rise for matins, but when the bell rang for lauds the following morning and I went to the chapter, the Abbess was not there. The sisters waited for one of them to take the lead and then Signora Pellegrina took it upon herself to start the office. It was the first time that the Abbess had not risen for lauds, but all I thought was that the Magistrate's visit had taken its toll on her mind and body and that she needed rest. I went about my daily chores until the bell rang for prime, which always comes soon after lauds, and I returned to the choir. The Abbess was still not there. I looked around the choir because I could tell that there were fewer sisters than usual and I saw that Signora Arcanzola and Signora Ursia were also missing. It was then that I knew something bad had happened.

After prime, I flew down the stairs and crossed the courtyard to the cell of the Abbess. I knocked on the door and a low voice said, 'Come in.' I opened the door and looked in. Signora Arcanzola was sitting beside the Abbess, who was lying on her mattress of straw. Her eyes were closed and her breathing was very shallow.

'Don't look so frightened, Oliva,' said Signora Arcanzola.

'What's the matter with her?'

Signora Arcanzola looked at me in a way I had never seen before. In the bright candlelight, she looked straight at me, without guile. 'I don't know,' she said. 'Listen to me, I need you to do something for me.'

'Yes, Signora. Anything,' I said, trying not to cry.

I went to the herb garden, as Signora Arcanzola instructed, and picked ginger, valerian, some root of gentian and wood of aloes. In the kitchen, I crushed the herbs in a mortar and poured in the last of the red wine I found in the barrel. I mixed the herbs into the wine as best I could and then carried it carefully to the cell. When I returned, Signora Arcanzola told me to put the mixture down in front of her. She then took a piece of linen from the *cassa* of the Abbess and started tearing it up. On the ground, she folded a piece of the linen many times over and then poured the liquid on it. From her pocket, she took out a small piece of amber, placed it in the liquid and wrapped it all up. 'Here, hold this,' she said, passing it to me. She lifted the Abbess's shift. Her skin was as white as alabaster. 'Put it on her stomach,' she said. I did so. She tore the rest of the linen into strips and, lifting the Abbess very carefully, she put the pieces around her body and tied the poultice to her stomach. Then she pulled the Abbess's shift down again and placed a blanket over her.

'Child, I have other things I must do. Signora Ursia has gone for the doctor. Stay here with Aurelia,' she said.

I said I would and Signora Arcanzola left the cell. I stared at the face of the Abbess. It was so calm and composed that it could have been a mask. The doctor had never been called in all the time I had been there and for him to enter our convent meant that it was serious, but I could see nothing in her expression that showed something was so wrong in her body. Signora Lucretia and Signora Agnesina came and went, but neither stayed long. Signora Ursia came and knelt by the bed and said a prayer. I remained by her bed all morning, ignoring the bells for terce and sext. I held her hand and would not leave her side.

I must have fallen asleep, for the next thing I re-member is the doctor entering the cell followed by Signora Ursia and Signora Arcanzola with their veils over their faces. The doctor introduced himself as Luigi Parigi and bowed to me. Then he quickly knelt down by the Abbess and pulled down the blanket covering her. She was still asleep. The doctor care-fully felt the Abbess's stomach for several minutes. Then he asked for a candle and, holding it near the face of the Abbess, he opened her eyelids and looked into her eyes. Signora Gratiosa entered the cell, wringing her hands.

'How is she?' she asked, but the others hushed her.

After some time, the doctor rose to his feet and turned to us. 'Physically, I can find nothing wrong with her, but she has obviously suffered a huge dev-astation of some kind. I cannot tell what.'

'What can we do?' Signora Arcanzola asked.

'Nothing, Sister. The mind is full of ruses and feints that elude us but cause havoc in the body. The hour being uncertain, all you can do is hold yourself in readiness and watch over her.'

The doctor said his goodbyes and left us to our woe. Signora Arcanzola told me to go and eat something, but I refused. It is not enough for me to give all that is asked of me, I must go beyond what they want. She thought about arguing with me, but she could see that I wasn't going to give in, so she sighed and said, 'Very well. I will get you some bread and soup.'

When she left, I was alone in the cell with the Abbess. I sat perfectly still. I could hear voices coming from across the canal, a man shouting a warning. In the cloisters, it was very quiet. The sunlight lit up a square of wall and I watched the motes of dust fall through it.

'My time here is coming to an end, my child. I feel it.'

I looked at the Abbess. Her eyes were still closed. She had not moved and I wasn't certain I had heard what I heard.

'Do not talk like that, Abbess,' I said.

She opened her eyes. 'You are very kind, but it is true, nonetheless.' When she saw my surprise, she said, 'Did I frighten you?'

I nodded and she smiled. 'You are not to be afraid of ghosts, Oliva. Some are more caring than you think.'

She turned her head and looked at me.

'Why do you look so astonished, child? There are many voices to be heard in this place. Our convent has had many sisters pass through it, but their stories remain long after they have gone. Like a palimpsest, their voices are laid down one on top of the other. I hear their whispers in the corners of a room when I enter, but I know they are faithful and so I am not frightened of them. All the petty squabbles and complaints of the sisters occupy my mind much more, but they are nothing compared to the worry I have over the Magistrate and Bishop. Until our old ways die out, they want us merely to be icons, not living, breathing women, as we used to be. The future of this convent lies in my hands, but my duties as abbess are arduous. I have tried to remain phlegmatic, but it is impossible to feel any contentment of either mind or body.'

'You have done your best, Madonna Aurelia,' I said.

She squeezed my hand. A few moments later, she said, 'I should warn you that, when I am gone, Signora Pellegrina is sure to become abbess. She has been here for many years, even longer than I have. She has been unkind to you, I know, but that is partly my fault. She knows how fond of you I am, my child, and so goes out of her way to make your life miserable. You are not the first, nor will you be the last, but there is nothing more I can do. She has put her name forward to become abbess many times but has never been elected, but it is her time. I have tried to protect you from her, but when she is abbess, I will not be able to protect you any longer.'

Her words made my hair stand on end and I fixed my eyes on her mouth, not wanting to hear those dreadful messages. But she seemed unaware of my terror. She closed her eyes. Her face took on the same fine expression, like the white stone facade of a statue.

Signora Arcanzola brought some bread and soup. I tried to eat, but could only manage a few spoonfuls because of the fear and tiredness I felt. She finally dismissed me, saying I could miss compline and matins. I thanked her and, taking one last look at the Abbess, left. I did not want to return alone to the dormitory, so I went to the infirmary. The lamps in the cloisters had been lit and the flames held steady. There was no draught this evening and it was warm. I walked through the kitchen, which had been closed for the night, and across the garden. The grass was damp after the rain. Inside the infirmary, the candles had also been lit. The room was small, just three beds. In the corner, Signora Lucia was lying as still as a log, but she was awake. I took a candle and placed it on her bedside table. I sat on a stool and took her hand.

'Is that my little sparrow come to see me?'

I smiled. 'Yes, Signora.'

'I should chastise you, child, you have not been to see me for some time now.'

'Forgive me, Signora, but I was with the Abbess.'

'Yes, of course. Sister Sordamor told me. How is Aurelia?'

'She will die, Signora,' I said.

'How do you know that, child?'

I could not tell her how keenly I felt it. I laid my head on her bed and wept for the soul of the Abbess. Signora Lucia put her arm around me, but I could not stop crying.

Eventually, she said, 'You know, Aurelia used to occupy herself by writing histories. She wrote a volume on the East and West Indies and a history of the kings of Persia. You didn't know that, did you?'

'No, Signora,' I said.

'How she enjoyed herself, but that all stopped when the Magistrate banned inkwells and quills for us nuns. All we have now is needles. How times have changed, Oliva.'

'Ottavia has run away to get married,' I said.

'I know. You must miss her,' she said. She waited a moment and then she said, 'Can you keep a secret?'

'It would not be a secret if you told me, Signora,' I said.

'Well, it would be our secret.'

'What is it?'

'I was married. In fact, I still am. That is why I could never become abbess of Sant'Alvise.'

'You're married, Signora?'

She laughed. 'Yes, I am. Oh, I haven't seen my husband for many years, but we are still husband and wife. He was a good man, but I got the calling and left him to marry our Lord. It was difficult at first because He does not like to reveal everything at once. He usually enlightens one gradually and so, for a long time, I wasn't sure I had done the right thing. I'm still not sure, but it is too late now. Do you think I will go to Purgatory?'

'Oh no, Signora, you won't go to Purgatory.'

She took my hand and squeezed it. 'I hope not,' she said.

I slept fitfully that night, dreaming of the Abbess and rising for prayer when the bell rang. There were very few of the sisters at matins or lauds, and Signora Pellegrina took it upon herself to lead the office again. She already thinks of herself as the new abbess. We chanted the psalms and said our prayers but my heart wasn't in it. The other sisters looked as if their hearts weren't in it either, for we had taken a battering from the Magistrate and they all looked weary.

Signora Arcanzola was caring for the Abbess so I was told to heat the water and prepare the breakfast. The kitchen and storeroom were empty as I went about cutting the bread and putting the cakes and biscuits on plates. I ate a slice of bread to fill up the hole in my stomach. As I drew water from the well, the sparrows arrived out of the sky and gathered in the courtyard. They bobbed and chirped, looking at me, expecting food to be thrown for them. They would have to wait. I filled up the vats and lit the fires under them. As today was a Friday, it would be a fast day and so I went to collect the eggs. It was already warm outside as I crossed the garden. The sun was breaking over our wall and the sky was already blue. The cold spring had finally gone.

When everything was prepared, I carried it all to the refectory and laid it out on the table. I got out the wooden cups and water jug. I returned to the kitchen, wiping my hands on my habit, and looked around in case I had forgotten anything before I was due to sit again for the painter. There in the doorway to the storeroom, he was standing, wiping his brush on a cloth. I had not seen him come in.

'Good morning, Oliva,' he said. 'I need a cup of water for my paints.'

'Very well, Signore.'

Richard Skinner

I filled a cup of water and gave it to him.

'Thank you,' he said. 'Are you ready for me now?'

He made way for me to enter the storeroom. 'I cannot stay long for the Abbess is ill,' I said.

Signor Avílo pointed to the window. 'When the sun hits my eyeline, you can leave. Please sit,' he said. I sat on the stool under the window and he unwrapped his looking glass and leaned it against the wall next to me. I avoided looking into it. He stepped behind his tripod and looked at me.

'I know the Abbess is ill. Will she die?' he asked.

'I think so, Signore.'

'Has her soul forsaken her body,' he asked, 'or has God forsaken her soul?'

'God has not forsaken her soul, Signore, I am sure of that.'

'How can you be so sure, Oliva? There are two sides to every story.' He had his paints and canvas ready and was just about to start when he said, 'For instance, should I draw what I know or what I see? Which do you think, Oliva?'

'I do not know, Signore,' I said.

'Painters have a habit of painting what they see rather than what's actually there, but seeing is dependent on looking, which is itself an act of choice. The objects we look at are not only things but also

116

the relationship between things, and between things and ourselves. Men know the distance between things, but women know the distance between themselves and things, which is probably a more important thing to know. Is there more to the world than we see?'

'Of course there is,' I said.

'That is where you and I disagree. Our eyes bring little bits of the real world to our attention, and from these shards I believe we build our world. It is all in the eye of the beholder, there is nothing more,' he said.

'You talk as if you are enslaved, Signore.'

'I am not enslaved, Oliva. My eye is not my servant, it is my ambassador. My eye is the sun of this world and you are the pupil of my eye.'

I closed my eyes and beseeched You to stop this torrent of words. I prayed to You, 'Take me, rather than let me stain my soul by the slightest deliberate fault. Let me neither look for nor find anyone but You and You alone. Let all creatures be as nothing to me and me as nothing to them. Let no earthly things disturb my peace. O Jesus, I ask only for peace – peace and above all love that is without measure or limits. Enable me to fulfil all my duties perfectly and let me be ignored, trodden underfoot and forgotten like a grain of sand. To You I offer myself.'

But the painter would not stop.

'You can never look at yourself except in the eye. I, however, can look at you in ways and places in which you cannot look at yourself, unless with a looking glass. The Egyptians used mirrors to reflect the soul, but I prefer the way the Romans used them – to reflect the body. Am I too much concerned with the body, Oliva? With my body? Your body? Am I a narcissist?'

He laughed a diabolical laugh. 'Your beloved Dante put narcissists in Purgatory along with the counterfeiters. Shall I go to Purgatory, Oliva?'

The Abbess has told me that the fire of love cleanses more than the flames of Purgatory. 'Yes, Signore, you shall,' I said.

Later that day, the bell rang for none. I climbed the stairs to the choir, too tired and wretched to think of anything. I stood by the door, handing out the psalters, and the sisters walked in one by one. They looked like careworn ghosts and the convent felt as though it was under siege. Signora Pellegrina led the office once more and it was during the recital of our vows that my vision clouded. It was as if a fine mist had descended and I could only see through a milky whiteness. Then, no sooner had it come over me than my vision cleared again, like a bubble bursting. I carried on with our chanting and, when the office was ended, I crossed myself. As the sisters were leaving the choir, I called to Signora Pellegrina.

'What is it?'

'The Abbess has died,' I said.

All the sisters turned and looked at me, but Signora Pellegrina stared the hardest. She nodded and, without another word, we all descended the stairs and crossed the courtyard to the cell of the Abbess. The door was open. Signora Arcanzola, who had been with her all the time, was standing by the bed, looking down at her. We gathered around the bed. On her face, there was an expression of wonder and she looked utterly at peace. Her arms lay at her sides. Signora Ursia fell to her knees and started praying. I heard sobs, but no tears came from me. Presently, Signora Pellegrina said, 'I will go for the priest. Prepare her body for unction.'

'You are not abbess yet, Pellegrina, so do not presume to issue orders,' Signora Arcanzola said with bitterness.

Signora Pellegrina said nothing and left the cell.

The others followed her one by one until it was only Signora Arcanzola and me.

'It is a bad day for our order, Oliva,' Signora Arcanzola said. 'Go and fetch hot water and soap.'

'I will, Signora Arcanzola,' I said. I went to the kitchen. The cloisters were unnaturally quiet and I wondered where the sisters were. In the kitchen, I put on a small pot of water to boil and fetched some soap from the washroom. When the water had boiled, I poured it into a bowl and took it to the cell.

'Put it down there,' Signora Arcanzola said. 'Help me to undress the Abbess.'

We pulled back the blanket and I held the Abbess up while Signora Arcanzola removed her shift. When we laid her back down, her white skin was without a blemish, just as her soul was. We washed her body carefully and dabbed it dry. Signora Arcanzola took up a large piece of linen and shook it out. We wrapped the Abbess in it. We did all this in a kind of dream, without speaking to each other. I wanted to forget myself through this work. I wanted no more sinking into the dark waters beneath me.

'Wait here and I will bring Signora Ursia and Signora Gratiosa,' Signora Arcanzola said.

'Yes, Signora,' I said.

She left me alone with the Abbess and the dream

turned into an agony, but I was not yet ready to shed a tear in case my reddened eyes gave me away.

When Signora Arcanzola returned with the others, the four of us lifted the Abbess and carried her out of the room. The bell was rung as we crossed the courtyard towards the chapter and placed the Abbess on a bier that had been put by the entrance. The sisters began to gather round. Prayers were repeated for the Abbess until there was a knocking at the front door. The sisters put their veils over their heads and six of them picked up the bier and carried it the short distance to the front door. Signora Gratiosa opened it and I saw a group of men waiting outside. They took over from the sisters and carried the bier into the church next door. The bell summoned us to the choir, where we all congregated. I looked through the grille and saw that the body of the Abbess had been placed on the altar, with the men waiting patiently either side. A priest came in. He said the mass and the nine psalms for the Abbess. When the mass was finished, the men took her away to be buried in a communal burial site.

As we were leaving the choir, Signora Pellegrina called me over. I felt my heart sink as I approached her.

'Oliva, I want you to pray for the soul of Aurelia this night. Go to her cell and spend the night there,' she said. 'You are excused from matins.'

'Yes, Signora,' I replied and left the choir.

After compline, I did as Signora Pellegrina told me and went to the cell of the Abbess. Her *cassa* was still there and her bed of straw. On the altar was a cross of gold and by the bed was her breviary, with its red and gold cover, its red velvet tassel and beautiful silver clasp. I took this up, sat on the stool in the corner and opened it. I ran my finger along the words. I recognised some of the prayers, but not all of them. I could not bring myself to hunt through the breviary for all the beautiful prayers. There are so many of them that I get a headache. The daylight was fading, so I looked for the candles on the shelf where they are kept, but there were none. I looked in vain in the *cassa*, for it was empty. I felt a pang of sadness as I realised that the Abbess's clothing had already been moved to the *vestiario*. There was nothing left of hers except the cross and the breviary. Thinking that one of the sisters had taken the candles by mistake, I resolved to get more candles from the storeroom, but when I tried the door, I could not open it. I tried again, but it had been locked from the outside. This could not be, for locks and bolts are forbidden in the convent, but try as I might, I could not open the door. It slowly dawned on me who had removed all the candles and barred me from leaving the cell – Signora Pellegrina. No wonder she had asked me to stay the night in the cell. She wanted me to suffer and this was her revenge. I am young and despised. What a cruel and wicked woman she is.

As the last of the daylight faded from the window, like a great eye slowly closing, the cell began to get bigger and bigger. The walls disappeared and the door shrank. I listened for signs of life on the other side of the door, but the cloisters were quiet as a grave. Within half an hour, I sat in complete darkness. For all I knew, I could have been sitting in an enormous cave, one whose walls I could not have touched had I thrown a stone. I did not know what else to do, so I started singing softly to myself. I missed our singing in the choir. I sang the psalms I could remember by heart, and those I didn't I tried to recall by screwing my eyes up and thinking hard. When I had gone through all the psalms I knew, my thoughts turned to Ottavia. Where was she? A part of me travelled away with her in the city to get married and have another life beyond these walls. I pictured her moving every day through the streets, amongst the traders and merchants with their milks and marzipans, oranges, cherries, musk melons, almonds and pine kernels. I imagined her in a warm, bright room, being attended upon by Jacopo. She had forgotten the sisters, her old ways and me, I was sure. Oh, dearest sister, why have you forsaken me? I began to feel very sorry for myself and started to pray. You know, God, that I have never wanted anything but to love You alone. Your love has grown in me, but now it is an abyss whose depths I cannot plumb, and rushing to fill the void, I can hear the dark waters flood in. Above the roar, I heard voices. They were far off at first, but they grew loud above the flowing waters. I remembered the Abbess telling me not to be afraid of the voices, but I didn't have her courage, and I could feel the strength ebbing from me, like water seeping into sand. All around me was a cauldron of waters and fires, and voices. Out of the darkness, I saw three nuns, wearing long mantles and veils. The tallest of them approached me. She lifted her veil and covered us both with it, but I could not see her face for it was not there. It was as blank and flat as a plate. Then I could feel something bite my ankles. I cried out and crawled along the floor to the Abbess's bed. No sooner had my head touched the pillow than a warm gush of something filled my mouth. I retched but swallowed it back down. My forehead was pricked with sweat and I knew my night in the cell would be like a crucible of inner suffering, a trial that I was bound to fail. I lay shivering on the bed. It was the darkest night of my life, and no night is dark enough to conceal what is deepest within us. You must travel through the same sunless tunnel to understand how dark it is. I lay with my knees tucked under my chin. Time drifted by, but I had no sense of it passing and my spiritual dryness increased as the night wore on. I could find no comfort in Heaven or earth, my love could vanish in the twinkling of an eye, like a drop of water flung into a furnace. Then a bell tolled for a long time and I didn't know whether it was really tolling or if I was dreaming it. I opened my eyes and realised that I must have slipped into sleep, but for how long? Minutes or hours? I couldn't tell. The bell continued to sound and I slowly became aware that it was ringing for lauds. I looked around the cell, expecting to see an apparition take off, the last of its flowing habit disappearing into the wall, but the cell was empty. I sat up slowly and held my elbows. It was cold. The first hints of day were creeping in through the window. I got up and went to the door. I held my breath as I pulled the handle and, mercy, it opened!

I stepped out into the empty cloisters and stood still for a moment. I tried to stand firm, but I felt as if I was standing on the brink of a cliff. Draw me, Jesus, and we will run. I would like to have fled the convent, like a soldier deserting a battlefield, but there was nowhere to go. There was a power at work that would harm me, but I could not tell where it was or when it would next fall upon me. The waters below me called out. To jump into their darkness and quietude appealed to me, but I could not jump. Daylight was only just beginning to bleach the sky. The bell was still ringing and I went to the choir.

There were only a few sisters there. Signora Lucretia and Signora Sordamor were missing and Signora Arcanzola. They had started the chanting of the psalms. I picked up a psalter from the pile and stood at the back of the choir, looking at the six sisters in front of me, all dressed from head to toe in white. The twenty allotted psalms came to an end and the sisters made to leave. When Signora Pellegrina turned and saw me standing at the back of the choir, she looked at me with unutterable astonishment. Her bewilderment was so great that it filled me with an indefinable feeling of the supernatural. I felt God was there, very near to us.

I left the choir and followed the sisters along the cloisters as they went their separate ways to start their day. The sky was not yet bright. I crossed the garden and entered the infirmary. It took some time before I saw that there was a figure in a chair. It was Signora Sordamor. As I approached her, I realised she was asleep. Signora Lucia was asleep, too, with her arms by her sides and her mouth open. She looked much worse. I sat by her bed, listening to her shallow breathing, and laid my head down.

Suddenly, I awoke. I looked up and saw that Signora Lucia was still sleeping and then I remembered where I was. Signora Sordamor had disappeared. My mouth was dry. I needed some water. I got to my feet and dragged myself to the kitchen, where I drank water from the trough. Signora Arcanzola was busy working. The fires were blazing, filling the room with oppressive heat.

'It is washday, Oliva, fetch the water,' she said.

I went to the well, put the stone in the bucket and dropped it into the water. I looked up. The sky was already blue and bright. It would be hot today. I heaved the bucket back up and went to the kitchen with it. It took me an hour to fill the vats and I was exhausted. Then I went to the infirmary and the cells of the Signoras and collected the bed sheets.

From a big pile in the kitchen, I put them one by one into the huge vats of water and, all the time I did this, Signora Arcanzola remained quiet. For her, this was just another day, with nothing out of the ordinary about it. She had no idea of the ordeal I had gone through the night before and so said nothing about it, and I didn't say anything about it either. Then the bell rang for terce.

'All love stories begin with looking. Words come later. To gaze at one's lover, as into a mirror, and out of this mirror a new madness comes upon men. Here hearts are changed; intelligence and moderation have no business here, where there is only the simple will to love.'

The painter kept up his monologue, like a pickpocket who distracts me while he steals something from me. After terce, there had been another delivery of wood and I spent an hour stacking it in the kitchen before sitting once again for the painter. My ordeal in the night had left me as no more than an empty, hollowed-out vessel but Signor Avílo was determined to pour into me his questions and riddles. He contemplates endlessly, but he is never sincere and I can feel my strength and courage to resist ebbing away.

'Whatever is the matter, my child? You look as if you have seen a ghost,' he said.

'I am quite all right, Signore.'

'But you are inscrutable at the best of times, Oliva. Your long forehead, lean cheeks, closed lips, the blankness of the expression – it betrays nothing but represents everything.'

'God is beyond all expression,' I said.

'But your face is an icon, so fresh, so transparent that a man's glance must pass through you as the sun's rays pass through flawless glass.'

It was hot in the storeroom and I could feel spots of heat on my cheeks. 'My face is other people's business, not mine, Signor Avílo, as I don't have to look at it.'

He laughed at my reply, as an indulgent father would laugh at his daughter. 'You are so fascinating, my dear Oliva, for you are a little flame of heat that warms up this dark, cold place. I can see clearly how the sisters all grapple with notions of pride, vanity and self-love, but you are not like them. There is an energy in you that you channel into something you believe in one hundred per cent. You know it could destroy you, yet you continue with joy. Your way of being is excessive, never giving up, right to the bitter end, and you radiate this heat without even knowing it. I feel it every time we are together in this room. Your only driving force is love, but your capacity for love will drive you into the ground. You can't live long like that.'

I was distracted from his words by a bell that kept on ringing. At first, I was alarmed – perhaps there was another quake to come – but then I realised it was ringing for the election of the new abbess. I stood up.

'I have to go now, Signore,' I said.

He nodded, as if dismissing me. 'I will see you again, my child, no doubt.'

I walked out of the storeroom and through the kitchen. A knife and some vegetables lay on the table, but Signora Arcanzola had already left for the chapter. I walked the length of the cloisters and saw Signora Lucretia and Signora Agnesina obeying the bell, too.

I had never before seen so many people in the chapter. My eye was drawn immediately to the Bishop, who was dressed in his white robe and was holding his crozier. All the sisters were there, too, but there were others who I didn't recognise, and I guessed they must be members of the sisters' families. All were milling around, greeting each other, gradually moving towards the Bishop, who stood in the room like a sun and received their benediction. Standing next to him was Magistrate Priuli. He was wearing his black cloak, which seemed even blacker next to the robe of the Bishop. If the Bishop was the sun, then the Magistrate was like the moon. The long table from the refectory had been brought in and three men were sitting at it, talking among themselves. There was a large wooden box, paper, a bowl of ink and a quill. All the sisters had their veils over their faces and approached the Bishop. One by one they kissed his ring. When they had finished, he raised his hand.

'Greetings from the Doge and the State of Venetia. It is a sad day for the convent of Sant'Alvise and we share your loss. The family of Abbess Aurelia Querini has performed glorious deeds for Venetia for many generations and has supplied many doges. She left the triumphs, delights and riches of the world, leaving even her own father, and offered herself to God and to us as a daughter. She set herself apart through her wisdom, honesty, saintliness and truth. Every praise shall be extended to her, every celebration, every glory and exaltation, such that no tongue could list them. We hold her up as a model Christian and an exemplary virgin and her stainless character is recognised by God.'

He turned to one of the men sitting at our table and said, 'Mark her name in the Book of the Dead.' The man took up a quill and wrote in our book. 'As a sign of our esteem for Abbess Aurelia Querini, the next girl to enter this convent and become a bride of Christ shall take her name.'

It pleased me that the Abbess was being so honoured. I remembered what she told me about how the voices of all the sisters who had lived in this place never die and now her name would live on as well. I smiled.

'May her soul rest in peace. Glory be to God. Amen,' the Bishop said and made a sign of the cross over us. We all said, 'Amen.'

'Sisters,' he said, 'as you know, a whole day should not be allowed to pass between the burial of the former abbess and the election of a new one. This morning, therefore, you will elect your new abbess by a secret ballot. You will each cast one vote. There will be no votes by proxy or by lay sisters, which means that there are nine sisters who may vote.' The Bishop gestured at the Magistrate standing next to him and said, 'Magistrate Priuli and I agree that, because there are so few sisters here at Sant'Alvise, the new abbess shall be voted in, not by the normal two-thirds majority but by a simple majority. Before the election is held, however, the State requires that each sister be communed and confessed. After that, please make your election with my notaries.'

Father Brittonio was already waiting by the grille and, one by one, the sisters went to it to receive communion and give confession. When they had done so, they each went to the table where they wrote on a piece of paper, which they folded and put into the box. The Bishop and Magistrate sat with their heads bowed towards each other, watching as the sisters went about their business. Signora Ursia was the last and when she had cast her vote, the three delegates opened the box and spent a few minutes comparing the pieces of paper. One of them wrote something down, then stood up and handed it to the Bishop. He looked at it carefully and then showed it to the Magistrate. He looked at us and announced the results.

'Votes for Signora Pellegrina, six. Votes for Signora Arcanzola, two. Votes for Signora Gratiosa, one. Before God and the State of Venetia, I hereby declare that Signora Pellegrina Malatesta, a very learned and excellent *suora*, has been elected abbess *con unione et pace* and, from this day forward, shall be addressed by you as Madonna Pellegrina. Abbess Pellegrina has the full confidence of the State and the

Church. Having been obedient for many years, the time has now come for her to rule. It is necessary to have only one figure in charge, and you should liken the rule of Abbess Pellegrina to the rule of God. The Doge sends his apologies that he cannot be here today to marry the new abbess, but he sends me in his place. Come forward, Abbess.'

Signora Pellegrina knelt before the Bishop and kissed his ring. From his robe, the Bishop took out a ring and put it on her finger.

'The Doge gives you in marriage this ring of topaz.'

He handed her a set of keys.

'Take the keys to this convent as insignia of your rank and position. *In nomine Patris, et Filii, et Spiritus Sancti.* Amen.'

We all said, 'Amen.' Signora Pellegrina sat on a chair next to the Bishop and he gave her the crozier. Holding the crozier in one hand, and the keys in the other, she gave a long oration in Latin. Her voice sounded far away and I did not understand a word of it. I tried to pray for Signora Pellegrina, who had caused me so many disturbances, but could not. I had tried to do as many things for her as I could, but she had nothing in store for me except trial and torment. Signora Lucia told me that I must be sanguine.

She said that whenever Signora Pellegrina taunted me, I was to remember that the devil was mixed up in it, for it was certainly he who made one see so many disagreeable traits in another. I must not let the devil do his work. I must set myself to do for Signora Pellegrina the same as I would do for one I loved dearly and so, whenever I was tempted to speak unpleasantly to her, I held my tongue. When she had finished her oration, we all stood and ended the election of Signora Pellegrina by singing a *Te Deum*. I sang with all my heart for the soul of the Abbess, for I knew that something had changed for ever and there was no going back.

The next morning, we had our first chapter meeting under the rule of the new Abbess. There was a hush among the sisters as we waited. Signora Pellegrina was late but I knew she had delayed her arrival to create such an effect. When the door finally opened, she came in as though she were floating on air. She looked at no one and sat in the Abbess's chair as though it were a throne.

'Good day, sisters,' she said. 'From this day forward, under my governance, I declare that this convent shall observe with greater devotion the hours of our office and our duty to the Bishop. Gone are the conventual ways of the former abbess. From now on, we shall give the Magistrate no more cause for concern.'

Signora Arcanzola and Signora Gratiosa received this warning without response, but in the silence, I could sense their reluctance.

'The Bishop and I have spoken and my first decree is that the portrait of the former abbess will be terminated. Oliva?'

'Yes, Abbess,' I said.

'You will no longer sit for the *tedesco*.'

'Yes, Abbess,' I said.

'The *tedesco* may keep the commission paid by Abbess Querini but he is dismissed and must not return to our convent. You may all now leave and carry on with your daily tasks.'

With that, the sisters and I left the chapter. As I walked along the cloisters, I felt a great weight lifting from my shoulders. Signora Pellegrina thought that she was wounding me further, but she was mistaken, for I was glad that I would not have to sit for the painter ever again.

As the sisters gathered in the choir for sext, I handed out the psalters and we proceeded to chant the twenty psalms. Signora Pellegrina stood at the head of the choir and led the prayers. It was as if nothing had changed at all. After the office, I went about my daily chores as normal, but nothing was at all normal. We had all passed through the eye of a storm and these days felt like the calm before another storm, one which was surely coming. I spent the rest of the morning working with Signora Arcanzola in the kitchen preparing the day's food and water. As we worked, Signora Arcanzola kneaded the dough with fury and I wondered what could be troubling her so.

'Shall I add more water, Signora?' I said.

'Yes,' she said.

I poured a little drop of water onto the mixture and said, 'The words of the Bishop about the Abbess were fine, weren't they?'

'They were, my child.'

'It is a pity the Doge could not be here. I have never seen him,' I said.

'The Doge will no longer attend any of our ceremonies, Oliva.'

'Why not?'

'Goodness me, child, do you not have eyes in your head? Because in the eyes of the republic, we at Sant'Alvise are all sinners and his absence is our punishment.' She continued to pummel the dough.

'Are we bad, Signora?' I asked.

'No, of course we're not. We are no worse than any other convent in Venetia, but he thinks we are all bad. He wishes to contain us, but we are not for containing, let me tell you!'

The Signora was in such a bad mood that I said nothing more. We placed the dough in six small tins and put them in the oven. I collected eggs and cleaned out the chicken coop. An hour later, the bread was ready. When we had taken it out of the oven to cool, Signora Arcanzola said that she had to attend to something and left me in the kitchen. I took a stool out and sat by the door, looking out into the garden. I was so used to being surrounded by white and dove-grey walls that it was always a shock to see how green the grass was. The walls were such cold, dead barriers, and I had taken on the colour of those walls, but the green of the grass seemed so alive. The colour cleansed and soothed my eyes.

'Oliva.'

I jumped out of my skin and turned around. It was the painter in his smock and enormous blue sleeves.

'Signore, the new Abbess has instructed me not to sit for you any more.'

'Yes, I know, but I am almost finished and need you only for a short while longer. Will you help me finish my picture?'

'But the Abbess, Signore,' I said.

'It will be our secret, Oliva. I need you only for a short time. Come.' With that, he vanished inside the storeroom.

I did not know if I should enter. Who was I to obey? Was I to incur the wrath of Signora Pellegrina, or the Bishop's painter? Unwilling though I was, I found myself getting up and following him into the storeroom. His stand and paints were at the ready, as usual.

'Sit, child,' he said. I sat under the window and assumed the position he had asked of me.

'I am sorry for your loss, Oliva,' he said as he leaned his looking glass against the wall. 'I know the Abbess was like a mother to you.'

'She was, Signore,' I said. I would not cry in front of him.

'It is a sad day when we lose those we love. When I was younger, I used to be visited every day by a young girl who attached herself to me. At first she was my model, but she wanted more than that from me and she soon became my mistress. She was young and very compliant, obedient even. The girls in Venetia are beautiful; also because, odd though it may seem in a city filled with painters, they consent much more readily to be your mistress than your model. They understand love better than art. One day, she presented me with a birdcage. Inside were two petals, one from a rose and the other a lily, three leaves and a flower. I grew to love this young girl and came to realise why a caged bird sings. That woman's heart was to me once a place of refuge, but now she is dead.'

'The Abbess always told me that death is a part of life,' I said.

'Such wise words, but do you really believe that? Is there a light brighter than the midday sun that guides you, that shines light on the truth in the depths of your heart?'

He waited for me to reply, but I was thinking of his dead mistress. How old was she? How did she die? What were her feelings and thoughts?

'Such attachments are an encumbrance to spiritual lightness, my dear Oliva. Once you go down that path, there is no return. And the older you get, the further away from yourself you drift, so you remake your world. Although a part of me died with her, I feel more alive now than ever. I have maintained my passion for her after death, and that is the essence of eroticism.'

The past few days had been in such disarray that I was still very drained. After sitting for the painter,

I went to my dormitory and, even though it was the middle of the day, I dived into my bed of straw as though it were oblivion. But I didn't sleep, yet I had a dream so vivid that I will never forget it in all my life. I dreamed I was by a lake, just like the one in the painter's picture. Clouds were moving quickly over the water and on the shore stood the painter. He was dressed in the Magistrate's black cloak. He opened his mouth to speak but a red rose bloomed out of his mouth and the petals dropped like tears. Let me pass through the door to Eden, I said. Horned dwarf, let me pass through the woodlands and the fields untouched. I want my freedom, I said, not this world or a dream. I want my human love, even if it only lives in a dirty corner. The dwarf was going to speak to me with words that would poison like tin or talcum, but I knew what to do with a rusty pin. There was a fir tree on the lake shore and then I was a leaf on the water. The fir tree was now very far away. I was in the middle of the lake, but the lake had turned into a rough sea. Its turbulent waves pitched me up and down, then night fell. The water continued to pitch me up and down when I woke up to see that Signora Ursia was stirring me from sleep.

'Wake up, child. We've been looking for you everywhere,' she said.

'What is the matter, Signora?'

'It is Lucia. She's fading.'

I stared at her.

'Come with me, quickly,' she said.

I put on my clogs and followed the Signora out of the dormitory. She walked ahead of me down the cloisters. The sun was shining brightly in the court-yard, which was alive with the sound of countless sparrows chirping and pecking at the ground. We walked across the garden and entered the infirmary. It was much brighter than usual inside for many candles had been lit. Signora Sordamor was watching over Signora Lucia. Signora Arcanzola and Signora Gratiosa were there, too. All were standing still, look-ing at her. I have heard that the dying gather things around them at the last. A kind of numbness gripped me. I walked up to the bed. She lay very still. I took her hand. It was cold. She moved her head a little.

'My little sparrow,' she said.

'Yes, Signora.'

'Good,' she said.

She raised her arm at Signora Sordamor, who picked up the breviary from the table next to the bed and gave it to Signora Lucia.

'I leave this to you, Arcanzola,' she said. Signora Arcanzola took it and crossed herself three times.

Signora Sordamor then picked up a wooden cross and placed it in Lucia's hands. 'This I give to you, Gratiosa,' she said.

Signora Gratiosa stepped forward and accepted the cross. She took Lucia's hand and kissed it. Signora Sordamor then gave Lucia the wooden baby Jesus that I had given her. She said, 'Ursia, you made this beautiful baby with your own hands. Keep it and do not give it to another novice until you find one as worthy as Oliva.'

'I promise, Lucia,' Signora Ursia said.

The Signora turned her head towards me and smiled. 'So, you see, child, I have nothing left to give, except for the most important thing I have to offer. To you I leave my heart, for, in you, my heart has found its faithful echo.'

At that moment, the flames on the candles turned blue and I knew there was a ghost nearby. She never took her eyes off me. It was terrible. We stayed like that for some minutes, and then Signora Sordamor bent over Lucia and gently closed her eyes. I could no longer stand upright for exhaustion and grief. But I couldn't believe it – she had died so nobly, without a shudder, without a gasp, without the life and the light of her soul even vanishing from the eyes looking on us to the end. I grabbed her hand

and sobbed on the bed. I felt the arms of the sisters on me, trying to console me, and I heard their voices in my ears, trying to comfort me, but it was no use. I was losing everyone I held dearest to me. They were leaving me for ever and I could not bear it, but angels do not stay on earth. I cried for Lucia and the Abbess. I wept for Ottavia, who may have forgotten all about me, but most of all, I cried for myself. What would become of me? Death was everywhere.

Today, my only guide is self-abandonment. I have no other compass. I found myself at the doorway to the storeroom, where I expected to see him, and I did. The room was dark, with only a single candle lit. He had his back to me and was looking into his mirror, but I could not see his reflection. He was standing there, as real as day, yet he had no reflection. How could this be? I stood quietly in the doorway so as not to be noticed. It was impossible for him to be a man and not have a reflection. I realised that there was only one possible answer, which was that he did not possess a soul. And then it all made sense to me – he did not have a soul because he really was the devil.

At that moment, he turned to me and said, 'My dear Oliva, I knew that you would come back to me.' His beard was the devil's, his smock and his blue sleeves. He had such gall. The floor moved like dark water as I walked to the stool and sat down. He placed his looking glass next to me.

'This is the last occasion you and I shall meet, Oliva,' he said. His voice was the trumpets of Hell, sounding the arrival of doomsday. 'And so we have no more time to waste.'

He swelled with pride before me.

'I will confess, Oliva, that I have an avid desire to possess you,' he said and put his maulstick against my chest. 'There are those who think that as soon as a young girl has put on a veil, she has neither passion nor desire and breathes nothing but piety and devotion, but they are wrong. It is impossible to change the heart as easily as the habit. I know, Oliva, that beneath your habit lies a heart full of appetite.'

He raised my habit with his stick and looked at my bare legs. I saw fangs in his teeth and his smile was that of a fiend. I knew nothing of evil, so I was afraid to meet it. I could not meet it but I had not yet found out that nothing can be unclean for those who have clean hearts and that a simple, virtuous soul sees evil in nothing, for evil exists not in things but in corrupt hearts. Is there a light that guides me, a light that shines like a star in my heart, guiding me more surely than the midday sun? No, there isn't. I am nothing more than an open book and You can read my every thought. In me, You have created a poor savage with no guide but natural law, and it is to my heart that You have not deigned to stoop.

I said to him, 'You stood before the Gates of Horn and Ivory and had a choice, but you chose to step through the Gate of Ivory. You do nothing but deceive and confuse. You would contrive matter till it is smooth to the eye, botched inside, but smooth to the eye. I cannot pray for you any longer. You should be certain that your diabolical art will not enable you to prosper. Your brother will break your neck in the end and put you prostrate in the bottom of an abyss with your ancestors in eternal torment.'

He reached out with his other hairy hand and touched me where in all modesty I should never have been touched. 'I will dress you in a yellow linen robe, paint two crosses on it and watch you burn at the stake, consumed by flames and devils!' The mists that had surrounded me sank into my soul and smothered it so. How I pity those who have lost their soul. All before me was a darkness as black as pitch, a night of annihilation. My suffering increased as I grew weary of the surrounding darkness, and the voice of the unbeliever came out of the darkness to mock me. 'I wish to possess you, Oliva,' it said.

Such a rage took hold of me and I lashed out at the looking glass. It smashed into a thousand pieces. I took hold of one of the slivers of glass and stood. I said to the voice, 'You wish to extinguish the light of the convent and turn us into a spectacle for the whole world, but you are the foulest blasphemer and denier of God and the saints and I will propel your soul into the heat of the fire and the light of the sun!'

I stabbed again and again and I felt something cold and sharp penetrate me. The centre of my being pushed up to my breast and a surge of blood filled my mouth. Bright red blood poured down the front of my robe and stained it for ever. When they arrived in my vision, his eyes looked at me in horror and exploded like drops of water on glass. The light in them was extinguished. Waves of delicious peace flooded my soul. I was free and need not fear anything any more. The strings securing my knees went slack and I collapsed.

Author's Note

Although *The Mirror* is a work of fiction, it could not have been written without the emerging body of research and writing on the lives of nuns in Renaissance Italy. In particular, I am indebted to the work done in this field by Dr Mary Laven and Professor Kate Lowe. For his help in the Courtauld Institute library, I would like to thank Mr Peter Wood. Thanks are also due to Sam Thorp and Chris Yandell for reading early drafts, to Jacqueline Crooks for her comments, and to Christian Patracchini for the Venetian proverbs. *The Mirror* is dedicated to all the nuns, past, present and future, of Sant'Alvise.

THE VELVET GENTLEMAN

The smallest work by Satie is small in the way a keyhole is small. Everything changes when you put your eye to it.

Jean Cocteau

He was one of those capricious plants which produces a strange, unique flower in some solitary and inaccessible place.

Louis Durey

Satie remains the pauper who can keep nothing, but always loses, in the end himself – and who thus possibly finds the truth.

Dieter Schnebel

Day One

I died yesterday. I was 59 years of age, which most people would consider old, but not me. All the years I was young people said to me: 'You will see when you are 50.' When I was 50, I didn't see anything. Growing old is a habit I never acquired because I was always too busy living.

My life was a neverending search for whiteness. But my search has, except for a few brief moments, been in vain. I wanted to live every day as if it were my first, & my last, but the exigencies of life kept me from the purity of my purpose. My death, however, was calm & well ordered, just how I wanted it.

After I died, I woke up to find myself standing in what appears to be a decrepit railway station. I can see no further than a few metres since the clouds swirl in, obliterating everything beyond the platform & the large building in front of me. There are many other people standing nearby, all ages & sizes. I wonder if there is another Frenchman among them? Two men are standing on the platform, watching us. One is wearing a grey three-piece suit, the other blue overalls. They don't move, they just point us up some steps. They don't look like station guards, but I suppose they must be sentinels of some sort. With the others, I walk up the stone steps & through a large door with an assortment of casement windows. I count the steps; there are 10.

In the large waiting area, the floor & walls are bare concrete & water appears to be dripping from the floor above. Our footsteps & the dripping water are the only sounds. Such dilapidation is delightful. A queue quickly forms at a counter, behind which an African woman is sitting. When it is my turn, I prop my umbrella on my arm & tip my bowler hat at her. She asks me for my name & I reply, 'Monsieur Satie, Erik. *Compositeur de Musique*.' I push one of my handwritten cards under the glass. The card seems to interest her & after inspecting it, she regards me with her round, rheumy eyes. Then she runs her finger down a list of names & points me to where, presumably, I am to wait.

The antechamber I enter is enormous & chilly. There are a dozen park benches made of wood along the walls, all of them occupied. I find a space & sit down, propping my umbrella between my knees. I count there to be 22 fellow travellers. The ceiling is fully five metres high, with a skylight. The clouds seem to hover just above it. The walls are grey plaster, with nothing hanging on them. I sniff the air but there is no scent. After some minutes, the man on my right introduces himself. He is a Turk from the Tyrol, named Serif. He, apparently, has also recently passed away, in a mountaineering accident. I polish my pince-nez & ask him if it is really true that the people from his land are fond of yodelling. He replies that it is indeed true, he himself knows how to yodel. A yodelling Turk. Imagine that. He is about to furnish me with an example of his yodelling when my name is called out. I say farewell to Serif & walk towards a young Oriental man standing by an open door. We shake hands. He ushers me through to an office & asks me to sit opposite his desk. Without another word, he sits & looks through a dossier.

The desk is huge, with nothing on it except the dossier. Behind him are three filing cabinets that are as high as the room. To my left, there is a window looking out onto the overcast sky. The walls are once again bare, but this time a grimy brown colour. The man looks up & tells me his name is Takahashi, & that he is from Japan. He explains that he is in charge of welcoming new arrivals & helping them during their stay. He seems extraordinarily sad as he says this. I ask him if he is sad. He smiles & says no. He pauses & then says it is only that he has done this many times & is getting very tired of it. I counter swiftly & say that boredom is deep & mysterious. One simply has to adjust. I expect him to parry but, somewhat disappointingly, he chooses to cede the point.

He folds his hands & says that my stay here is limited to seven days, no more, no less. In that time, I am required to select one memory of my life above all others. This memory, he says, has to be chosen carefully because it is the only memory I will be allowed to take into the afterlife. This is the purpose of my week here & it is his job to aid me in any way he can during my stay. He stops & sits back, waiting for me to speak. I narrow my eyes at him & grin. This is an excellent joke. How superb his delivery is, so po-faced & sincere.

'Mister Satie, I am not joking,' he says.

Well, that makes me sit up.

'Are you sure?' I ask.

'Quite sure,' he says.

I look at Monsieur Takahashi again, in a new light. He returns my gaze, inscrutably.

'Are you God?'

He smiles & shakes his head.

'Is there a God?' I ask.

'I really don't know.'

'Why not?' I ask.

'Just because I work here, I don't have access to any greater knowledge than any of the guests. I strongly suspect someone like you would know more about that kind of thing. Everyone here, including me, just follows their instructions.'

Now, in my experience, one can tell if a person is being truthful or not & I know he is telling the truth. I nod for him to continue.

He informs me that the station has its own film studio. There is a separate set of staff who work there & whom I will meet in good time. Is time ever 'good', I wonder? When I have selected my memory, he says, I am to describe it as exactly as possible to one of the members of staff from the film studio. Their job is to recreate it as accurately as they can, so it is important that I pay great attention to the details. I tell Monsieur Takahashi to rest assured, I am very good at details. When everything is ready, he continues, they will put me in the set, into my memory as it were, & film it. I express my excitement at the prospect & tell him that I was once in a film. He nods & says, 'I know, it's in the dossier. It should make things easier for everyone.' I ask him what day it is. Monsieur Takahashi seems nonplussed by my question but, nevertheless, tells me it is Thursday.

'Ah,' I say.

I am shown to my room for the week. Again, it is bare, except for a cot in one corner, a table & chair. Splendid. I hate ornament. Even the cot is of a better quality than the one I slept on for 27 years. Monsieur Takahashi announces that he will leave me alone for a few hours, to come to terms with the task ahead.

'It's usually a good idea,' he says; 'there's a meeting arranged for this evening in the main hall.'

I wave goodbye to him & sit down. The chair is perpendicular to the single square window, so I get up & move it so that I am facing the window. I gaze up at it. The sky is still leaden. The walls too are grey. The wonder of monochrome.

The table in front of me is made of worn-out wood. It was evidently once stained red to make it seem like mahogany. But gradually, as time went by, as it always does, the red dye has been rubbed away. I once had an old red trunk. Beneath its russet stain, the wood was a very white almond. To open it was to experience an event of whiteness. I run my finger over the table & see that the grain is still stained with red lines. The table suddenly takes on a red hue. I'm sitting at a red table. If only all the tables in the world were red.

My heart beats a little faster whenever I see red. Thursday is red. It's my preferred colour, apart from black, to write & draw in. When I was a young alchemist, I learned a recipe for making red ink: Take a small amount of ground Brazil wood, half a litre of diluted acetic acid & a quarter of a litre of alum, boil slowly for one hour, strain, add a pinch of gum & allow to cool. The resulting colour, a bright vermilion, was perfect for drawing the gules in my heraldic pictures.

One of my favourite authors in my youth was Alexandre Dumas *père*. He used rose-coloured paper for his essays & letters. But I am digressing, forestalling, because I am aware that I am not entirely ready for the work asked of me. A single memory? How on earth does one go about separating the wheat from the chaff? No doubt I shall find my way as I go. My week will be one of extemporisation. Where to begin? Childhood?

I have come to the conclusion that childhood is the period in our lives we analyse the most only because it is the period we have the most time to analyse, but no matter. Some are born old, some die young. Some people, young people, are very old for their age. In my particular case, I never grew up. I had quite an unremarkable childhood & adolescence, with no features worth recording in serious writings. So, I will not talk about them. Let's move on.

At that time in my life, I began to think & write music. Wretched idea, very wretched idea. I was enrolled at the Paris Conservatoire when I was 16 years of age. The Conservatoire was a vast, highly uncomfortable & rather ugly building; a sort of local penitentiary. I slaved over Bach, Chopin & Liszt, but got nowhere. According to my teacher, I was 'gifted but lazy'. I did not enjoy playing the piano & could not sight-read music to my examiners' satisfaction. My teacher called me a 'thoroughgoing delinquent' & I was dismissed. I countered this failure by simply making lists, which, as everyone knows, is a cure for listlessness. I made lists of my future achievements, my friends & enemies, of books to read & music not to listen to.

I went on holiday to Honfleur, where I had grown up. Honfleur is a little town washed together by both the poetic waters of the Seine & the stormy waters of the Channel. There is never any sun in this fine northern town, but this is a good thing because I hate the sun, it is a brute. One morning, I climbed down the sea wall & ran across the white sand beach. When I reached the sea, I stood as still as a heron & looked out to the hinge where sea & sky met. The little waves lapped onto my shoes. I imagined they were hands trying to rub me out & I knew that I had momentarily lost my way in life.

It was then that I remembered a story told to me about my grandfather's grandfather who, according to family folklore, divided his time between boats & horses. He was walking home from a race meeting one day & took a short cut through a forest. He carried on in the same direction, but got nowhere. The trees were like bars preventing him from reaching the immense horizon & he was soon completely lost. He leaned against a tree & saw chaos in the branches above him. The sun set & night closed in. It got colder & colder. As all the poor people slept, the stars came out in clusters. He looked up at them & felt the full weight of the atmosphere bearing down on him from on high. When the sun eventually rose, he felt humbled, chastised almost. There was dew in his hair. He started walking to warm himself up &, unexpectedly, he came across a path. It was only a few metres from where he had spent the night. He said it was the loneliest night of his life.

Although this happened in the Past before I was

born, I continue to relive this story in my imagination, & my oldest memories are therefore 100 years old, perhaps more. I knew I was closer in spirit to my grandfather's grandfather than to any of my teachers. By reaching into my atavistic Past, I would be able to make my mark on the world. I decided that it was time to make a few promises to myself for the future. I surmised that the earlier in life one makes a promise to oneself, the greater the chance of it being fulfilled.

Standing alone on the white expanse of sand, I promised that I would attain the dignity of solitude that had been achieved by my fine ancestor. I would live alone in my cosmos, which was that of childhood. I, who came from a happy, gentle people, would cultivate courage in order to confront a world that was harsh, destitute & cold. I vowed to change the spelling of my Christian name from Eric to Erik, in honour of my ancient Viking ancestry. I composed my first piece that night, which I entitled *Allegro*. It was the first of my giant steps.

I returned to Paris to discover that Victor Hugo had died. Just as I had made my bargain with life, he had made his deal with death. In his will he wrote: 'I give 50,000 francs to the poor. I desire to be carried to the cemetery in one of their hearses. I refuse the prayers of all churches. I ask for a prayer from all living souls. I believe in God.' Well, he wasn't going to get a prayer from me. I never liked his dreary books. His death & Wagner's, a few years before, were a breath of fresh air. Hugo's remains were collected in an urn & placed for 24 hours underneath the Arc de Triomphe. There was even a guard, consisting of young children in Greek vestments. Such pandering to one man was obscene. Commemorative ceremonies are both false & dangerous, as are statues of famous men. Long live forgetfulness! I was glad to see the back of all the brass bands & howling women.

With my new resolve, I decided henceforth to view education merely as training, & I had to confess to myself that, at 19 years of age, I was not trained nearly well enough. Therefore, somewhat humbly, I readmitted myself to the Conservatoire, to an intermediate piano class. It was here, thanks to one of those seemingly insignificant events which chance uses in order to bring together kindred beings, that I met Contamine de Latour. His real name was José Maria Vicente Ferrer, Francisco de Paula, Patricio Manuel Contamine, but I called him 'Patrice', *le Vieux Modeste*. He was a swarthy, hairy Spaniard who claimed to be related to Napoleon & was therefore entitled to the throne of France. I admired him for his unfailing sense of humour, his generosity, his whimsy, & for the respect he never showed me.

We were inseparable. Literally so, for we only had one pair of trousers & shoes between us & had to take turns to venture outside. I can see us now, squabbling over whose turn it was to wear them. We didn't eat every day, but we never missed an aperitif.

I explained to him my plans to inaugurate my own Church, & professed with gusto my love of plainchant. All this I had to do before I was 25 years of age, because I was convinced I would die then. I used to tell him he should write *Erik Satie, His Life & Works* after my death. How I laughed. In turn, Patrice introduced me to alchemy & Gothic art. When I was alone, I spent my days at the Bibliothèque Nationale, studying plainchant & Viollet-le-Duc's books on Gothic art. Or else, I would wander into Notre-Dame & spend hours daydreaming & gazing up into the gloom. The lancet arches let in the light crossways. The musty air smelled of antiquity. The only sounds were soft footfalls & murmuring, echoing voices. I could almost hear the Gregorian chant coming down through the years & I composed my four *Ogives* in response.

During those days, I realised I could never be a philosopher because philosophers are logical. I am a daydreamer & daydreamers, like poets, must follow their own illogical thought patterns. My childhood was uneventful because I had not realised that I am incapable of following other people's rules. I am a man happy to know only 13 letters of the alphabet & create my own language out of these. This is much easier than to admit my deficiency & therefore be at the mercy of others. My mind is an old, dusty hotel full of empty rooms waiting to be filled with ideas. I like things in order, but dust doesn't bother me. I decided to leave the Conservatoire.

My escape from academic life was enabled by volunteering for military service. When I was 21 years of age, I found myself serving with the 33rd Infantry at Arras, in Pas-de-Calais. I was issued with a rifle, a dark blue tunic with two rows of brass buttons, a kepi, hessian trousers & a magnificent pair of black boots. At first, I threw myself into the routine of drill marches, runs & hard labour, so much so that I was promoted to the rank of corporal. But I soon began to suffer. Every day, I had to readjust my poor, sensitive organism to the rigours of duty. My mind & body began to rebel, but there was no way out. I decided that I would have to become ill in the hope of being discharged so, one winter's night while my compatriots were sleeping, I ran topless into the night & lay down in the snow. It did the trick. I contracted bronchitis & was hospitalised for two months.

My mad dash into the snow was a great event in my life. It allowed for a period of convalescence, during which I found my calling. For days, I did nothing except lie among the white sheets, coughing & looking up at the high, white ceiling. I ran my fingers over the bed-linen, following the Beethoven & Bach pieces I had tried to master at the Conservatoire. When I had tired of their complex progressions, I tried Schumann & Chopin, but I soon grew frustrated with their vapid romanticism. I ceased my finger movements & cast my gaze down the length of my immobile body.

How large the sheet was, how it enveloped me in its lavendered whiteness. What dreams & images were open to me if only I could return to such a state of purity, antiquity & tranquillity? How sick I was of the sublime. Damn Wagner! I wanted something altogether less grandiose. What I needed was to create my own images, not recreate someone else's ideas. Images are so much more demanding than ideas. What I needed was repetition, not progression. This was the door into my world & I had found the key. It was so simple, yet often the simplest things are psychologically the most complex. Locks are nothing other than psychological thresholds.

With this in mind, I began composing in earnest. I pictured Hugo's children in Greek vestments guarding his urn. What if I composed pieces that were as limpid & inescapably plastic as a Greek vase or urn? I began running my fingers over the bed-linen again. What if my left hand looped like an ostinato, rather than progressed? Then there would be a cycle & not a development. If there was a cycle, the passage of time would be defeated because it would be made to recur. There is grace in curves, but straight lines are so inflexible. My pieces would be complete in themselves, but the cycle they followed would extend to infinity. They would not be heard, they would be overheard. Our lives would be shorter than theirs, & the only thing that would remain mysterious about them would not be their form, but their formation. They would seem found, not made.

I composed three white-key melodies over the remaining weeks I lay in bed. I had to commit tours de force to get one bar to stand up, but I managed it in the end. They were three versions of the same theme, like walking round a piece of sculpture & viewing it from three different angles. They were subjects for infinite meditation. The first I indicated to be played *douloureux*, the second *triste* & the third *grave*. Collectively, I named them *Gymnopédies*, after the dances performed by the naked children of Sparta in honour of Apollo. Purity, antiquity & tranquillity. I had found my way at last.

I wake from reverie. I know that I have not been asleep, but in a kind of half-sleep, populated by my former selves talking with old friends. I don't carry a pocket watch, nor ever have, & so I do not know the time, but I instinctively feel that I am late for the meeting down below. I hate being late. I stand & straighten my wing collar & waistcoat. I grasp my umbrella. Time to go.

Downstairs, I seek out the auditorium & find it already full of my fellow travellers, dotted here & there among 12 rows of wooden chairs. There is a huge stage, above which is an enormous clock. It is as big as an oculus window in the nave of a church, but it has no hands. I take a seat on the end of the back row. Sitting next to me is a very old woman who is knitting a voluminous scarf. She introduces herself as Madame Higginbotham, from England. I tip my bowler at her &, as I have heard that people in England only ever speak to each other about the weather, remark on the chilliness of the evening. She agrees emphatically & says her lumbago has been much worse since arriving. I polish my pince-nez. She asks me if I find myself in the same peculiar position that she finds herself in. Indeed I do, I say.

'I don't know if I'll be able to manage it at all,' she says. 'I've not done anything of note.'

'He who strives ever upward shall be saved,' I quote, but she ignores me. To hide my embarrassment, I comment on the scarf. Apparently, it was for her grandson, whom she describes as a good-for-nothing layabout, but now she doesn't know what to do with it. Nevertheless, finding grace in her project, she continues to knit. Several awkward moments pass. To break the silence, I mention that I am half Scottish.

'Oh, are you? That's nice,' she says.

'Yes, indeed,' I say, 'my mother was Scottish – from the Leslie clan. Do you know them?'

She shakes her head & carries on knitting.

'I love all things Scottish,' I continue, 'the tartans, the dancing, the castles. Everything.'

She momentarily ceases her knitting & looks directly at me. She smiles sweetly. 'What about the unemployment, the drinking, the weather? Do you like those as well?'

I am speechless.

I am saved by the fact that four black men have appeared on stage. Three of them are carrying instruments: a clarinet, a trombone & a trumpet, while the fourth sits at an upright piano. Monsieur Takahashi arrives in front of a microphone & taps it. The taps echo around the great hall, like popping fireworks. He welcomes us all & says he hopes our task will not prove too difficult or unpleasant. 'We aim to please,' he announces. Madame Higginbotham raises her eyebrows at me. Monsieur Takahashi then introduces the four men on stage as a ragtime band called the Rhythm Kings of New Orleans. Their names are Luther, Ulysses, Tommy Pride & Joe Sapp. We all applaud. He goes on to explain that they were all killed yesterday whilst travelling by rail from Sacramento to San Francisco & that they would like to play some ragtime tunes for us. We applaud again & off they go with 'The Maple Leaf Rag'. I adore ragtime.

After the performance, I am filled with heartiness & hope for my week's stay in this halfway house, this sweet hereafter. All is possible & nothing impossible. Onwards & upwards, as I always used to say.

Looking around the hall, I see that the other travellers are also quite animated; it seems the music has breathed the life back into us all. I know that any decisions I shall make will not be found among these people. I am addicted to making decisions, but they must always be made solely by oneself. In my experience, this is a cruel fact of life, but a true one. I shall retire for the evening. I tip my hat to nobody in particular & take my leave.

I climb the broad, shallow stone steps to the first floor but, instead of returning to my room, I decide to explore the floors above. I am deeply attracted to corridors & find wandering down their labyrinths intensely invigorating. What will one find? Perhaps, one day, I shall come face to face with the Minotaur & he will finish me off once & for all.

The floor above mine is, somewhat disappointingly, exactly the same. The floor above that is also correspondingly similar. Disaster. But I can hear voices somewhere down it & decide to explore. I come to the door behind which there are voices, & stoop to listen. I can hear Monsieur Takahashi's voice, in amongst others. It must be a staff meeting of some kind. I listen more closely.

I hear Madame Higginbotham's name being mentioned. Somebody says, 'Not a problem,' to which there is general consent. There are other names, which I do not recognise, that don't seem to cause too much concern. Then I hear my own being read out. A silence falls onto the meeting. Someone says something too low for me to hear. There is a murmuring among them, followed by a long pause. I smile to myself & tiptoe away, so that I am not heard.

Day Two

When I awake, I sense three heads bent over me, expecting me to say something important. I'm afraid I will have to disappoint you, I think. When I open my eyes, I am alone. My room is chilly.

I lie & reacquaint myself with my body. Arms. Legs. Toes. I feel light & clear. I have slept surprisingly well. Slumber always appeared as a rather elusive state in life to me. I never really needed, or wanted, 'unconsciousness'. I was always late to retire & early to rise. I fetch my pince-nez, which is lying on the red table next to my cot. I breathe on it before shining it, but no breath comes out. The sound makes a little impact in the room. Phonometrics. Sounds.

Anyone will tell you that I am not a musician. They are right. I am, or was, a composer of music. There is a difference; a musician is a know-all, whereas a composer of music is a humble servant. My work is pure phonometrics. In fact, it gives me more pleasure to measure a sound than to create one. With my phonometer in hand, I work with joy & with assurance. On the phono-scales, a common-or-garden F sharp gives a reading of 93 kilograms.

There are sounds everywhere, waiting to be weighed. But a sound's weight depends on the medium through which it is transmitted. For instance, water has the greatest sound efficiency of any medium & sounds are therefore heavier in it. An ocean is really nothing more than a simple space filled with water. The fish, along with every submarine & diver, bore holes through this space, or rather, this body of water. If the water didn't immediately close up behind them, an enormous tangle of empty tubes would go through it; the sea would be made of holes & would hardly be there at all.

Then there is the sky. I imagine the atmosphere as a body of air that fills space. Sounds are either a dent or a hole in that space. If it's a dent that's bashed into this body of air, it's going to burst at some point. If sounds make holes in space, they pierce the air & their weight is easier to measure. Also, they make way for other sounds. The earth is the worst conductor of sounds, but it too is full of holes, dug by little moles.

My modern-day experiment was to reduce music

so that it aspires towards the point of zero. Complete silence. An inevitable failure, but a noble one for, although sounds become fainter & fainter with age, & therefore become lighter & lighter, they never disappear. One day, I envisage an instrument so sensitive at measuring the weight of sounds that we will be able to hear the remains of Christ's Sermon on the Mount, or Pontius Pilate's troubled mutterings in his sleep.

But let us move on. If yesterday was Thursday, today is Friday, as sure as eggs is eggs. I get out of my cot & walk around the day ahead, by myself. Friday is green, the colour of envy & limes. Friday is the day of fish & furlongs. I have the idea that my task here will not be entirely easy. How can I be sure I will be able to remember everything? Surely it's not possible to remember everything that has occurred in one's life? If it were, one's time would be spent increasingly in the struggle to remember everything &, at a certain point, life would cease to move forward altogether because of this effort. Who would want that? I feel a scuttling in my chest. What a ghastly, grisly task! I need air & an open space. I must go outside.

With my bowler & umbrella, I leave my room, turn right & wander down the corridor. It is like the corridor of a hotel, with doors along it at regular intervals. I've only stayed in a hotel a few times in my life; not very pleasant. I take the stone steps buoy-antly & come into the reception area. All is quiet. Outside, the day is mercifully sunless & rather cool. The railway platform is empty. I recall Monsieur Takahashi informing me yesterday that no new ar-rivals will come until we have departed. Well, at least I can remember something.

I stroll along the façade of our station, then stand still to let its shape sink in. There are water stains running from the flat roof down the grey walls, & windows running in lines, like a government build-ing. Lawns stretch away to a bank of louring clouds. To one side of our building, more lawns lead to an area enclosed with tall, neatly trimmed hedges. Curi-ouser & curiouser. As I pass through a gap in the hedges, I see it is a garden, cultivated & manicured by careful hands. It is a large rectangle, 50 or so metres long & 10 or so metres wide, with only two entrances through the hedges. Around the inside perimeter, there are flower beds. Beside those is a gravel path with iron benches, & the centre of the rectangle is made up of a shallow lake with a stone fountain in its middle. Wonderful.

The flower beds are arranged in neat groups, yel-low alternating regularly with red & white. They are too numerous to count. I bend down to smell the little yellow flowers – pansies, I believe – but there is no smell. Oh well. I decide to take a circuit around the path 24 times – one for each hour that I have been here – then sit down & contemplate the water. I stride purposefully.

Now, how best to move forward? I have surmised, somewhat before the fact admittedly, that I will almost certainly not be able to remember everything that has happened to me in my life. If my memory were perfect, I would forget nothing, but as there are things I'm certain to have forgotten, my memory must be quite bad. Do we suffer from remembering, or do we suffer from forgetting?

This question causes me great consternation. It is an impasse & I have no idea where next to go. Maybe ideas are not the answer. I am not used to ideas, I deal in images & imagination. Perhaps that is a better way? Perhaps in daydreams I will be able to reach into the great domain of the undated past? It is an appealing notion. I look down at my lace-up boots as I stride round the rectangular lake. Very well, I will endeavour.

A pair of black, hobnailed boots. This was the only thing I kept when I was demobilised from the army & I wore them for many years to come. After my period of convalescence, I decided to shed my skin

& to reinvent myself as a Montmartre Bohemian. I would wage war against those who fouled the air with their expressive Romantic notes. I announced to my family that I was leaving to brandish my *Gymnopédies* as a call to arms against Wagner. My father, although bemused, gave me 1600 francs & sent me on my way.

I rented a mezzanine apartment at 50 rue Condorcet, which lay at the foot of Montmartre. For a modest 60 francs, I had made for me a table, a seat, a chest & a wardrobe, all of bleached wood stained with walnut juice & carefully polished to make it seem like oak. My bed was three planks resting on trestles, with a straw mattress & woollen blanket. I installed my piano & bought myself a top hat & priestly frock coat. I had arrived.

The Butte of Montmartre was really only a village in those days, no horse-drawn carriage had ever managed to negotiate its winding alleys. There were apartment buildings overlooking Paris to the south, but once you had climbed the 323 stone steps, you entered another world facing north, where everything was ancient, peaceful & rural. Cows, goats & sheep lived on the open slopes, among the windmills. None of the roads were cobbled, & ragged children played in the streams that ran down the muddy tracks. The old, ruined walls were draped in ivy & wisteria.

I completed my *Gymnopédies* & started copying them onto sheets & spent the rest of my time surveying my adopted home on the Butte. I tipped my top hat at all who passed by. Patrice lived on rue de l'Abreuvoir & we met every day. Whoever got out of bed first visited the other & we spent the rest of the day together.

As I was walking to his room one day, having just suffered a rather unexpected welcome from the most massive dog I ever saw, I spotted a white cat disappearing round a corner. I considered myself very lucky to have seen such a rare & magnificent beast & decided to follow it. Needless to say, the lightning-quick cat soon outstripped me. Minutes later, I passed a hitherto undiscovered bistro called The White Cat. I stopped & went pale at the coincidence. I decided that it was not a coincidence but a sign, an augury for things to come. I went on my way again & was so lost in thought that I hardly noticed an acquaintance of mine. He called to me &, as he approached, he said, 'My dear Satie, you look like a large, invisible white cat!' I was so taken aback that I could do nothing other than run in the opposite direction. Too much good luck is a bad thing.

Another kind of cat entered my life during this period, a black cat – Le Chat Noir. It was Patrice who first told me of this place. He dragged me to a café one morning & ordered two expresses & two plum brandies. I was a willing victim. He told me of this small cabaret, full of *fumistes* – perpetrators of tall tales & hoaxes, who regularly held literary evenings & published a weekly paper. 'We have to go,' he said & indeed we did, that very evening.

The Chat Noir was on rue Victor-Massé. Patrice & I were met at the door by Rodolphe Salis, the founder & Master of Ceremonies. I looked into his bloodhound face with its hangdog expression & introduced myself: 'Erik Satie, *gymnopédiste!*' He didn't bat an eyelid, but bowed deeply & replied, 'That's a very fine profession,' & waved us inside. As we walked in, a huge Swiss guard knocked his halberd three times on the wooden floor & announced our arrival.

The interior was gloomy, with chocolate-brown tables, benches & chairs. The wood was battered & scratched. The chipped walls were painted olive green & had either large murals on them or clusters of paintings & framed pictures. Hanging from the ceiling were muskets, swords, caskets & cups once used by Charlemagne.

There was a little theatre, which put on shadow plays & puppet shows accompanied by a harmonium. A small podium was where the *fumistes* came on to recite filthy poems or sing dirty songs. The main entertainment of the evening was the humorous sketches performed by all & sundry. While all this was going on, Salis welcomed every guest, subtly insulting them as they entered. Then he prepared glasses of absinthe & poured bocks of beer, which were served by waiters dressed as academicians. I looked upon all this with glee & gratitude. Here was my spiritual home, at last.

My modus vivendi had revealed itself to me & I let loose my pent-up exuberance on the world. In the street with Patrice the next morning, I took off my clothes, rolled them into a ball & stamped on them. I dragged them through the mud & poured dirty rainwater on them. I punched my hat to put a dent in it, ripped the soles off my shoes & tore my tie to ribbons. I decided to stop trimming my beard & let my hair grow wild. I was free.

Salis nicknamed me 'the Greek musician' & gave me employment at his marvellous establishment as the accompanying harmonium player. It was there I met another of my *vieux frères* – Alphonse Allais, who also hailed from Honfleur & whose family knew mine. When I wasn't playing, I would sit with him in a gloomy corner with an absinthe & listen as he talked about his paintings. He belonged to the group Les Incohérents & had exhibited all his monochromatic paintings in their shows. He described one as being entirely red, entitled *Tomato Harvest by Apoplectic Cardinals on the Shores of the Red Sea*. He talked about himself in the third person, in a style that was vainglorious & florid, but also deadpan. My young, burgeoning life was brightened by his sagacious ideas.

After these meetings, I got out my sheets of music & set about substituting all the standard tempo marks with my own made-up neologisms. *Dolce* became 'Gird yourself with perceptiveness'; *mezzo forte* became 'Grandly forgetting the present'; *pianissimo* became 'Like a nightingale with toothache'. I indicated certain of my pieces as 'Blackish'; 'Quite blue'; 'White'; 'White & immobile'; 'Very white'; 'Whiter'; 'Even whiter if possible'. Next to them, I wrote that these performance indications must never be read out aloud because they were the pianist's reward for playing my music. I decided it was time the outside world knew something of my glorious achievements & so, in edition VIII of the *Chat Noir* newspaper, I published an advertisement:

At last! Lovers of cheerful music can give themselves endless pleasure. The indefatigable Erik
Satie, the sphinx man, the wooden-headed composer, announces the appearance of a new musical
work which, up to now, he says, is the greatest. It
is a series of melodies conceived, in the mystico-
liturgical mode beloved of the author, under the
suggestive title *Ogives*. We wish Erik Satie a success
comparable to the one he has already attained with
his *Gymnopédie* No. 3, currently under everyone's
piano. On sale at 66 boulevard Magenta.

Unfortunately, after many uproarious evenings at the
Chat Noir, my capital began to dwindle. Drinking
absinthe means killing yourself sip by sip &, piece
by piece, my furniture went back, except my beloved
piano, which I kept though it remained untouched.
The piano, like money, is only pleasant to those who
have the touch. It soon became clear, to my creditors
as well as myself, that I would have to find less costly
accommodation. In springtime, I found an uncomfortable room on the summit of the Butte with a
tremendous view. On a clear day, you could see
Belgium. The houses on the summit were set together like superimposed boxes. A room that is experi-
enced, however, is not an inert box, for inhabited
space transcends geometric space. So high up near

the roof, all my thoughts became clear & ethereal. I felt as if I were on the top of the world & certainly above my creditors.

I am drawn back to earth by a presence beside me. I turn & see that a young girl is sitting next to me on one of the iron benches in the garden. She is as thin as a twig with a round face & cheeks the colour of raspberries. She says hello. Despite her wanness, there is something of a minx-cat about her. I lift my bowler hat to her & ask after her health.

'So-so,' she says.

I tell her I have been contemplating the furrows on the water caused by the slight breeze that has developed. She says she often sits here & does the same thing. She brushes her fair curls from her face. A pretty thing. I turn my frame slightly & introduce myself: 'Monsieur Satie, Erik. *Compositeur de Musique.*' She shakes my hand & tells me her name is Loulou. I wonder aloud at all the admirable cultivation I see before us, to which she quickly replies that it is she who has tended to them. I point to the flowers & ask, 'You've done all this?' She nods.

I tell her I am very impressed, which indeed I am. Then it occurs to me, & I ask her, how long she has been here.

She sighs & says, 'A long time.' She goes on to explain that she has been unable thus far to decide on a single memory & has to remain here until she does so. 'All the staff here, all the people who run this place are like me.'

I enquire about Monsieur Takahashi.

'Yes, even him,' she says.

Well, this news puts an altogether different complexion on my stay here. If I fail in my task, I will remain in limbo. Perhaps not such a bad state to remain in, but is it desirable? I elicit from Loulou that she is, or was, 19 when she arrived & that her passing away was due to a virus. There was no name for what she died of & this perplexes her. She asks after the reason for my transition from the last world to this. I smile & raise an eyebrow at her.

'Have a guess,' I say.

She looks at my face, my forehead & cheeks, & hazards at old age.

'Very true,' I say, 'but greatly aggravated by a prolapse of the liver & pleurisy.'

She tells me her father used to drink horrible amounts every evening. She is clearly disgusted at the memory. An old saying comes to mind: 'Birds are entangled by their feet & men by their tongue,' & so I remain silent & still, with my hands on my umbrella & my back straight, gazing at the splendour before us.

The breeze has become a small wind, causing bigger ruffles on the water. They come in towards us like galloping horses. Loulou, a mere slip of a thing, wraps herself up in her drab black coat. The stone fountain is actually a lion spitting water from its upturned mouth. I ask if she likes animals.

'So-so,' she says.

I inform her that I was born in the year of the tiger. She looks at me. I raise my arms in the manner of paws & open up my face & roar like a tiger. 'Very apt, don't you think?' She grimaces & her face takes on the sweetest roseate glow.

It seems that Loulou spent most of her life helping her parents at their café-restaurant, located on a countryside crossroads just to the south of Paris. During the dreary winter days, she tried to keep warm & washed the dishes & table linen. In the summer, she tended to the garden & longed to travel. The most exciting thing that ever happened there, she says, is that the Tour once stopped at the restaurant for lunch. None of the riders gave her a second glance. How sad. Her predicament is that she didn't live long enough. Her short, green life has not had the time to turn her memories golden.

Loulou's dilemma goes some way towards easing the burden of my own. Back in my room, I feel somewhat chastened & rejuvenated. I must tighten my belt & buckle down. Like Madame Higginbotham & Loulou, I must find grace in my project. To get out, one has to go in deeper.

Where was I? Oh yes. Well, my time at the Chat Noir didn't last long. The inimitable Salis & I soon fell out. Over what? Don't ask, for I cannot remember, but the man was a self-important buffoon. Let's move on, I will come back to that.

With my newly gained experience as an accompanist, I quickly found alternative employment as a hired key-thumper at the Auberge du Clou, located on avenue Trudaine. This was just as well, for my finances were unspeakable. It was there that I met my greatest friend, & the composer of music I most admired in my life, Claude Debussy.

At the time of our meeting, I was explaining to a group of bourgeois ignoramuses the need for us French to prise ourselves away from the Wagnerian adventure, which did not correspond to our natural aspirations; that we needed to have our own music – with no sauerkraut if possible. The group took offence at this, but I kept to my viewpoint with alacrity. The debate turned into an argument, at which point I called each member of the group an asshole. One of them was just about to throw a punch when a man, who had thus far remained impassively listening with his arms folded, stepped forward. It was Debussy. The others settled down, for Debussy already had a reputation far in advance of theirs since winning the Prix de Rome. I thought, for a moment, he wanted to throw the first punch. Instead, he said he understood the curious stamp of my musical personality & the hopes it gave rise to for the future. It was the beginning of a beautiful friendship.

Let me describe him; a kind of thumbnail sketch, if you like. Physically, Debussy took after his mother. His hair was the colour of chestnuts & he had a paunch. Overall, he had the air of a slightly confused badger. His character was, most of all, charming, & his flashes of bad temper proved purely 'explosive' & were not followed by any lingering ill-feeling. As soon as I saw him, I was drawn to him & wished to live constantly at his side. For 30 years I had the good fortune to be able to fulfil my wish. We understood one another implicitly, without complicated explanations; we had known each other for ever, it seemed.

We took to meeting twice a week for a coffee & a conference. Debussy presented me with a copy of his *Cinq poèmes de Baudelaire* with a dedication inside: 'to Erik Satie, a gentle medieval musician lost in this century'. One Monday evening, I brought with me a de luxe edition of my *Gymnopédies*. I played them for Debussy but my playing was, as ever, abominable. I can see his impatient grimaces even now. After some minutes of sufferance, Debussy pushed me aside & said, 'Come on, I'll show you what your music sounds like.' Enabled by his profound comprehension of the keys & the dextrous movements of his digits, my little Greek pieces shone with a bright white light. 'The next thing', I said, 'is to orchestrate them *like that*.' He absolutely agreed & said, 'If you don't object, I'll get down to it tomorrow.' Imagine my joy.

After these meetings with Debussy, I would return to my cupboard to warm myself in the corner of my cold. I ate nothing but bread & soup thickened with potatoes & copied out my *Gnossiennes*. I was happy to prefer my Art to myself. I knew that I had to serve it with self-denial. I was putting myself in order; that way I could bring my sensibilities to be at one with magnificent privations. You know, inconveniences are part of every living thing. A true musician must be at the service of his Art; he must place himself above human miseries; he must draw his courage from within himself, himself alone, & there was nothing more sincere in me than the spirit of renunciation.

Poverty had long ago arrived in my life & was never to leave. Not that I minded, on the contrary – instead of fighting poverty, I learned to nurture it, since I knew that poverty would cause me to sin less. My space was to receive none of the riches of the world. Intense poverty has with it a felicity. As destitution increases, so it gives us access to absolute refuge.

These religious sensibilities found an outlet: I became known as Monsieur le Pauvre & became affiliated, albeit briefly, with the Rosicrucians. Much to my personal dismay, I couldn't actually see the great works of the Middle Ages, that great age of solitary patience, but this didn't stop me from imagining that my soul could be bathed in the peace of those times. I took to my room & let small things evolve slowly in my imagination during those long periods of leisure. The contemplation of the minute detail of the world would allow for flights of fancy that would otherwise be denied by philosophers.

When I was not in my cell, or rather my 'abbey',

I spent my days at the Bibliothèque Nationale per-
fecting my calligraphy. The intense concentration I
invested in my handwriting was to be the perfect expression of the beauty & contemplation of Middle
Ages Christianity. I was determined that the formation of the letters should be perfect in every way: the
joins, the down & up strokes, the dots, the crosses.
It was full of serifs & ampersands. I took a full 30
minutes to compose & finish three or four lines &
passed hours practising my signature.

I had printed some notepaper, embossed with two
interlocking crosses in a red seal. On this paper, I
wrote my *pneumatiques* to arrange or cancel meetings. I received many letters from admirers & acquaintances. I left most unopened, but still replied
to them; one must never waste an opportunity to
spread the word. In Gothic script, I wrote two
pamphlets. I wrote manifestos on art & aesthetics.
I drew heraldic signs in gules & sable. I composed
business letters, which was the best kind of writing
because it had a definite meaning; you had
something to say & you said it. I wrote postcards
to my enemies – heretics, infidels & miscreants who
had spurned the Ideal. One recipient was a cur who
had failed to find subscribers for one of my pamphlets. I sent him a postcard of flaming red hearts &

swords, in the middle of which I wrote, 'In the name of the Rose-Croix, be damned!'

At that time, I was also doing a lot of alchemy. Alone in my laboratory one day, I was having a rest. Outside the sky was pale, leaden, sinister: quite horrible. I was sad, without understanding why; almost fearful, for no apparent reason. I had the bright idea of cheering myself up by counting slowly on my fingers from 1 to 260,000. I did so; all that happened was that I got very bored. I got up, fetched a magic nut & placed it gently in an alpaca-bone box adorned with seven diamonds. Immediately a stuffed bird took flight; a monkey's skeleton ran off; a sow's skin climbed the wall. Then night came to cover the objects & destroy all shapes.

Night has come to cover objects & destroy all shapes, once again. I sit up in my cot & shake my head clear of flights of fancy. O my soul. Against the grey walls of my room, the little window is now a square of indigo. It positively hums in its frame. The indigo seems to spill over into my room & remain suspended in space. I put my hands to my chest & feel my bony corpus. I touch my head & feel my goatlike cranium. I reach for my bowler.

Downstairs in the great hall, the face of the clock

still has no hands. There are six tables laid out, at random, with people sitting at them in threes & fours. I spy Madame Higginbotham by the multi-coloured trail of her knitted scarf. With her are two men, one of whom is in a dark uniform. I stand at her side & bid her good evening. She returns my greeting & introduces her companions. The soldier is a compatriot, Monsieur Armengaud, who has a dreadful wheeze. The other is a bear of a man, a Polish peasant called Andreij. I sit & place my bowler on the table.

Andreij crosses his arms & asks if I have managed to select my memory yet. 'Unfortunately not,' I say, 'it is uncommonly difficult so far.' Monsieur Armengaud concurs. 'If I had to choose a bad memory,' he says, 'it would be easy. But a good one?' He shakes his head & coughs. 'When I realised that I could forget almost everything, I thought this really must be heaven.'

It transpires that Monsieur Armengaud was in the Great War, but died of emphysema. He tells me that it was only by chance that he was in uniform when he died. He was a civilian, but was attending his battalion's annual reunion & thus was wearing his dress uniform. He & his comrades were toasting absent friends when he collapsed.

Andreij, on the other hand, has had no such difficulty. He tells me that, without question, his happiest memory was the day of his daughter's birth. 'Monica,' he says. I think it is a beautiful name & tell him so. He is silent for a moment & then tells us that the day she was born, he felt as if he also had newly entered the world. He wipes his face with his hand. 'She looked like a prune,' he says, 'but she was suddenly my life.' Apparently, she is three now. Andreij died in an accident on the farm where he laboured. A beam from the roof of the barn hit him on the head while he was loading hay bales for the winter. I say nothing to this, but inwardly I think, 'What a banal way to die.'

A middle-aged woman dressed in a night-blue gown approaches our table & asks if I am Erik Satie. Her dark hair is short & she has big marsupial eyes. I say that, indeed, I am he. She points across the hall & tells me that Monsieur Takahashi has just mentioned this to her. Everyone looks to where she is pointing. 'My name is Biljana,' she says. I take her slim hand in mine & attempt to repeat her name. She laughs & corrects me: 'Bil-jána.' She emphasises the second syllable. 'I am from Slovenia,' she continues. 'I have heard your music.' How delightful. I ask where & when, & she tells me her story.

When she was 19, she had a lover, who used to play records on a phonograph during their trysts in a hotel in Ljubljana. He had taught her how to listen to music with the body as well as the mind. One day, he made her lie on the bed & close her eyes while she listened to my *Gymnopédies*. Afterwards, he said, '*Douloureux, triste, grave*,' & they made love. 'It was almost like an instruction of how to live,' she says, '& from then on, I listened to music as if I were a tuning fork.' She touches my cheek & says, 'Thank you.'

Well, I am lost for words. What better moment could there be for a composer of music & his craft? I stand up & bow deeply to her. She is about to leave when I feel compelled to ask what became of her lover. She smiles & replies that she doesn't know. He was on his way to study music in Vienna & just disappeared one day. She says this without a hint of bitterness.

'You never saw him again?' I ask.

She shakes her head.

'Did you miss him?'

'I never married; that's how much I missed him.'

Biljana's story reminds me of my own *affaire du cœur*, for which I was ill-equipped & from which I never fully recovered. I'm certain that one never fully recovers, one merely learns to replace.

In either event, Marie-Clémentine Valadon was, in consecutive order: a trapeze artist whose career was cut short by an accident, a model for Renoir & Degas, a professional painter, the mother of an illegitimate son & the wife of a banker. Somewhere between mother & wife, I came in. She was known to everyone, for some inexplicable reason, as Suzanne, but my name for her was Biqui. She was as timid as a mouse, & rarely spoke. I drew a castle for her & called it Hôtel de la Suzonnière. It had 93 gable windows & a steep sloping roof.

After five painful months, I pushed my little Biqui out of a window & onto the courtyard below. I then walked to the local police station & accused myself of murder – wrongfully, however, as my little Biqui's remarkable deftness for acrobatics meant that she escaped from the fall, & my life, unscathed. Once she was out of my life, I wrote a notice & posted it on the front door of my abbey. The notice was smudged by my own tears & I pinned a lock of Biqui's hair to it. It read:

On the 14th of the month of January in the year of grace 1893, which was a Saturday, my love affair with Suzanne Valadon began, which ended on Tuesday the 20th of June of the same year.

On Monday 16th of the month of January 1893, my friend Suzanne Valadon came to this place for the first time in her life & on Saturday 17th June of the same year for the last.

In the spirit of my present task, I ask myself if I have any feelings about this episode. To be sure, the answer is a tall order. If nothing else, my task has taught me not to trust entirely what I remember. I am certain that I am not remembering my life exactly as it was, but merely as it appears to me as I retell it to myself. If what I remember is good, my memory is complicit. If what I remember is bad, my memory is complicit. There is nowhere to turn, nowhere to run. Every time I run away from memory, I run into it. It's rather like talking about the weather; you can make all the predictions you want, but the weather will come along in any case, whatever you say. Which is wrong? The weather or our calendars?

With some degree of certainty, however, I can say that Biqui meant a great deal to me. No one will ever know how much, especially since I will not allow them to know. My life was destined, from the first, to be singularly devoid of drama or romance. Love is a sickness of the nerves. It's serious, yes, very serious, but for myself, I was afraid of it & avoided it. Now, I find it comical.

After my torrid affair, I craved a return to my own 'moral' world, a landscape which could open up vast perspectives, filled with new clarities. I wanted to receive, as one only can when one is alone, the immensity of the world & transform it, through means of my icy solitude, into the intensity of my intimate being. To this end, I broke with the Rosicrucians & founded my own order of chivalry, based upon the model of those in the Middle Ages. I named it L'Église Métropolitaine d'Art de Jésus Conducteur, & named myself the order's *parcier & maître de chapelle*.

As penance for momentarily breaking my 'vow' of chastity, I made a pledge to myself that I would compose a piece that would require the patience of a saint to play. I attended to the matter for five months, & eventually shaped 152 notes on a single music sheet, which I entitled *Vexations*. I tried to make the piece as unmemorable as possible, by which I mean I arranged the notes in a particularly pallid, illogical way so that there would be no strong melody for the pianist to latch on to.

However, to add to the difficulty, I decided to lay a little trap. I added a performance indication thus: 'To play this motif 840 times in succession, it would be advisable to prepare oneself beforehand, in the deepest silence, by serious immobilities.' Yes, I demanded that the piece be played very slowly 840 times without interruption, which, by my calculation, would take 28 hours.

I made such an instruction to show the pianist that he needed great preparation to perform the piece. This is because the pianist, even after repeating it many times over, will have difficulty in remembering it because of this unmemorable, illogical arrangement of notes. But the real joke of such an instruction was that the best & only preparation would be to perform the piece itself. In the inhuman struggle to do so, it would be necessary for the pianist to turn himself into a machine, a machine that would experience the true depths & mysteries of boredom.

My piece was designed as a musical *koan* to be meditated upon, a mantra to be repeated. Each cycle brought the piece back to zero. As in a maze, one had to fail & fail again in the hope of succeeding, one had to endure trials & tribulations in order to find one's way to the centre.

Inevitably, however, he will fail, because he is not a machine; he is human. In failing, he realises he will never be able to perform the piece, no matter how well he prepares himself, but he may be consoled that falling short brings one nearer to God. If a pianist does manage to succeed, then he must really be a saint.

Here at the waystation, I want for nothing, need no money, yet my time is limited. Time & money are, according to most, the axes of life. The one is inversely proportional to the other. It is a kind of trap, for the acquisition of money should result in more time to oneself, but being rich requires time to manage one's fortune. On the other hand, if one is not careful, the time one spends when poor can be consumed by the pursuit of the next meal. Best not to enter the race at all. For me, time was always my capital, not money. The poor man is not one who has little, but one who always wants more.

With these thoughts in mind, imagine my surprise when, after completing my spiritual conundrum *Vexations*, I inherited 7000 francs. It was a fortune. I didn't know what to do with it. I thought it best to spend it as quickly as possible, so as to dispense with the troublesome issue of its supervision. I decided to dump my ragged soft-brimmed hat & frock coat, & to kit myself out with a new uniform, as befitting my newly turned-over mind. To this end, I visited a store called La Belle Jardinière & had myself measured up for a velvet corduroy suit & hat. After an hour of standing like a scarecrow while the shop assistant took my measurements, I stipulated that he should make seven such suits & hats, each identical & in exactly the same colour. The assistant didn't believe me at first, but, after I had reassured him several times, he shrugged his shoulders & took down the order.

My plan was to wear the suits in rotation, one per week, for seven years. I chose the colour of these suits very carefully. I studied the fashions of the day, pored over men's attire in the streets, only so that I could be sure to violate them. The colour I decided upon caused much consternation among my friends. Most thought it 'mustard-yellow', Vincent Hyspa called it 'chestnut-coloured', Patrice plumped for 'grey', Grass-Mick settled for 'beige'. All wrong. The colour was indisputably *écru*.

I showed off my new reincarnation by traversing Montmartre quadrilaterally, from rue Caulaincourt to avenue Trudaine, & from place de Clichy to boulevard Barbès. With my double-knotted black cravat & my trusty army-issue hobnailed boots, I am positive I looked like a walking disaster. Nevertheless, my apparel must have impressed, for I quickly became known in Montmartre as 'the Velvet Gentleman'.

I deposited the remainder of my windfall in a branch of the Société Générale, & set about spending it. I organised huge groups of friends to eat at my expense in the best restaurants. I tipped regally, so as to ensure the best service. Waiters bowed with respect. I visited the Société to withdraw money once a day, sometimes twice. Within six months, it was all gone. What a relief.

In the midst of all this prodigality, however, I had singularly failed to make sure my rent payments were up to date. I had fallen several months behind & my landlord threatened to evict me. Mercy. After a calm negotiation, I agreed to move, from the second floor to a small room on the ground floor, which was much cheaper. The evening before I was to change rooms, I sent a note to myself, which read: 'Tomorrow will be the day, milord. Yours humbly.'

My new room was three metres high, two metres long & one & a half metres wide. I put my planks & trestles along one wall & jammed my piano in next to them. I couldn't open the door properly & had to climb in through the narrow gap by standing on the bed. There was only one window, near the ceiling, far too high up to look out of. It was triangular. A fanlight allowed light & air into the room from the landing. A shelf acted as my work space, as well as my altar. I covered the walls with my pictures of medieval castles & knights in armour. I hung up the five portraits of me, including the one by Biqui, & christened my room 'the cupboard'. It suited my need for secrecy. It was my hiding-place, a symbol for my pent-up soul.

My cupboard was too uncomfortable, however, to remain in for any great length of time. I could only stay in the room by lying down. In summer, I sweltered; in winter I froze. I would sleep fully clothed, but ice would form on the tip of my nose. During the day in winter, I wore six shirts, one on top of the other. As they didn't have buttons, I used to do them up with an enormous hatpin, with a cork on the end so as not to prick myself.

To relieve this discomfort, I took to spending inordinate amounts of time with Debussy. He had finished orchestrating my Greek masterpieces, *Gymnopédies*. In the end, though, he only scored the first & the third. These he had premiered at the Salle Érard one cold February night. What joy! Such lush orchestration that my heart bloomed with love for my honourable friend. That moment was the closest we ever were, my dear Claude & I.

When I wasn't with Debussy, I walked the streets. I wrote nothing of consequence for nearly two years; a strange feeling had its grip on me. A torpor full of spleen. An inept stupor. When I descended from the Butte, I walked all day in circles, parabolas & figures of eight along the smooth & efficient lines of Haussmann's designs. Paris had been shaped in a certain fashion, governed by a strict regularity. His new perspectives promoted new monuments & directed the gaze away from those much older monuments that were symbols of my beloved Middle Ages.

No, no. I much preferred the haphazard Brownian motion of Old Paris, that lay now on the periphery of the city, where the ragpickers & the city's poor lived in lean-tos with glasshouse roofs. Around its muddy tracks & back alleys, the loud cries of the street merchants harmonised together into a continuous symphony. These cries of the vendors & pedlars were directly descended from medieval polyphony.

In Montmartre, the squares were like overcrowded stages, where the public were the actors & shop signs acted as the titles of their everyday dramas. Each morning, I walked on stage & played my role, but I wanted to be less centre stage. I wanted to remain in the wings. I have always been more interested in culling images from the margins. Profligate Montmartre was consuming my deep spiritual struggle, sucking the life out of me, the life I needed for my work, my Art. I needed to withdraw into a private universe, where a shabby rented room would become my own world theatre. It slowly dawned on me during these perambulations that, if I was going to continue my work, it would be necessary to relocate once again, far away from the centre of things.

Day Three

All last night, I heard sobbing coming from the next room. It was the sobbing of a woman who was trying hard not to be heard. I have been sitting at my red table all morning, trying not to let the sound disturb me. I cannot help thinking of it, however. Obviously, I like obsessions, my own as well as other people's, but this grisly task I have before me has set my nerves on edge. So much so that my mood this morning is quite black. A mood I'm rarely in, somewhere between restless & anxious, choleric & melancholic. Moods are tiresome.

Through the little square of my window, the sky is mercifully overcast once again. My room is quiet. Nobody's stirring. I place my hands on the red table & try to sit as comfortably as I can. I stare at the walls of my room for such a long time that they seem to fragment into their constituent parts before my very eyes. My poor, wrecked body has always been at the service of my Art, & my Art has always been at the mercy of the Room.

The impressions of spending large amounts of time in different places disappear when one spends all one's time in a single place alone. Space transcends Time. The bounds of a space can be made beautifully limitless if one ignores the huge amount of time spent in that space. The trick is to let the room outgrow the walls. The trick is to contain oneself physically so that one can release oneself emotionally in one's work.

I spent 27 years, the last years of my life, in one room. It was at 22 rue Cauchy in the southern suburb of Arcueil-Cachan. The house had four chimneys & my room was above a café called Au Rendez-Vous des Bretons. The room itself was quite large, much larger than any I had lived in before, & smelled of raisins. There was a window looking out on a cottage belonging to a lord of the region (a Freemason, I believe) & some trees. A veritable paradise compared to the streets of Montmartre. The previous tenant, a *clochard*, was clearly a man of disgusting habits, for I had to scrub the floor with washing soda & then wax it before it was habitable. It was the only time in my life, thank God, that I cleaned anything.

In my room, I made sure to cover up the window, to stop prying eyes from entering. I then installed my straw mattress, planks & trestles, my red trunk, a bench & my two pianos, one on top of the other, as well as hanging my portraits on the cold plaster walls. When all was ready, I sat for days taking in my new surroundings. Every corner of my room, every angle, every centimetre of secluded space was for me to hide in, to withdraw into myself, into my imagination. I was alone before God. My room became my universe. What would I have done if I hadn't had that room, as deep & secret as a shell? Ah. Snails don't realise their good fortune. I closed down my Église Métropolitaine & withdrew completely from the world.

My first winter in my new domain was abominably cold. I gathered together all the empty bottles I could lay my hands on & asked my landlady to fill them with hot water. I then placed them under my planks & lay down, stiff as a board. The bottles looked like some strange kind of marimba. Steam drifted upwards & warmed my ears. I must have looked like some fiery spirit in repose.

When I was perpendicular, I set about creating my own world for contemplation. I made countless drawings of houses, manors & châteaux. In one such fortress, there was a central square, around which a single street ran four times; first in squares, then in octagons. All the doors & windows along this street faced towards the central square, so that the backs of the houses formed a continuous wall. A secret symmetrical world perfectly protected from the outside world.

The production of these drawings would absorb me for hours, days. Certainly, they meant nothing to anyone except me. For myself, these tiny creations were sites for infinite meditation. I pictured belles with their beaux disappearing pell-mell along colonnades, corridors & into doorways or mirrors. They were imagined worlds every bit as real as the 'real' world. In fact, I felt more at home in these miniature worlds, because I could dominate them. My dreaming self could live in them without fear of dissolution in the surrounding world. I could be conscious without risk. For me, the size of an object was inversely proportional to its significance. The miniature is the refuge of greatness. After all, look through a telescope or a microscope & you'll see more or less the same thing.

When I wasn't drawing, I took to books. Reading to oneself is internal – as internal as can be; while reading to others is external – as external as can be. I read to, & for, myself. Lewis Carroll's *Alice in Wonderland* was always my favourite book for its daydreaming, its non-Euclidean geometry & its nonsense. These things fitted in with my own sensibilities. How I would love to have grasped the tiny golden key & passed through the little door, hand in hand with Alice. I would have seen off the hookah-smoking blue Caterpillar & his impertinent quizzings, & listened to the Mock Turtle's story with rapt attention. I could even have mastered the Lobster Quadrille. Because I am half Scottish, I am the only Frenchman who understands British humour & the only composer whose music understands Alice. It was always one of my ambitions to write a ballet of *Alice in Wonderland*, & I tried to muster a collaboration throughout my life, but to no avail. It was one of my many disappointments.

But those days of dreaming had to end, albeit solely through necessity. I was destitute once again. I was glad to be in Arcueil, but Death must have loved these suburbs all so filled with herself. If the dead go fast, money, which is no more stupid than anything else, goes equally fast. I was dying of boredom: everything I began timidly failed with a certainty I'd never known till then. All this was no fun. I got completely fed up with it; an empty stomach, a parched throat, gave me no pleasure whatsoever. Exhaustion

& anaemia. I saw poverty, that old bitch, giving birth to one endless series of monstrosities & all these things would turn out disastrously for me, perhaps for everyone.

As luck would have it (doesn't luck always have it?), a new form of earning a crust came my way. In the dawn of the twentieth century, John Philip Sousa brought his civilian band from Amerika to Paris for the Universal Exposition, where they played every afternoon for a month at Les Invalides. Tired of my failures in Arcueil, I was intrigued to hear this New World music & strode purposefully from my hovel one afternoon to see his band perform there. Nothing was to prepare me, however, for what I heard that day. As soon as the band started the first piece, which Sousa introduced as 'At a Georgia Campmeeting', I was transfixed. Sousa called the piece a 'cakewalk', & explained that cakewalks were the imitations slaves in the South did of their masters, the best of which was awarded with a cake. I listened in awe as his band went on to play 'Smoky Mokes', 'Hunky Dory' & 'Bunch o' Blackberries'.

Well. This irresistible concoction of Amerikan minstrel songs & European military marches was completely new to me, but its rush & odd rhythms

perfectly matched the style of playing I had performed at the Chat Noir for years. Almost overnight,
the music caught on & a new fashion swept through
Montmartre. To cash in, my old friend from our
Chat Noir days, the *poète-chansonnier* Vincent
Hyspa, suggested we team up. For no reason other
than being penniless & bankrupt of my own ideas,
I agreed. Nightly, we toured the cafés-concerts &
cabarets on the Butte: him singing waltzes, marches
& cakewalks, & me accompanying him as pianist.
We were a great success. I realised that this was a
way of establishing contact with an audience that
was severely lacking for my classical pieces. It was a
chance to experiment with new & popular forms &
I seized the opportunity with both hands. To meet
the demand for these songs, Hyspa & I collaborated
even more closely. Together, we wrote 28 waltzes &
cakewalks including, for our own amusement, many
ditties too dirty to be performed in public.

As a result of being offered this work of apparent
lowliness, I wasted valuable time but earned some
money from this trade. But, in order to attend these
nightly performances, I had to walk the 10 kilometres from Arcueil to Montmartre every day. I set
out in the mid-morning, making my first stop at
Chez Tulard in Arcueil for a morning coffee, before

carrying on towards Porte d'Orléans & thence through Montparnasse.

This part of the city couldn't have been more different from Montmartre. Here, the landscape was made up of grand boulevards, department stores & mass transportation. The small, local *vitrines* had given way to modern shop displays. For the most part, kiosks had replaced wandering pedlars. The few remaining tradesmen were left immobile in the huge, empty squares, where they were forced to stay longer & cry louder just to make a sou. The deep old ways of Montmartre were fast disappearing; everything now revolved around flat displays of wealth. It disgusted me & I was glad to be out of it.

I walked slowly, taking small steps, my umbrella held tight under my right arm, stopping intermittently to jot down ideas in my *carnet*, which I carried with me everywhere. I made many other stops en route at various cafés & bistros for replenishment, arriving in Montmartre for my appointment with Hyspa in the late afternoon. When we finished for the night, at around 2 a.m., I had obviously missed the last train or tram back to Arcueil, & so I set out to make the return journey on foot, stopping under street lights to make a note of some thought or other before it dissolved into the inky ether.

Hyspa, & many others, were astonished at the distance I covered every day & night, but I enjoyed it immensely. In the first place, it was invigorating exercise & helped my wretched body keep some modicum of shape. The only dangerous areas in my *marche bourgeoise* were the wild & barbarous quarters of la Glacière & la Santé where street thieves were not unheard of. That is why I often carried a hammer in my pocket. If I spotted some evil-looking type, & didn't have my hammer, I lay down in the gutter & pretended to be drunk. Besides that, I loved being outdoors, especially when it rained or was cold. If it was sunny, the journey was a descent into fiery hell, for the sun is a lout. If only my legs were long enough to give him a good kick in the eye! No, no, sunless days are certainly the best.

Often, after too many iced beers, too much Calvados & too many stories in Paris, I would get to Arcueil around dawn. As I went through the woods, with the birds chirruping all round, & saw a large tree with its leaves rustling, I would go up to it & throw my arms round it, & as I did so I would think: he at least has never harmed anyone. Then, I would return to my cell, rub myself down with a sponge & set out once again for the mountain.

To the casual perambulator, the routine of these

endless walks back & forth across the same land-
scapes must seem like a kind of torture, but Habit
is merely a compromise between an individual & his
organic sensibilities. It consists of a perpetual adjust-
ment & readjustment of those organic sensibilities
to the conditions in which he finds himself. If one
fails through negligence or inefficiency to make the
necessary readjustments, one suffers; but if one per-
forms those readjustments adequately, one is merely
bored &, as we all know, boredom is deep & mysterious.

Once my organic sensibility had readjusted itself
to perform these walks automatically, my mind was
left in a state of detached boredom, free to observe
totally the very limited & narrow environment I
passed through. Day after day, I passed along the
same route, but every day it seemed different. A
building took on a lighter hue; an overcast sky gave
a little square a gloomy aura; the verdigris of a statue
became more intense. This idea of variation within
repetition is the aim of my compositions. During
these walks, I was 'beating' time in both senses of the
word. As Alice says to the Mad Hatter: 'I know I have
to beat time when I learn music!'

Why, since one takes up so much time in one's life,
should one not take up a lot of space as well, even

though the terrain may be mental? I've spent my whole life looking for precious images for my work. It is Space, not Time, that leads to eternity. In my search, the same images kept on returning, ancient & tranquil, & I realised that the eternity open to my view is made up of time that repeats itself, not time that goes on & on for ever. It seems to me that memory records spaces, not time. Memories are motionless, & the more securely they are fixed in space, the more solid they are. Maybe there's something to that.

In any case, Hyspa & I were in great demand & the *valse-chantée* we wrote together, '*Tendrement*', was a big success. I wrote another waltz, '*Poudre d'or*', which was also a great success, so much so that both of them were registered with the Society of Authors. Fame at last. My publisher informed me that it was now time to approach Paulette Darty, the famous 'Queen of the Slow Waltz', with a view to her recording some of these songs.

On the day arranged for such a meeting, we were admitted to her magnificent house by her secretary, who told us to wait in the drawing room, as Madame Darty was having her morning bath. We could hear her splashing about in the next room. While we waited, my publisher & I 'warmed up' by running through a waltz I had completed. No sooner had he finished singing it than the indefatigable Madame Darty sped out of the bathroom & asked me what enchantment I was playing. 'A little trifle called "*Je te veux*",' I said. She demanded to sing it there & then. Flexing my unwieldy paws, I played the tune once again &, even now, I can see her superb pink décolleté rise & fall as she belted out the words. When she finished, she exclaimed that she simply must put '*Je te veux*' in her repertoire for the music halls. I made a little bow. 'It would be an honour,' I said. In the following few years, I wrote many waltz-songs for her. Perhaps this brief flirtation with fame should be the memory I choose? I could do worse, surely? Who knows? Certainly not I.

I place my pince-nez onto the bridge of my eagle nose & straighten my wing collar. I stand up. I have no idea what the time is, but I sense things are happening outside my room.

Sure enough, on the main set of steps, some of my fellow travellers are learning to play the instruments belonging to the Rhythm Kings of New Orleans. Serif is getting to grips with the trumpet; Monsieur Armengaud is trying his hand at the clarinet. Luther & Joe Sapp are instructing them. Anything to pass the time, I suppose. I stay & watch Monsieur

Armengaud's dreadful wailing: the sight cheers me
up no end.

I corner Ulysses, who has nothing to do as the
piano is in the great hall. When I ask, he confirms
that he is from Amerika. I mention that I never went
to Amerika & then offer that I have heard it is a land
of new opportunities. He looks at me askance.

'Don't know what you heard, but there ain't many
opportunities for a black man. Just trouble,' he
replies.

I shake his hand. 'Good old Ulysses,' I smile. He
wanders off.

I leave the musical mayhem behind & make for
the gardens. I stride over the grass, wet from the
night's rain. I adore the smell of the rain but, cruelly,
the air smells of nothing today. All about me are
myriad drops of water hanging from blades of grass.
In each drop the world is contained in its entirety.
Sometimes, the sheer multitude of things is too over-
whelming to take in.

Quite soon, the noise seems far away. The station
sits squatly, like a frog. I pass through a gap in the
hedges & my steps crunch on the gravel. I come to
the beautiful, shallow lake. The yellow, red & white
flowers tremble slightly. I sit & place my umbrella
between my knees. Today is a day like any other. No

better, no worse. I am far away from everything, but no nearer towards what I am supposed to arrive at. It is easy to calculate what the days have taught, but not the years. I have only a few days to learn the lessons my 59 years are alleged to have provided, but the perspective of years obliterates everything. Oh yes, I have composed many things, quarrelled with many people, but the results were never those I expected. I was always mistaken, & the results of my life are therefore incalculable.

'What do you mean, "cannot choose"?' I am sitting in front of Monsieur Takahashi's enormous desk. 'Do you mean you are unable or unwilling?'

I consider my response. He is leaning calmly on his arms & waiting patiently for me to answer.

'Unable. Perhaps unwilling too,' I say.

'Believe me, Mister Satie, I understand the difficulty of the task . . .'

'Impossibility, more like.'

'. . . but I must insist on its necessity.'

'Why?'

Monsieur Takahashi opens his hands. 'Do you want to stay here for ever?'

'It could be worse,' I say. 'In fact, it's perfectly pleasant here.'

'Not after a while. It soon becomes intolerable. Take it from me, you don't want to remain here unconditionally.'

'Undyingly?' I raise my hand to my mouth to hide the chuckle there.

Monsieur Takahashi looks at me for what seems an age. He leans back in his chair. I think he's trying to hide a smile too.

'Tell me in what way you are finding it difficult to select a single memory,' he says eventually.

'Ah yes, I've thought about this.' I take my *carnet* out of my jacket pocket & flick it open. 'No. 1: I had no objectives in life, so I can't tell if it was of any use. No. 2: My life wasn't a matter of happiness or sadness, I was just born at the wrong time. No. 3: I've never thought of my life in terms of memory. Since it is true that the more one remembers, the closer perhaps one is to dying, I've always done my best to forget, to live.' I snap my *carnet* shut.

Monsieur Takahashi sighs. 'Mister Satie, you're going to make my life very difficult, aren't you?'

'Why not? Mine was difficult enough.'

We agree to adjourn, but Monsieur Takahashi has informed me that, preferably, I should select a memory before nightfall on the day after tomorrow. Only then will the film studio have enough time to do a more than adequate job at recreating it.

I endeavour to do as he says & resolve to tour the back of the building, which I haven't yet explored. Outside, the sun has no more power to it than an ornament or a sponge. As I turn round the corner, I look up: the walls of the station are high & stained, & the corner of the roof sticks out brazenly. Behind our station, the grasslands roll away unevenly downhill. At the bottom, there is a tiny copse of perfectly formed trees, with their heavy burden of innumerable leaves. I make a beeline towards them.

Decidedly, they are fruit trees. Maybe cherry, or plum. I wonder if they blossom in summer? Then I wonder if there *is* a summer in this halfway house. I'm not at all certain. Perhaps they are pear trees. Now that would be serendipitous, since pears have figured prominently in my work. Let me explain.

In amongst all the success of my popular music-hall songs, I was at work again on my own classical composition. But, as well as striving for simple classical melodies, I also struggled to bring into this classical piece something of the waltzes, ragtime & cabaret songs that had recently filled my head. It took many months to do but, once I had finished it, I knew that it was my first piece as a serious composer.

I named my composition *Three Pieces in the Form of a Pear* although, in reality, there were seven separate pieces.

I played my *Pieces in the Form of a Pear* to friends & colleagues whenever there was a piano available in the café in which we sat. I was wild about this latest creation. I talked about it a lot, & spoke very highly of it. I thought it was better than anything that had been written up to then. I might have been wrong, but if anyone had told me so, I would not have believed it. Generally, my friends & colleagues were pleased with my efforts but, without exception, everyone was puzzled by my title. One such colleague was so earnest in his inquisitiveness that I decided to let him in on it.

'You do know', I said, 'that I visit Debussy quite often; I admire him immensely & he seems to think much of whatever talent I may have. Nevertheless, one day when I showed him a piece I had just composed, he remarked, "Satie, you never had a greater admirer than myself. I liked your *Gymnopédies* so much that I orchestrated two of them. You have some kind of genius. Now, as a true friend may I warn you that from time to time there is in your art a certain lack of form." So, when I finished my *Pieces in the Form of a Pear*, I brought them to Debussy who asked, "Why such a title?" "Simply, my dear Claude," I said, "because you cannot criticise my *Pieces in the Form of a Pear*. If they are in the form of a pear, they cannot be formless."' Hah. Well, he was dumbstruck, then he chuckled a little.

Talking of food, I remember being invited to dinner one summer's evening by a group of young musicians who called themselves Oeil de Veau. The more musicians we have, the more madmen we have, but no matter. This group apparently held me in great esteem & so it was my honour to attend. They had prepared a special meal in which each course was named after a musical allusion. We passed a perfectly delightful evening munching our way through dish after musical dish. Imagine my exhilaration when the dessert was announced as 'pieces in the form of a pear'.

Does one eat to live, or live to eat? For myself, most certainly the former. If I had my way, I would dispense with food altogether; think of all the work one could do if one didn't have to eat. But our poor bodies need sustenance. As far as was possible, I ate only white victuals: eggs, sugar, grated bones, the fat of dead animals, veal, salt, coconuts, chicken cooked in white water, fruit mould, rice, turnips, camphorised sausage, pasta, cheese (cream), cotton salad &

certain kinds of fish (without the skin).

When there was good food to be had, however, I was a hearty eater since I was usually so ravenous that I devoured anything put in front of me. I looked forward to my evening meal most of all & would get very angry if it was delayed for any reason. I didn't like rich food as much as I preferred simple dishes. In art, I like simplicity & the same goes for cookery: I was a gourmet, not a gourmand, although I did once eat 150 oysters at a single sitting. On another occasion, I ate an omelette made of 30 eggs. At the end of every meal, I would cut off the crust of a piece of bread & eat the bread with my coffee. This was an old custom I'd picked up in my youth from the finest gastronomic experts in Honfleur.

In the old days, cafés were very different: they were more like cabarets; & the drinks had nothing to do with what is sold these days in bars, bistros, 'tea-rooms' or the other places one can find when walking around town. Even so, people drank 'seriously', very 'seriously'; & one of my great-uncles recounts in his 'ancient memoirs' that he often sank 'manye cuppes' with Rabelais at the Pine Cone, the famous cabaret. What a cabaret. Villon came to the Pine Cone long before Rabelais became a regular along with my great-uncle.

Among my favourite beverages were Calvados, which is a brandy from my native Normandy, quetsch, which is an Alsatian plum brandy, & absinthe. I used to alternate these with iced beer. Very pleasant. One fine evening, I left the Bœuf sur le Toit to catch my tram back to Arcueil. I was accompanied part of the way by a young caricaturist named Jean Oberlé who, when we reached the boulevard Saint-Michel, suggested a nightcap before going our separate ways.

'I accept, young man,' I said, 'but as I shall have to leave you abruptly when I see my tram, perhaps with no time to say good night, we'll say our good-byes now, then it'll be done.'

I raised my bowler hat. 'Good night, my dear sir, it's been a great pleasure to get to know you.'

'Good night, *maître*,' he replied.

'Farewell, my goodly friend. I give you my old hand to kiss.'

He kissed it.

'And now,' I said, 'let's have that beer.'

It's odd. The bars were full of people quite happy to offer you a drink. But none of them ever thought of standing you a sandwich.

Two figures are striding down the slopes towards me.

I realise I am still standing under the fruit trees. I must look very forlorn. I rouse myself. It is Serif, accompanied by Loulou. I bid them good day. Serif shakes my hand & tells me he's been looking for me.

'Monsieur Serif asked me where he might find you & I told him to look outside,' Loulou says. 'It seems you like being away from the centre of things, Monsieur Satie.' I put my hand to my mouth to hide a smile. Beautiful creature.

We walk on the green, green grass. Serif appears to be quite animated. He tells me that he has succeeded in selecting a memory. 'Indeed,' I reply, 'that's cause for celebration.' Serif doesn't seem so sure. I plead with him to tell me of it & he does so.

It transpires that Serif travelled to the Tyrol from Turkey with his parents, sister & grandmother in order to escape Ottoman rule. The whole family spent years working in the olive groves around their village in the mountains. When they had enough money, they left the village one night without telling anyone. Serif remembers having to carry a huge bundle of clothes on his back. They walked for three weeks until they arrived at the great port of Izmir. From there, they paid for passage on a freight boat across the Ægean Sea to Piræus, & then another up the Adriatic Sea to Trieste. The voyage didn't agree very well with the grandmother. They had to walk slowly for three days to Udine, & then headed into the mountains. They didn't realise how cold it would be the higher up they climbed. The grandmother got very ill & Serif's father had to carry her on his back. One night, the grandmother died in her sleep. His father said she had died of homesickness. They buried her &, the next day, reached the top of the pass. They looked down into Austria & said a prayer.

'That is your memory?' I ask.

Serif nods. 'Standing in the clouds & looking down into the new land. Yes,' he says.

'A beautiful sentiment, my dear Serif,' I say. There is an awkward moment. I suspect Serif feels he has revealed too much of himself.

He smiles. 'I never got to show you how I can yodel.'

'No, that's true,' I say.

'Allow me to take this opportunity.' He stands tall, braces himself & lets out the most ear-piercing sound I have ever heard a human utter. It is enough to scare the demons from one's soul. My eyes widen in fright & my toes curl. It is truly astonishing!

After Serif has hurried off for a rendezvous with Monsieur Takahashi, Loulou & I walk towards the garden, which has become our home from home. I ask her who is staying in the room next to mine.

'Biljana,' she replies. 'Why?'

'Oh, no matter,' I say. I tell her about my meeting with Monsieur Takahashi.

'He's right, monsieur, you don't want to stay here for ever,' she says.

'Is it so bad?'

'No, not bad, but everything's on hold. Sometimes I feel like I'm suffocating here.'

'Ah. That's bad,' I say.

The clouds are still low today. I can see that the atmosphere here could be a little oppressive.

'Have you ever seen what lies beyond the clouds?' I ask.

'Oh yes,' Loulou says, 'there's a mountain range. Far away.'

'Have you ever climbed a mountain?'

'No,' Loulou says.

'Me neither. I wonder what it's like to be so high up? There's no breath up there, you know. Maybe mountains are the heroic door to heaven? Sometimes I wish I could have flown in an aeroplane. There's more truth in an aeroplane than in Art. But, you know, my nerves could never have coped with something as aggressive as an aeroplane.'

Loulou smiles.

I point my umbrella upwards. 'When Blériot flew across the English Channel, all Paris celebrated.'

'Everyone outside Paris too,' she replies.

'It seemed like the dawn of a new age. Imagine flying through the clouds. How extraordinary.'

'Monsieur, have you ever been in love?'

It's as if the pretty little Loulou has just given me the slyest, subtlest, most delicate slap on the face. 'Well, yes. Once.' I'm blushing.

As we pass through the hedge into the garden, her earnest face looks up at me. 'What's it like?'

'What a question, my dear.' The fountain is functioning. The lion is still roaring. The water falls in graceful curves.

'Try,' she says.

We sit together. I place my umbrella beside me & brush down my trousers.

'It's cruelty & comedy, like the two sides of the same coin. It's the source of all sorrows & all joys.' I look down at Loulou. She is wrapped up in her little coat, looking into her lap. 'You know, one must never talk sincerely about these things other than to oneself, or to the person one loves. To all other people, one must talk with irony, or in metaphors.'

Loulou frowns. 'Why?'

'Because, like dreams, talking about love to one outside the equation is banal.'

'Sometimes you talk in riddles, Monsieur Satie.'

'Never a truer word spoken, my dear child,' I confide.

We sit in silence, each in our own thoughts. I stroke my nose.

'Ah yes, I have it,' I say. 'Did you know that oysters open their shells when there is a full moon?'

Loulou shakes her head.

'It's true. Through instinct alone, oysters on the beach sense when it is a full moon. In the dead of night, they open their shells & reveal their most hidden treasure – a pearl – to the silvery disc in the sky. They have a secret language with the moon, one which no one else is privy to. Maybe that's what love is.'

I can see she is taking this in. Her coat is jet black.

'What day is it?' I ask.

'Saturday,' she replies.

'I thought so. Saturday is the colour of your coat, did you know that?'

'I don't understand you, monsieur.'

'You're in good company, let me tell you.' I hum a few bars of Saint-Saëns. 'Have you ever been in love?' I ask.

'No,' she says, 'I haven't.'

'Do you wish you had been?'

She looks at me & shivers a little. 'Of course I do. Doesn't everyone?'

'Rest assured, my dear, it's overrated.'

Day Four

Often, I regretted having come into the base world; not that I hate the world. No, I like the world, the social world & even the twilit world, being myself a sort of twilight *demi-mondain*. But what did I come to do upon the earthy, earthly Earth? Did I have duties to perform there? Did I come to carry out a mission – a commission? Was I sent to enjoy myself? to have a little change of scene? to forget the hardships of a world beyond, of which I remember nothing? Wasn't I an intruder there? How could I answer all these questions? Thinking it was the right thing to do, almost as soon as I arrived down there, I started playing snatches of music which I made up myself. All my troubles stemmed from this.

I was approaching 40 years of age. What in heaven's name did I think I was doing? Apart from my *Pieces in the Form of a Pear*, I was writing crude rubbish & it was not good for me. I was tired of producing 'Outsider Art' that no one heard. It was time

to take stock, time to go back to square one. To facil-
itate this, I was considering returning to education.
I thought that a school could be like a crucible for
me. Or like a lens, concentrating the rays of light into one bright spot.

I decided to talk things over with Debussy; he was
the only one to whom I could express my meagre
thoughts. The opportunity arose when I attended
the first public performance of his latest piece, enti-
cingly entitled *La mer*. After the performance, Debussy asked me for my opinion. I looked him in the
eye & said: 'My dear Claude, in the movement called
'From dawn to midday on the sea', there was one particular moment between half past 10 & a quarter to
11 that I found stunning.' I do believe it was the kind
of remark he was not in the habit of hearing from the
sycophantic group of *debussystes* that had gathered
around him & he tried to hide a smile.

I told him I was contemplating studying counter-
point at the Schola Cantorum. He seemed shocked at
the idea & pleaded with me not to. He argued that I
had learned everything I needed to learn. 'Nonsense,'
I said, 'one can always learn new things.'

Despite Debussy's protestations, I went ahead &
enrolled myself in October. I can't forget my first
day at the school. My fellow pupils were all young &

pimply, but of a goodly sort. They tittered somewhat when I propped my umbrella on the back of my chair & shoved my gangly legs under the small wooden desk. My tutors were very surprised to see me; one even asked if there hadn't been some kind of mistake. I assured him there hadn't.

As befitted this hoped-for metamorphosis, I felt I needed a change of attire. I decided to abandon my velvet suits. I'd been wearing them for 10 years; three years longer than intended. I could no longer bear the sight of velvet, not even in paintings. I wanted to cast them off, like skins, & bury them. He who buries treasure buries a part of himself along with it. What was once so precious to me was no longer of value: I wanted to emerge afresh, like a butterfly from a chrysalis, to a bright new world. Besides, the suits were starting to give me indigestion.

My new armour was to be a dark grey three-piece suit (as worn by minor civil servants), a bowler hat, starched white shirts, high wing collars, grey cotton gloves &, of course, my omnipresent umbrella. By then, I had a collection of more than 100 umbrellas. Whenever I had some spare money, I bought a bouquet of umbrellas. Along with my pince-nez, an umbrella is the very stuff of modernity. My new uniform looked appropriately subfusc.

After three years of hard labour, there I was with a diploma in my hand, one which bestowed on me the title of 'contrapuntist'. Proud of my learning, I set out to compose new forms. My first work in this style was *Choral & Fugue* for piano duet. I showed my piece to my tutor, Vincent d'Indy. I have certainly been yelled at in my poor life, but never have I been so looked down on as I was that day by d'Indy. I had written pieces before with such rich charm, & now? What a drag. What a bore. I'd had enough of composition.

Composing music is an odd profession, to say the least. Whereas in most other professions you begin to acquire a sense of certainty about what you're doing, in composition one acquires a sense of uncertainty the more one does it. Whoever was so foolish to pursue that jewelled egg was welcome to it. I decided to retire.

My room is still chilly, but I realise, since I've been here, that I have not been cold once. Strange. I can tell that everyone in this station is still horizontal, dreaming stories to themselves in their heads. So each day begins. Perhaps the world does not take place once & for all time, but is created anew every day? Perhaps the world is nothing but a slippage between dreaming & waking? Dreams, of course, are made to be forgotten. Is the world thus as well? If an alien being came to Earth, what strangeness he would find.

I have a slight cramp in my fingers, due to a lack of industry. I get up from my cot & inspect the four corners of my room. Everything is as it should be. I close the door quietly behind me & tiptoe down the corridor to the stairs. Biljana's room is as quiet as a grave. My steps ring out in the stairwell.

I poke my nose about downstairs. The foyer & antechamber are empty, as is the great hall. On the stage, the upright piano stands, well, upright. I approach it as I would an old friend: with careful enthusiasm. Clambering onto the stage is a little indelicate, but managed, eventually. I place my umbrella on the top of the piano & sit on the stool. What a sight my umbrella is on the top of the piano. I open the lid & the white keys shine brightly at me, all at once. The black keys give the whole keyboard the look of a shapely set of teeth. It is my palate. My palette.

I crack my fingers & begin to play No. 4 & No. 1 of my *Gnossiennes*. I marvel at their clarity, brevity & simplicity. When I composed them, I knew I had to leave out whatever was not necessary, whatever was merely anecdotal or decorative. Art is the discovery of what is necessary – that, & nothing more. Art is Form, & I formed my *Gnossiennes* to discipline the emotions at the same time that it aroused them. Yes, that's right. I move on to my *Cold Pieces*.

When I finish, there is a soft clap from the back of the great hall.

'Very pretty, Mister Satie.'

It is Madame Higginbotham.

'Oh, that was very nice,' she says.

I stand up & take a little bow. 'If I'd known I had an audience, I would have paid more attention to play them better,' I say.

'You played them beautifully, Mister Satie.'

I bow again & fetch my umbrella. I hesitate slightly at the edge of the stage & clamber down equally inelegantly, but no matter. Striding up the aisle, I take a seat next to the good lady. Her scarf trails by her like a comet.

'How are you today?'

'Middling.'

'How is your lumbago?'

'No better, no worse,' she replies.

'It seems we're the first up.'

'I'm always the first up. I'm an early riser, like you. First to get the water on the boil.'

'Indeed,' I say.

'How are you managing with our little task, Mister Satie?'

'In essence, not very well. It seems my lifelong habit of amnesia has to be dismantled in a matter of days.'

'Dismantled?'

'Yes,' I say. In conversation, I fear Madame Higginbotham will always get the better of me. 'What about your good self?'

'Oh, it's all settled.'

'You've succeeded in selecting one?'

'Oh yes.'

'Well, congratulations,' I offer.

'I wouldn't say that exactly, but at least I can finish this scarf.'

I look at the said scarf on the floor, coiled up like a sleeping anaconda. 'Don't you think it's long enough already?'

She smiles. 'Perhaps,' she says.

'May I ask what your memory is?'

'Certainly. It's the day my dog died.'

'Your dog?'

'Yes. A stupid dog. His name was Spanner, because he kept on confusing my husband's tools with bones.'

I put a hand to my mouth to hide the smile.

'Terrible time, it was.' She stops knitting for a moment. 'You know, I felt more for that daft dog when it died than I did on my wedding day, or the day my daughter was born. Strange, don't you think?'

Madame Higginbotham has just gone up in my estimation. 'No, not really,' I say.

Madame Higginbotham's story brings to mind the day the giraffe at the zoo in the Jardin des Plantes died of pneumonia because of the floods in Paris. How terrible. There is no doubt that of all God's creatures, animals are by far the most intelligent. Carrier pigeons are not prepared for their mission at any time, yet they manage perfectly well. Fish are kept from studying oceanography, yet they survive.

It is rumoured that a horse has recently had its first communion in a parish near Vienna. This is the first occurrence of this sort of religious phenomenon in Europe; there are references to a jaguar in Australia which acts as a Protestant vicar, & is said to be managing very well. Such intelligence begets modesty. Why is a man good-looking? Because of all the animals, man is the only one that says so. You would never catch a polar bear looking at itself in a mirror.

I love all animals, particularly zebras, penguins, pandas, & those splendid cows from the thin sliver of land called Frisia. An acquaintance of mine once described me as a zebra among horses. I couldn't have agreed more. In all my 27 years in my cell in Arcueil, I opened my door to no one except the odd stray dog. The more I know about men, the more I admire dogs.

Andreij has come to join us. We exchange pleasantries & he sits down. His face is as round as a pie. He seems to be self-sufficient, wherever he is. I envy this. He asks after my health.

'Very good, kind sir,' I reply, '& yours?'

He makes a face, but says nothing. For a minute or two, the only sound is the clicking of Madame Higginbotham's knitting needles.

'Have you chosen your memory?' I venture.

'Yes. I told you. The birth of my Monica.' He crosses his arms.

'Ah, yes,' I say.

'They will film me today,' he says.

'Really?'

'Yes. To save time.'

'Good idea,' I say.

Madame Higginbotham perks up. 'Mister Satie played some of his tunes this morning,' she says.

'Musician?' Andreij offers.

'Composer,' I say.

'A musician played in my town once. He played . . .'
He searches for a name.

'Chopin?'

He shakes his head dismissively. '. . . mazurkas,' he
smiles.

'Ah, dances.'

'It was my last night as mayor of my town. We
celebrated the harvest.'

'I can play mazurkas. Polonaises too,' I say, but
Andreij is lost in thought.

'It was a good party,' he says finally.

Like Andreij, I was once involved in civic duties. My
retirement from the life of composition meant that
I had free time & no good use to direct whatever
meagre abilities I possessed. I wished to put my en-
ergies to some useful employment &, as is always
the case, found the answer close to hand. In Arcueil,
I saw all about me opportunities for improvement
& I decided to throw myself into the civic life of
my adopted home. The local council was more than
receptive to my suggestion. I began conducting the
local choir. I founded the Amis du Vieux Arcueil for
the study & preservation of local ancient buildings. I
joined the local Radical Socialist party.

But most of all, I devoted myself to Arcueil's Lay Association &, under their aegis, assigned myself the title of 'superintendent'. On Sunday mornings in the town hall, a group of children would gather & I would teach them the rudiments of sol-fa. I can see them now, their faces upturned like bright poppies, hanging on to my every word. On Thursday afternoons, I took the children on outings into the surrounding countryside. In that vast arena was housed a museum of seemingly insignificant things which I was impatient to place under the magnifying glass of imagination for them.

As we approached the forest, I told them the story of the Pigeon in *Alice in Wonderland*, & how vigorously she protected her eggs. There is nothing more beautiful in all Nature, I said, than the sight of a nest with its eggs. Birds have neither the hand of a squirrel, nor the teeth of a beaver; they use their own breasts to make their homes, constantly turning round & pressing back the walls on every side to form a contoured hollow. They make nests so skilfully that it would be impossible for any mason, carpenter or builder to make a house so perfectly. I quoted the old proverb: 'Men can do everything except build a bird's nest.'

Little Antoine was the first to spot a nest in the

branch fork of a tall oak. As his prize, I promised he could look inside it. I laid down my umbrella & pulled up my sleeves & mounted the first branch. I hauled little Antoine up with me as the other children stood gawping below. I pushed the little boy up to the next branch & climbed up there myself. With me holding onto him, he crawled along the branch. I feared for his safety, but children are hardy creatures. He peered inside & said there were three pinkish-grey eggs. He reached out a trembling hand, but I called out, 'Don't touch them, don't touch them!' The little boy froze for a minute, & then made his way back.

Afterwards, we hunted for snails in order to examine their world. As we marched through the forest, looking under rocks or round the trunks of trees, I shouted out that life begins less by reaching upward than by turning in on itself. 'The mollusc', I shouted, 'exudes its shell. It is the embodiment of the mystery of slow, continuous formation!' When we actually found a mollusc, we crowded round & one of the children tickled the snail with a blade of grass, whereupon it withdrew into its shell. I pointed out that its shell is built on transcendental geometry. I told them that a crystal, a flower or a shell are privileged forms that are more intelligible for the eye, even though more mysterious for the mind, than all others we see. I know they understood me. Children have natural wisdom: they know everything.

I have always loved children, all children, perhaps because they are the only people I understood & who understood me. Children like new things. It is only at the age of 'reason' that they lose their taste for novelty. They have an instinctive hatred of 'old ideas': they guess that they are the ones that will be a drag in the future. When they take possession of all their intelligence, tiny children observe Man, & they know him. You can be sure it does not take them long to see what a dummy they are looking at.

I came into the world very young, in a time which was very old, & I performed every contortion in order to remain a child throughout my life. We have to grow old in order to free youth from its fetters & live according to its original impulse. In the realm of absolute imagination, we remain young late in life. I can share with children their joys, their hopes & also their fight. I wished to compose for children, & I used children's songs & popular tunes as the inspiration for new pieces. They, in turn, would write songs like mine if they could master composition at a young age. Think of Mozart's *Twinkle, Twinkle, Little Star*, composed when he was just three. I would have been very proud if I had composed that song at 33. I should so much like to know what kind of music the children who are now four years old will write in the future.

Let me tell you a little story. Once, a certain man called Georges Auric sent me a copy of an article he had published in a musical journal, in which he was very enthusiastic about my compositions. I immediately wrote a reply, saying that his article was 'far too complimentary & is a veritable study'. I asked him to suggest a date for a meeting. When I arrived at the man's house at the appointed time, five o'clock, the door was opened by a boy of 14 or so. I said, 'Could I see Monsieur Auric?' & the boy replied, 'That's me, yes, that's me!' I cannot describe my immediate delight that one so young had understood my music. But we later fell out over a hole in my umbrella. The young Auric had wrecked it.

I decide to spend the afternoon touring the uppermost floor of the station, which I have not yet explored. Things in this halfway house get tattier the higher up you go. The top floor is in an even greater state of disrepair than the lower ones. The plaster walls are dreadfully stained, the paper hanging from the ceiling, & bits & pieces all over the floor. It's one thing to be unadorned, quite another to be shabby.

The first room I enter has a dozen wooden desks in it. They are tiny desks, obviously intended for children. This place must have once been a school. I'm back at school. I spy an exercise book on the floor – rather similar to the ones I used all my life. I open it & put my nose to it to take in the scent. Usually, in my experience, books smell of mushrooms, but this one has no scent at all. Page after page is filled with a script I do not recognise. Hebrew? Aramaic? The squiggles are fastidiously neat. How I wish I knew what the squiggles meant.

Looking around, I see there is a map of the world on the wall. The colours are mainly red, pink, yellow. A globe is on a table by a window. It has the same colours on it. I spin it & watch all the countries in the world blur into one whitish streak.

The next room is equally dishevelled & is empty except for two leather chaises longues. The leather is the colour of chestnuts. The staff room? There is a large, framed photograph on the wall. It is of a young man whose torso is naked. It's hard to say if he is European, Arabic or Asiatic, but he is a handsome fellow wherever he's from. The photograph has been carefully hung in the centre of the wall. He takes pride of place in the room. I wonder who he is. Maybe he is Adam? I have often considered myself a man in the manner of Adam (he of Paradise).

I, too, had my photograph taken for posterity, but only on a handful of occasions. The first of these was when the town council of Arcueil-Cachan recommended that I be awarded a medal for 'civic merit' for the sol-fa lessons & outings I had organised. The Minister of Education named me an *officier d'Académie* when I was 43 years of age. I had always scoffed at & ridiculed those who accepted the Légion d'honneur, only because they probably didn't merit it, but this was different. I was proud of the honour bestowed on me, because it was bestowed by a committee that had nothing to do with my work. I accepted with as much grace as I could muster, though I nearly cried when the decoration was pinned onto my lapel.

I was so proud of this little piece of ribbon that I visited a local photographer's atelier & had my photograph taken with it on. I can recall the acrid smell of the chemicals wafting about the place. I wore my stiffest, whitest wing collar & brushed my bowler hat. For the first time in my life, I felt that this moment had to be recorded. Up to then, I had never sought to record my own life – the idea repulsed me – & any painting made or photograph taken of me was somebody else's doing.

Photography is an elegiac art, an art full of nostalgia & pathos. To take a photograph of someone is to submit to their mortality; you acknowledge Time's relentless march just in the taking of it. You're smiling, & that smile is for everyone else now, for ever, even if you don't like it. Quite the wrong feelings to evoke, let me assure you. A little piece of you disappears when you have your photograph taken, & so you must set limits to such occurrences & be quite sure the moment is the right one. It took me a great deal of mental effort to transfer from the age of the daguerreotype to the age of the photographic print &, from then on, I contrived to have my photograph taken only if I deemed an event worthy of such attention.

This award made me something of a celebrity in Arcueil. Fame at last. In my honour, the council invited me to perform an evening of songs for their annual Matinée Artistique. I was glad to accept. As my collaborators, I invited my old comrade in arms, Vincent Hyspa, & my representative in the world of variety, the inimitable Madame Paulette Darty. The evening passed off most pleasantly, with Madame Darty filling the town hall with her veritable boom of a voice. What a pair of lungs the woman had. She brought the house down with applause.

When the citizens of Arcueil discovered that I was a composer of 'art' pieces as well as a café-concert pianist, they were astonished. But the evening had an adverse effect on me. Its success only emphasised how impecunious I remained. Poverty had entered my room like a miserable little girl with green eyes. To put it bluntly, I was hard up, cleaned out, broke, bust, destitute, without a bean. I was sick of it. I knew I had done all I could in the municipality &, rather than taint the children with my righteous indignation, I resigned immediately from all local involvement in Arcueil.

As we are halfway through our stay at this halfway house, a general meeting has been called in the main hall. We all gather & take our seats at the appointed time, though no one has the faintest idea what the time is. Monsieur Takahashi arrives late. There is an air of expectancy, of excitement almost; as though everyone knows full well how this meeting will go. It is bemusing, to say the least.

The general murmuring dies down when Monsieur Takahashi calls the meeting to order.

'Ladies & gentlemen,' he starts, 'I wanted to speak to you all today, at this midway point of your stay here with us. First of all, let me say that I'm very happy with the good work done so far. All but a few of you have managed to choose your memory . . .'

There is light applause.

'. . . & those who haven't yet managed to still have until tomorrow night. Filming for some of you will start this evening & will continue for the rest of the week. You will be assigned a member of staff from the studio, who will be personally responsible for putting your memories onto celluloid.

'For those of you who haven't yet managed this difficult task, I have a few words of encouragement. In our experience, the memories most important to past travellers have been of significant moments in their lives – births, deaths, marriages. This may seem obvious, yet it is worth mentioning again. But many memories have been of seemingly less significant moments. My predecessor, for example, quoted the memory of one of his most illustrious guests – Leo Tolstoy – as being the sight of a rainbow arcing over the steppes of Russia. It was, apparently, quite difficult to recreate, but they managed it to everyone's satisfaction.

'So, ladies & gentlemen, for those of you who have chosen your memory – well done. For those who haven't – keep trying & good luck. I'm sure you will succeed. Don't forget, we're here to help.

Are there any questions?'

Madame Higginbotham raises her arm. 'Do you have any dogs here?'

Just when I had resigned myself once again to a life of anonymity & starvation, that good lady, Chance, reached her hand into my life & turned everything upside down. Some say there's no such thing as chance; that happy accidents happen because of good intentions. Well, I'm all for that. I spent my life trying to develop good Habits, not in the hope that it would lead to some great reward, but only because I didn't know how else to live. I am certain many thought I was my own worst enemy – maybe so – but the course that my life took was the only one open to me. Forgive me.

In any case, at the tender age of 44, I was 'dis- covered'. The perpetrator was a young composer, whom I had met years before during my days in Montmartre, called Maurice Ravel. From time to time, I had received a missive from him assuring me that he owed me a great deal. From such humble beginnings, Ravel had cultivated for himself a quite formidable reputation, & always he had championed my music. He said I was 'a brilliant precursor . . . a disturbing inventor of neologisms who, a quarter of a century ago, was already speaking the daring musical language of tomorrow'. Good heavens.

His standing was such that he was invited by the illustrious Société Internationale de Musique to organise an evening of music in my honour. Ravel proposed to play my *Sarabande* No. 2, my *Gymnopédie* No. 3 & the Prelude from *Le Fils des étoiles*. Of course, I was unable to attend. I wrote to him saying that, to my great regret, the evening would be too moving & beyond my strength. I sent a representative in my place, & he informed me that the recital was a huge success.

As if all this weren't enough, Debussy then proposed to conduct his orchestrations of my *Gymnopédies* at the Salle Gaveau only a matter of weeks later. This, too, was a great success. But what should have been a high point in my life was, in actuality, a turning point in my friendship with Claude. He was, by all accounts, very surprised at the success of my *Gymnopédies* & this soured our friendship. What was it that surprised him so? Why couldn't he allow me a very small place in his shadow? I had no use for the sun.

The memory of such an act of betrayal still pricks me. For one who seemed to have everything, it appeared so uncharitable. Surely he believed in me all along? I have an idea to find out. I clutch my umbrella & leave my room. On my way down the staircase, I pass the good Madame Higginbotham, but I am too preoccupied to acknowledge her somewhat cursory greeting. At the bottom of the stairwell, I hurry down the corridor, turn right & knock on Monsieur Takahashi's office door. I hear a chair scrape, & the door opens.

'Can I help you, Mister Satie?'

'Monsieur Takahashi, I have a somewhat odd request,' I say.

He makes way for me & indicates a chair.

After agreeing to my entreaty, Monsieur Takahashi leads the way out of his office. There is a connecting passageway from the main building to the film studio, down a long corridor with lightwells. The circular skylights form soft discs of light on the floor. We pass through a set of swing doors, then enter a space the size of a cathedral. It is the film studio. I spy a group of naked mannequins in one corner. Somebody cover up their immodesty! There is equipment everywhere: poles, trestles, spotlights & light rigs, cloth backdrops painted in sunset colours, cardboard trees, material bushes, huge clusters of cotton clouds hanging from wires, benches, beds, bureaux, life-size models of planes & trains, even a whole house.

We disappear through a door in the wall, where Monsieur Takahashi takes me down a spiral stair-case. Another door opens into the basement, which holds the studio archives. He flicks several switches & we stand for a moment in the darkness. Two or three lights flicker &, in the gloom, I see that the space is filled to the ceiling with aisle upon aisle of iron frames, all stacked with different-sized film cans.

'Let's hope the alphabet still prevails here,' Monsieur Takahashi sighs.

My memory resembles a library like this, albeit in alphabetical disorder. We locate the rows for D & search. Most of the cans are covered in dust & have been stacked higgledy-piggledy. Each has a hand-written name & number on it. I have no luck.

'I think it may be up there,' Monsieur Takahashi points. 'Give me a leg up.'

I put down my umbrella carefully. I clasp my hands together & strain as Monsieur Takahashi puts his foot in. I hoist him up.

'Hold on,' he says.

I have never lifted anything so heavy in my life, or afterlife, for that matter.

'Steady,' he says.

My puff is going & I am starting to perspire.

'Got it!'

I take a seat on the back row of the auditorium. The seats are covered with red velveteen & are surprisingly uncomfortable. Well, I reflect, they're not made to sit in for long. There are 10 or so rows in front of me & the pale screen above them. It is dark. I wait. Monsieur Takahashi is having a word with the projectionist. Presently, a door opens & he comes in, silhouetted against a block of white, & takes a seat next to me. 'All set,' he says.

The screen flickers with scratches & flecks of dust. Numbers count down from 10. A title appears:

PASSENGER No 583,776: ACHILLE-CLAUDE DEBUSSY

NATIONALITY: FRENCH

PROFESSION: COMPOSER

BORN: 22 AUGUST 1862

DIED: 25 MARCH 1918

Then the screen goes black. It fades up to reveal what looks like the living room at Claude's magnificent mansion on the avenue du Bois de Boulogne. There

he is, sitting in one of his splendid upholstered armchairs, smoking a cigar. Behind him is the mantelpiece supporting a tall mirror. There are two other
people with him, also sitting in armchairs. One is a
mere slip of a man, wearing big round spectacles & a
floppy beret. The other is dressed very properly, with
a bowler hat & umbrella. It's me. The three of us are
talking, but there is no sound. In slightly speeded-up
motion, legs are crossed & uncrossed. We gesticu-
late & become animated. Claude puffs away on his
cigar, occasionally adding something wordless to the
conversation, but mainly smiling at the scene before
him. Claude & I get up suddenly & stand by the
mantelpiece. The other man holds a camera to his
eye & we look at it. He takes a picture.

How could I ever forget that day, the day I met
Igor Strawinsky? I used to visit my dear Claude at
his home every Friday for lunch. Soon after my 'discovery', Claude wrote to me that he was inviting
someone who wanted to meet me. It was Strawinsky.
He was as thin as a pole. In addition to his floppy
beret, he wore striped trousers, an ornate black
jacket with silk lining & a blisteringly white chemise.
His eyes were full of disdain, although they could
turn quickly to affection. His fingers were the longest
& most delicate I have ever seen. He reminded me

of a mischievous imp. He shook my hand politely &
said, 'You & I will get along, no doubt.'

Later on, we spent the afternoon in Debussy's vast
garden, drinking *thé à la Russe*. A friend of Strawinsky's had just brought over from Amerika some
78 discs by 'Jelly Roll' Morton. We listened to them
on Claude's phonograph. Like me, Strawinsky delighted in the rush of their odd rhythms. Through
the iris-like horn, a man shouted, 'Catch a water-
melon,' above the music. What delighted me above
all, I told Strawinsky, was that Jelly Roll Morton put
into his rags the sounds of the street & the night life.
I was reminded of my days among the street pedlars
in Montmartre. It is truly of & for the people. Jazz
told the story of the people's pain – that is why it is
beautiful & real. He agreed wholeheartedly with me
& said, 'Did you know that Jelly Roll Morton was
the first jazz musician to write down all his pieces of
music?'

'Quite right,' I said, 'scoring one's music is the
composer's attempt at minimising the unwanted
chance of human error in the performance of the
piece.'

'Do you believe in improvisation?' he asked.

'Absolutely not,' I replied. 'Improvisation is not
knowing what it is until you do it. Composition, on

the other hand, is not doing it until you know what it is.'

Strawinsky smiled. 'But imagine if you could only hear a piece of music *once*. Imagine the intensity you'd have to bring to listening. Don't you think it might concentrate the ear?'

This was more like it. 'I'm not interested in performers expressing themselves, because I'm not interested in expressing myself,' I said.

'But your denial of self-expression is the ideal that all chance music aspires to. In any case,' he said, 'I believe totally planned things & totally arbitrary ones have a similar place in the shaping of a piece.'

'I'd prefer a Jelly Roll Morton 78 to a Wagner opera every time,' I proclaimed.

How he laughed at that. Many people, superficial people, compared me to Strawinsky. It was unholy, of course. Strawinsky is a magnificent bird & I'm a fish. It was nonsense to compare birds to fishes.

'Mister Satie?' a voice says.

The lights in the auditorium have come up & I see that the film has ended. Monsieur Takahashi is sitting next to me.

'Yes, here I am. What do you want?'

'Was the film any help?'

Did the film aid me? Does it jog the memory? Sitting here in this empty auditorium, how do I feel? It is nice to see my good friend again. Fancy him choosing that day! I have not forgotten it, but to Claude it was clearly a day to remember. Therein lies a great difference. To his earth & fire, I was his water & air. We were two halves of the same self. Only in death can I see what I was in his life, & he to mine. Only by seeing this little film, this brief projection of his consciousness, have I realised this. My dear Claude, I am silenced.

'Yes,' I say & get up to leave.

Day Five

At around this time, I began to write. Or rather, I had been writing for years, but began to collect together my automatic descriptions, my meditations, my disagreeable aperçus. Much to my astonishment, the Société Internationale de Musique continued to champion me & called on me to provide them with some of my writings.

Of course, I had many ideas about writing. Opinions even. Like my compositions, I thought that my writing should be a distillation of ideas. Before writing a work, I walked around it several times, accompanied by myself, choosing what was necessary & what was not necessary. For me, thinking in images & writing were both instruments of discovery, not reference. I decided to call my collection *Memoirs of an Amnesiac*.

It is hard to remember everything, but it is generally accepted that remembering is healthy, & that we suffer above all from forgetting. Isn't that so? What nonsense. If one were to have total recall, it would be close to having complete amnesia. Remembering everything must be a kind of madness. Perhaps our minds are just the world gone mad with remembering? Life is hard, & some of its moments can be unbearable. To remember unbearable moments, one has to make them bearable somehow. A slight refraction of the truth to make them palatable. Either that, or consign them to history.

Today is the fifth day, Monday, which is pale & priestlike, a cool grey. The colour of doves & Jesus' eyes. The fifth day. Five. The pentad, one of the mystic numbers, being the sum of the first even & odd numbers. One is God, two is diversity, & three is the sum of unity & diversity. These are the two principles in operation since creation. What did God create on the fifth day? Wild animals, cattle & every creeping thing, of course. But he also made human beings to have dominion over the fish in the sea, the birds of the air, the cattle, all the wild animals on land & everything that creeps on the earth. What a shame. The fifth commandment is: Thou shalt not kill. Well, the Great War put paid to that. I wonder what Monsieur Armengaud has to say about it all? I resolve to find him & find out.

He is loitering in his room on the second floor & invites me in when I knock. He is fiddling with Luther's clarinet. 'Can you play this thing?' he asks.

'I'm afraid not.'

'I always wanted to learn an instrument, but I never had the time,' he says.

'A common problem, monsieur,' I reply. 'There are hundreds of instruments I would have liked to play. But at least the clarinet is quite safe.'

'Safe?'

'Oh yes, there are some instruments that are deadly. The octopus's, for example. Instruments from the wonderful family of cephalophones, with a range of 30 octaves, are completely unplayable. An amateur in Vienna tried, but the instrument burst, snapped his spine & completely scalped him.'

By the look on his face, Monsieur Armengaud has clearly not understood a word of my discourse.

'Anyway, monsieur,' I say, 'you're not missing much. Tell me, have you chosen your memory yet?'

'Yes.'

'May I ask what it is?

'The night of the Armistice. My two friends & I spent that night very drunk & extremely disorderly.'

He laughs. 'We ended up in a bordello &, well, you can guess the rest.'

'Yes, I certainly can. How's your cough?' I venture.

'I have good days & bad days. Today is a good day.'

'Did you contract your cough from the war?'

He nods. 'Just a little mustard gas in your lungs wreaks havoc. But at least it got me out of the front line.'

'Ah,' I say, 'what did you do then?'

'Do you really want to know?'

'Certainly, monsieur.'

He tells me that, along with other partially wounded men, he had to bury coffins. A lot of men were dying from dysentery. Some people came from a medical college to do post-mortems, but nobody wanted to sew them back up again, & so they had to. The coffins reminded him of orange crates: you could see through the wood. They put them on a hearse crossways, about 10 high. The old horse that pulled the hearse looked as though it was going to fall down at any minute. On the way, women used to come out of their cottages on their knees. There was a trench dug as far as the eye could see across the field, deep enough to take two coffins. He used to hate seeing that trench & knowing that they were going to fill it in. Then the priest would say his litany none of them could understand & they'd put a handful of soil on each coffin before shovelling the earth into the trench.

It takes me some time before I am able to assimilate Monsieur Armengaud's dreadful tale. I do so by walking round the waystation five times. During this march, I can recall the day that the Archduke Ferdinand was assassinated. I was at the house of Misia Edwards, who had arranged a meeting between myself & Sergei Diaghilev, the Russian impresario. Like me, Diaghilev had recently found that bonny bride, success, as well as that withered witch, fame. His ballet company, the Ballets Russes, had had scandalous performances of Strawinsky's *The Rite of Spring* & my dear Claude's *Prélude à l'après-midi d'un faune*. All Paris was up in arms. Of course, I held him in even higher regard because of all that.

Diaghilev was benign & rotund. He had a white patch in his hair & highly polished shoes. He reminded me of a preening skunk. When I met him, I saw holes in the soles of his shoes. Diaghilev noticed my gaze & said sadly: 'Never become a ballet impresario – it never pays.' I had just finished playing my *Pieces in the Form of a Pear* to Diaghilev when a friend of Madame Edwards's ran into the room & told us of the Sarajevo assassination. We all knew it meant war.

The response of many of my young friends was to leave for the front one after the other. I saw them off by sending each of them a note exclaiming what a beautiful thing a flag is & instructing them to love their officers. Although I was too old to join up, the Socialist militia of Arcueil-Cachan enlisted me with the rank of corporal. We were armed to the teeth & I led nightly raids around Arcueil, tirelessly scouring the streets in search of the Hun. Death was in our pockets, but the authorities ordered us to stop since we achieved nothing except to wake up sleeping residents.

Paris was emptying out. I can remember how haunted the city seemed. Most of those who remained were either foreign, on leave or wounded. Many left for Amerika. Good luck to them – they would need it for we all know that the Statue of Liberty is really just an ice-cream lady.

With nothing to do in Arcueil, I caught a train to the Gare de Sceaux in the morning & spent my days at the Dôme & Rotonde cafés in Montparnasse. I met & befriended many painters, whose company I enjoyed infinitely more than that of 'musicians'. I had many interesting conversations with these learned gentlemen. For instance, I learned that the most primitive colours are black & white. Then red. Then either green or yellow. The Greeks, they said, only knew four or possibly five colours. André Derain compared his colours to 'sticks of dynamite'.

As most of the theatres & galleries in Paris had been closed down because of the war, the talk shifted to the city's circuses. My cubist friends were addicted to the circus. They admired the double act of Footit & Chocolat, the grace of the three Fratellini brothers. But their favourite of all was Grock, the 'musical eccentric', who presented slapstick numbers & parodies on the clarinet of Amerikan marches & cakewalks. They thought the sight of a clown playing a mandolin whilst atop a teetering tower of chairs was cubism in the flesh.

There is a fellow here at the waystation who reminds me of a clown; he is short, stocky & sad. I can remember once seeing a drawing of a clown; a kind of metaphysical joke at the clown's expense. In it, the clown has happily stepped along a series of blue cubes, only to be faced with a single red sphere. He is standing on the last of the blue cubes, looking at the red sphere in complete perplexity. He does not know how to proceed. He is intensely sad. Ah, how I know his suffering.

Coming to, I find myself statuesque by an outhouse. It is a low shed, leaning against the back of the main building. It is a dishevelled affair, not even worth storing coal in. I know I have been standing here & staring at it for a good amount of time. These daydreams will have to cease if I am to succeed in my efforts. Let's look for the clown.

I'm suddenly very taken with the idea of ascertaining whether this man was a clown or not. After discreet enquiries, I come across the man in question in the main hall. He is deep in conversation with another fellow I haven't yet met. As I approach them, they look up. The man is indeed as wide as I had thought. A veritable bull of a man. I tip my hat to them & introduce myself.

'Monsieur Satie, Erik. *Compositeur de Musique.*' I hand the man a card.

He takes it & gazes at it. He seems suspicious.

I try to catch his eye. 'Excuse me, monsieur, but I have a question for you.' I clasp my hands in front of me, in supplication. 'In the previous life, were you by any chance a clown?'

The man looks at me aghast.

'A clown, monsieur, were you a clown? It's quite simple.'

Looking quite perturbed, he almost shouts at me, 'No, no. I was a baker.'

Well, we all get things wrong. Liberty must allow for mistakes. All I asked for was to be free enough to be wrong. That's a kind of definition of liberty, don't you think? Let's move on, I'll come back to that.

One evening midway through the war, I was scheduled to perform (yet again) my *Pieces in the Form of a Pear*. After the recital – very boring – my *chère grande fille*, Valentine Gross, told me that one of the 'young guard' was desperate to collaborate with me after hearing my pieces. His name was, apparently, Jean Cocteau. Well, that was fine by me, but what I did not want was to use something old in a new venture. The very idea of presenting old wine in new bottles was deplorable. I asked Valentine to relay this to the young man.

Cocteau assented & very soon afterwards came up with a folder of notes entitled *Parade*, which he defined as 'a burlesque scene played at the door of a fairground theatre to attract customers'. His notes proposed three numbers presented by barkers, who shout ballyhoos about a Chinese Conjuror, a Little Amerikan Girl & an Acrobat. He called it a 'realist ballet', because he wanted there to be in it the sound of steam engines, sirens, dynamos, klaxons, whistles, typewriters & the odd pistol shot. I agreed to compose the music for *Parade* but, secretly, I decided to tone down such noises in the finished score.

To everyone's amazement, Cocteau managed to persuade Pablo Picasso to design the sets. The project took on an altogether more promising aspect with this news. Picasso had ideas I liked better than our Jean's & we worked very closely together. Picasso had eyes of black marbles; hooded, like a cobra about to strike. He didn't suffer fools gladly. He confided in me that, in his opinion, it was going to take the whole of his life for him to learn how to draw like a child. He was my master & I was proud of being his pupil.

Cocteau, on the other hand, bored Picasso & me. He was an arriviste & I loathe arrivistes. I simply question myself politely, saying: 'Where do they want to arrive at? Arrive at what? At what time? In what place?' Cocteau, with his blanched face & rouged lips, was not an *homme*, he was an *hommelette*.

Diaghilev, whose Ballets Russes was to stage *Parade*, proposed to take Cocteau, Picasso & myself to Rome in order to marry stage design, music & choreography. I spent most of the advance I had received from *le bon* Diaghilev on a set of handsome suitcases, but I didn't go. Travel is calamitous for me. My mind is a crystal glass – perfect & clear when left untouched, but easily shattered if manhandled. I needed to stay in my hovel in Arcueil & finish the music.

I quickly completed the opening piece: the 'Prelude of the Red Curtain'. It was a fugal exposition, very meditative, very serious, even quite 'crusty'. For the ensuing short pieces, I drew on my days as a music-hall pianist. I filled them with quick shifts & harsh juxtapositions. For the Little Amerikan Girl, I included a 'rag', similar to an Irving Berlin rag I'd once heard. I marked the whole ballet in a constant pulse of 76 beats per minute: the exact beat of my daily march to & from Arcueil.

Every now & then, I visited my dear Claude to show & discuss with him what I'd done. His health at that time had taken a nosedive & he was too ill to leave his room. I had to endure many painful teasings from Debussy on these occasions. He couldn't believe that I could possibly have had so many recitals entirely for my own music. He thought it must be some kind of practical joke. Perhaps it was also the depression he felt for the state of things in the world at that time, but the rancour with which he treated me was alarming.

One day, just like that, I'd had enough. I wrote a note to his wife telling her that Claude's derogatory remarks were unbearable & that I would no longer be visiting.

While the cannon roared over Paris, *Parade* was staged at the Théâtre du Châtelet, the largest theatre in the city. I had my photograph taken to mark the event. During the performance, everyone talked about Picasso's cubist costumes – hybrids of cabinets of curiosities & automatons. I, however, wasn't the slightest bit interested in the spectacle, I was only interested in the sounds, my sounds. I was pleased that Picasso & I had managed to oust Cocteau's libretto altogether, though I was outraged that Cocteau's typewriter was left in. Cocteau really was an imbecile.

The performance was a scandal. At the height of the Great War, its renegade modernism was seen as an act of aggression against the traditional values the soldiers on the front line were fighting for. Diaghilev raised the red flag on the stage to celebrate the deposition of the Czar. Scandalous. Picasso was a 'cubist' – dirty word! – & under contract to a German art dealer. Scandalous. Apollinaire wrote that the ballet was an act of *sur-réalisme*, a word which no one could make any sense of. Scandalous.

But, of course, for those people who really mattered to me, it was a great success. I was praised to the skies; I was famous. The one person from whom I desperately wanted approbation, however, refused to give it. Debussy, still ill, managed to drag himself to the Théâtre du Châtelet that night. After the performance, he sought me out & informed me that his opinion had not altered one jot. There was nothing more to say & we bade each other good night.

Parade separated me from a great many friends & acquaintances. This work was the cause of many misfortunes; none worse than my libel trial. I was wrongly accused & my good name was dragged through the mud. I was afraid for my life & liberty during the whole unpleasant affair.

After the première of *Parade*, a critic named Jean Poueigh came to my box to congratulate me. We shook hands; it all seemed so courteous. Imagine my shock & surprise when, in a newspaper article the following week, he attacked my ballet in the most wounding of fashions. Hypocritic. I had no other recourse but to respond. Can you blame me if I wanted to vent my indignation? I sent a postcard to him:

My dearest Sir,

What I know is that you are an asshole, &, if I dare say so – an unmusical asshole. Above all, never again offer me your dirty hand . . .

Erik Satie

There was no reply. I still hadn't received full satisfaction, & so I sent another postcard:

Monsieur Fuckface Poueigh, Famous Gourd & Composer for Nitwits,

Lousy asshole. I shit on you with all my might.

E.S.

The humourless Poueigh's only response was to sue me for libel & defamation of character. I was dumbstruck. How dare he! At my hearing, I stood before the judge with my bowler hat pressed to my chest, & my umbrella over my arm. I was filled with fury that it wasn't the numbskull Poueigh standing in the dock instead of me.

Seven of my goodly friends testified on my behalf, but the prosecution really had it in for me. They railed against all modern art & artists, labelling them 'Boches'! This caused an uproar from the public gallery, which was crammed full with my cubist friends & fellow composers. I hoped the judge would see sense, but it was no good; I was found guilty & was sentenced to eight days in prison, a fine of 100 francs & damages of 1000 francs to the despicable Poueigh. When the verdict was read, the public gallery really exploded & all my friends were thrown out of the court. Every last one of them. My lawyer gave notice of an appeal.

I was escorted to the police station, where I learned that Cocteau had slapped Poueigh's lawyer twice. He had been taken down for a night's stay in prison. To the authorities, I begged leniency for all my troublemaking friends. I was overwhelmed at such support & I thanked each one of them before they all went home. Eventually, I too was released & I returned on foot to my hovel. I was crushed. They'll put me in prison, I thought, an unhealthy prison, with no air. No doubt I shall fall sick. No one will come to see me. My publisher won't pay me any further royalties. No theatre will play my compositions. I'll be bankrupt, with my reputation in tatters. I was finished.

My friends urged me to apologise publicly to the ignoramus Poueigh. I tried, believe me, I tried. I started several letters of apology to him, but could finish none. A few months after my court case was heard, my appeal was denied. My friends tried to arrange for a stay of execution. The very phrase filled me with dread. I, on the other hand, gave a lecture entitled 'In Praise of Critics'.

In it, I wrote that critics were 'misunderstood' & that 'they have a certain usefulness'. 'All critics', I said, 'are of *importance* . . .'; but 'importance', for me, was full of irony. To my eternal relief, my lecture did the trick. The Minister of the Interior suspended my sentence, 'on condition of good conduct & not receiving any prison sentence during the next five years'. The kindly benefactress Princess Polignac paid my fines & damages since I was, as usual, without a bean.

I had, at last, regained my liberty, but it was most bittersweet for, just 10 days later, Debussy was dead. I wrote to him – fortunately for me – a few days before his death. Knowing that he was doomed, alas, I didn't want to remain on bad terms with him. My poor friend. What a sad end. His wife told me that he read my note, crumpled it up & then said, 'Forgive me!' with tears in his eyes. When all is said & done, *ce bon* Debussy was something else again than all the others put together.

Some time after his passing away, I was asked to compose a work in his memory. I tried to imagine him lying flat out on his wooden table with all the mirrors in the room covered with sheets, but it was too much. I decided to set to music some lines of Lamartine's verse. They said more than I could about our tender & admiring friendship of 30 years:

What to me are these valleys, these palaces, these cottages,
Vain objects from which for me all charm has been taken
    away?
Rivers, rocks, forests, solitude so dear,
A single being is lacking & everything is empty.

Day Six

Tuesday is quite blue. The rarest colour in nature. The hue of the heavens &, at the same time, the depths. André Derain once told me that the fifth colour to enter any language is blue, but that the word 'blue' does not exist in every language. It is the colour with the least shape, the most immaterial. It is nothing, nowhere & endless. Ah.

This morning, I am crotchety & rickety. I fear Madame Higginbotham's lumbago is catching, for my back is chronically sore. A pain radiates, like filaments, down my arms to my fingertips. I must be getting very old. If you want to live long, live old.

Thinking of the colour blue reminds me of Biljana's night-blue gown. During my stay here, Biljana has seemed like a sphinx. On the odd occasion that I have seen her, she has had a slight smile on her face, as though possessing a secret. I brush my bowler with my sleeve, polish my boots by rubbing them on my trousers & stand up. I am somewhat unsteady on my pins today, but I shall survive.

I step into the grave-quiet corridor & knock on Biljana's door. She opens it immediately, as if she had been standing just behind it, waiting for this very moment. The effect is quite disconcerting. I tip my hat to her.

'Good morning, mademoiselle. You are well, I trust?'

'Oh, Monsieur Satie. Yes, thank you.'

I hold my hat to my chest & smile at her. She smiles back at me. We stay like this for a few moments.

'Won't you come in?' she says, taking a step back.

'Thank you. I will,' I say.

Her room is much like mine. The same monotonal walls & spartan furnishings. But she has put up a silk scarf on one wall & a Japanese fan on another.

'Charming,' I say.

There is a phonograph on the wooden table. Biljana puts a record on it & invites me to sit in her only chair, while she sits on her narrow bed. The music starts: a piano piece. A sonata perhaps.

'Monsieur Takahashi has lent me this phonograph for the week,' she says, noticing my interest.

'Delightful,' I say. 'Really, it is.'

This seems to please her. I'm glad.

'Did you pursue a career in music?' I ask.

'No, I was a painter.'

'But that's magnificent.'

'Well, that depends. I was never very well known, so you could say I didn't succeed, but I enjoyed what I did.'

'In the words of the great St John: "It's not what happens to you that's important, but how you react to it."'

She cocks her head & gazes at me. 'You were successful, weren't you?'

I have to chuckle at that. 'Not a sou, I assure you.'

'But you had commissions, collaborated, had your works published?'

'Granted, I did.'

'So it's easy for you to say. Not so easy for those who didn't have the choice.'

I raise an eyebrow at this. I am piqued.

'Would you say you know yourself well?' I say.

'Know myself?'

'Yes. Who you are.'

'I suppose so, yes.'

'Would you say you made good choices for yourself in your life?'

'No, I'm sure I made very bad choices for myself in my life.'

'Knowing oneself is about making choices, don't you think?'

'What do you mean?'

'Everything in life we decide to do or not do makes us who we are. As we get older, so we become more & more unique. One can be haunted by wrong turns, but one can never regret anything.'

She looks at me strangely. 'It's a nice idea, but I'm not sure if it works,' she smiles.

I sense that I will get nothing more out of her on the subject, & so choose a new tack. 'We haven't seen much of you.'

'No,' she says, 'I'm as quiet as a mouse. People hardly ever notice I'm there.'

'Surely not. You created quite a stir last Friday. You told me then that you never married. Is that true?'

'Oh yes, but that doesn't mean I was never asked,' she smiles.

'Naturally,' I say. 'But if you were asked, it means that you must have declined.'

'Even so, every woman likes to be asked at least once. Or so they say,' she laughs.

'Were you ever asked?'

'Actually, yes, more than once. I always seemed to attract much more attention from men than I wanted. When I was in Paris, I once shared a taxi with Picasso. He pulled me onto his lap, stroked my fur coat & called me his little bear.'

I roared with laughter. It was just like my dear friend.

'He said I was *charmante*, but he wouldn't help me. Eventually, I met a count in Rome who fell in love with me & asked me to marry him. I said no, but he allowed me to live with him. I stayed with him for many years.'

She seems distracted by the memory & stares into thin air. The music punctuates the silence. It is very beautiful. The music, I mean.

'May I ask what this music is?'

She seems quite alarmed by my enquiry. She stares at me. 'You must be joking,' she says, 'it's your sonata, of course.'

Well, I leave Biljana's room in a state of great confusion. For the life of me, I don't know how I could have forgotten my own piece of music. It's so absurd that when I am well down the corridor I let out a yelp, full of panic & fear. My only explanation is that it is a very old piece of mine & has therefore grown up. All my compositions are my children & my duty is to send them on their way into the world. The older they are, the better they can look after themselves. My sonata is so old it must have its own grandchildren by now. A timely reminder of how my memory stumbles, but let us move on, I will come back to that.

Where was I? Oh yes.

The proximity of my libel trial & the passing away of my dear Claude had put me in mind of a fellow I admired greatly: Socrates. I had always wanted to do something on Socrates. It's such an unjust story. Like me, when faced with an unfair charge, he refused to apologise. He had acted in good faith, as I had, & knew so, which gave him courage (which I lacked) when facing the court of 500 Athenian citizens. Of course, events turned out very differently for him; even so, I felt a strong affinity with him.

Like me, he had to sing for his supper & I learned many things from reading Plato's reports of Socrates' dialogues. All humanity has. I tried to live according to his honourable teachings as best I could, which, alas, was never quite enough. I believed in his assertion that it was only composite things that decayed. Non-composite things, like the soul, however, remained constant & unchanged, invisible, immortal, indestructible & for ever true to themselves. As the old Indian proverb says: 'The music continues, it is we who walk away.'

Most impressive of all, perhaps, was the fact that, far from preaching abstinence, he could drink any of his friends under the table, though no one ever saw him drunk. A man after my own heart.

I decided that I was going to write some music for Socrates. I suppose I had known for a long time that I would, but it had taken years for the idea to mature inside me. I also knew that this work would have to be completely detached from my personality, completely apart from me. I wanted to make it singular & something other than all my other work.

I found a fine translation; the one by Victor Cousin. His version was heavy & dull &, for those reasons, more to my taste. Next, I needed a commission &, after discreet enquiries, the most generous Princess Polignac came to my aid once again, giving me carte blanche to do as I pleased. I was swimming in happiness. At last, I was free, free as air, as water; as the wild sheep. Long live Plato! Long live Victor Cousin! I was free.

From the very outset, though, I have to confess I was frightened to death of bungling this work. I wanted it to be as white & pure as Antiquity. Aesthetically, this work was dedicated to clarity. It was not Russian, of course. It was not Persian, either, or Oriental. It was a return to classical simplicity, with a modern sensibility. I owed this return to my cubist friends.

Plato was the perfect collaborator, very gentle & never a nuisance. After reading his dialogues again & again, I chose those extracts that best suited my purpose & joined them up in order to make three entirely new texts. These new texts now became the three panels of a triptych, rather like an altarpiece, which told the story of Socrates' life. The first panel painted his portrait, the second described a walk beside a river with a disciple, & the third told of the circumstances of his death.

I had envisaged that these texts should be recited, as though read, by four women dressed in white robes. There were to be no sets. I wanted a 'symphonic drama', not an opera; one in which the voices followed the prose as normal speech would. I wanted beauty to be absent, so that lyricism was born of its opposite. There was never to be any extra emphasis on words like 'death' or 'love' or 'soul'. Originality through platitude.

I chose my instruments carefully: flute, oboe, English & French horn, clarinet, bassoon, trumpet, harp, timpani & strings. In writing *Socrate*, I was composing a simple work, without the least idea of conflict, without *fortissimi*. The music I wrote was never to raise its voice above the text. It was flat, but fluid & utterly white. Its marble-smooth surface was designed to resemble a Grecian urn, or the Ægean Sea on a bright, airless day.

After one & a half years of toil, I finished the score for piano & voices. The notes had coursed through me & poured out of me. I knew I had managed to create something different; it was time to bring my etiolated work into the light of day for people to view. Before a hand-picked audience, Jane Bathori, that wonderful *mezzo soprano*, recited part III, 'The Death of Socrates', whilst I accompanied her on the piano. I felt naked sitting there in that extraordinary drawing room &, when we had finished, I became aware once again of our audience, seated not two metres away. Every person present was in tears.

The première of the orchestrated version, two years later, was a pitifully different affair. An outright disaster, to be blunt. At the Salle du Conservatoire, in front of an audience of musicologists, composers & *criti-queues*, I presented my austere drama with the utmost seriousness. I entrusted my colleagues, if not the critics, to receive my work in the spirit in which it was given. The audience seemed distracted during the performance & they continued to become more & more animated. At the moment that Socrates drank the cup of hemlock, there were titters, & when he lay down to die, they positively howled with laughter. What on earth were they doing?! I just didn't understand.

In the paper the next day, one reviewer said that rigor mortis had set in; another wondered if *Socrate* wasn't a work of 'supreme irony'. Idiots! I knew my reputation was that of a humorist, but could no one understand the deadly seriousness with which I undertook *Socrate*? Why did they laugh so? My music was badly received, which didn't surprise me; but I was surprised to see the audience laugh at Plato's text. Strange, isn't it? People seemed to believe that the great Socrates was a character invented by me – & this in Paris.

I had always believed that *Socrate* would be my lucky star, my financial saviour. Instead, it plummeted into the enormous Ægean sea with nothing more than a fizz. Another failure, the most bitter of all. This was too much suffering. I felt damned. My beggar's life disgusted me. 'I *shit* on art,' I said to everyone; it had brought me too many problems. What was I to do?

All is quiet as I sit at my red table. I have been listening carefully to the sounds here ever since I first arrived. Each morning, at what I think is about the same time, I hear a soft boom from somewhere deep in the waystation. Heaven only knows what it is. Perhaps it is the fires started up to heat the water. There is a bath house here, but I haven't used it. The sound of running water, though, is perfectly pleasant to the ear.

Then there is the sound of silence. I have lain in my cot, at the dead of each night, trying to listen for the faintest stirring of a shoe on stone, or a whisper along a wall. Nothing. Usually, it would be true to say that there is no such thing as silence; no matter where you are, you will always hear the sound of your heartbeat & the blood rushing through your veins. Not here though. It is perfect bliss to exist in complete silence.

I was a sound pioneer. As the alchemist mixed material & chemicals in the hope of creating new substances, so I mixed sounds & silences in the hope of creating new sites for infinite meditation. New forms. *Socrate* was an utter catastrophe for me. Never again would I attempt anything like that. Instead of marshalling sounds into an arrangement that required attention, I began to think about the sounds themselves. I began to think of the future.

One day, I was lunching with my cubist friend

Fernand Léger. We were sharing a succulent pheasant at the Nègre de Toulouse on boulevard du Montparnasse, which he paid for of course, whilst trying to ignore the deafening music in the restaurant. Our conversation about painting progressed in fits & starts until we couldn't bear the loudness of the music any longer. We got up & left, but the whole incident got me thinking.

Over our coffee & Calvados at a nearby café, I explained to Léger that there might be room for 'furniture music', a music which would be part of the noises around it & would take account of them. I imagined it to be melodious, softening the noise of knives & forks without dominating them or making itself obtrusive. It would fill in the silences that can sometimes weigh heavily between dinner guests. It would spare them the need to make small talk. At the same time, it would neutralise the street noises that tactlessly force themselves in the picture.

Intrigued, I set about the problem of how to compose my Furniture Music, music which must be played so as not to be heard. As always, I started the process by making a list, which gradually transformed itself into an 'advertisement', as though Furniture Music were a consumer product like anything else:

- Furniture Music is fundamentally industrial.
- We wish to establish a form of music designed to satisfy 'utility' requirements. Art does not come into these requirements.
- Furniture Music creates vibration; it has no other purpose; it fills the same role as light, warmth & comfort.
- Furniture Music advantageously replaces marches, polkas, tangos, gavottes, etc.
- Insist on Furniture Music.
- No meetings, assemblies, etc. without Furniture Music.
- Furniture Music for lawyers, banks, etc.
- No wedding should be without Furniture Music.
- Do not enter a house which does not use Furniture Music.
- A man who has not heard Furniture Music does not know happiness.
- Do not go to sleep without listening to Furniture Music or you will sleep badly.

Instead of composing my own score, I would use extracts of other people's work. But who? I decided to use the work of those composers I disliked the most: Ambroise Thomas & Camille Saint-Saëns.

I arranged to test my Furniture Music during the interval of a play put on by my friend Max Jacob at the Galerie Barbazanges. I made sure to insert a note into the programme warning the audience not to pay any more attention to the music during the intermission than they would to the candelabra, the seats or the balcony. Just before the interval, I placed the three clarinettists in different corners of the theatre, the pianists in the fourth corner & the trombonist in a box on the first floor. I had instructed them to play the Furniture Music *ad lib* & repeat it *ad infinitum*.

The first act finished, the audience clapped & the house lights went up. Just as the audience started to leave, my ensemble started to play, but as soon as they did so, to my utter horror, the audience began to go back to their seats. I ran around the auditorium, shouting, 'Talk, for heaven's sake! Move around! Don't listen!' But it was no use, they settled into their seats & listened without speaking. They must have thought I was a madman. The whole thing went completely wrong.

No, no, the world did not want my Furniture Music; the big, fat, wide world wanted my Very Boring Music. A case in point: after the débâcle at the Galerie Barbazanges, the incomparable Paulette Darty expressed a desire to see me again &, to this end, a reception was to be held at her country residence in honour of our 'reunion'. On the evening in question, I was implored to sit & play at a great white whale of a piano. Well, that was fine by me, but what did they want to hear? My *Pieces in the Form of a Pear*, that's what. Very Boring Indeed.

Actually, if truth be known, it was a perfectly splendid evening. In fact, I was quite moved by the affection with which Madame Darty apparently held me. We hadn't seen each other for years – 20 at least – & the glorious evening was made complete when the resplendent Madame Darty sat on my lap while I played a couple of rags. She weighed a ton.

Madame Darty had, by now, actually become Madame Dreyfus, after marrying her wealthy admirer, Édouard. Subsequent to our little get-together, I accepted their kind invitations & spent many a pleasant Sunday at their country house. To all intents & purposes, it was in actual fact a château, built in the eighteenth-century style, with a well laid-out park, raked paths & a stream winding its way between the lawns. There was a birdhouse, ducks & a huge mastiff from the Pyrénées.

In order to get to this splendid location, I went to Paris, crossed it on foot & then took another train to the tiny station at Luzarches. From there, I walked three dusty kilometres to the house. I always made sure to arrive at midday on the dot, neither late nor early. To keep good time, one has to keep up with it.

Before lunch, Madame Dreyfus would suggest a tour of the gardens. Most probably feeling that I ought to have some kind of activity in order to keep my attention, she would give me bits of bread to throw for the ducks. I confess, I sometimes took a nibble myself. Madame Dreyfus often carried a folding chair. She would set it up by the stream & proceed to fish. I stood behind her & congratulated her whenever she caught something.

Such pastoral scenes were in stark contrast to the freneticism of my life in the city, although I must admit I never paid much attention to setting. I decided very early on that living in one place & experiencing many lives is more suitable to me than living the same life in many different places. Life's choices are not unknown to me, just unexplored. I stayed put in one location until either my finances or my moods got the better of me.

Nevertheless, I did make longer sojourns away from the fine city of Arcueil-Cachan. My *Socrate* was mustering interest in Brussels (imagine that) & I was invited to attend a performance there. My Belgian champions put me up at the Hôtel Britannique in the place du Trône. It was an aristocratic hotel, very swish, much too swish for a poor man like me.

On the first morning, I was to be introduced to the

singer, Évelyne Brélia, who was going to interpret the role of Socrates. I paced up & down outside the hotel waiting for her arrival. When she finally appeared, I gave her a severe look & said: 'You're late, dear lady.' She was quite shocked. After such an inauspicious start, though, things got better. She & her companions proceeded to show me the sights & sounds of the city. Here I was, in Brussels, like Cortez surveying the new-found land. But Brussels looked & sounded much like Paris.

When left to my own devices, I drew a rough plan in the back of my exercise book of the city's main streets & buildings. I coloured all police stations in red, pâtisseries in black & pissoirs in blue. I then set about discovering the city's cigars, its beer & its restaurants. What excellent cuisine. I managed to dine three times a day on mussels, *frites* & other white delicacies, all washed down with delicious Trappist beer. I'm afraid I rather overdid it; after my four-day stay, I was quite crimson with indigestion & returned to Arcueil in a dreadful state.

No sooner had I returned than the infernal Cocteau was up to his old tricks again. This time, his publicity stunt involved gathering together a group of six young musicians, whom he called Les Six. They apparently held me up as their mentor, calling me *le bon maître*, & espoused my 'aesthetics': Cocteau wanted to introduce them to me. It was all wrong, of course, for any 'aesthetics' I may or may not have had were solely mine to espouse; I had none to spare. I was dead against being anyone's fetish, let alone their emblem.

There is no school of Satie. *Satisme* could never exist. It would find me against it. In art, there should never be slavery. I have always made an effort to put followers off the scent, by both the form & the essentials of each new work. My music had to be made by me alone. That is the only way for an artist to avoid becoming the head of a school. My life was a series of sidesteps to avoid 'schools'. The 'logical' way forward has to be avoided at all costs, till the very end. Also to be avoided at all costs is satisfaction with one's achievements. I was not weighed down with prizes of Rome or any other town. That path leads only to the death of the possibility for change. I would gladly start all over again if I were shown anything new.

The only club I was happy to join was the Socialist Party, which I had first joined the day after its leader, Jean Jaurès, was assassinated. When the Socialist Party split into two factions, I had no hesitation in joining the more radical group & I thus became a

Bolshevik. I took much more delight in the title 'Erik Satie the Arcueil Soviet' than in the term *le bon maître*.

The last few years of my life were a flurry of masked balls & theatre collaborations. I mixed with the elite of high society but, you know, it was all very tiring. Entry into those salons was exclusive, & I'm sure I was the envy of many a young composer, but it was never where I was headed & it meant little. Besides, a nagging pain had started in my abdomen, which distracted me.

What it did make possible was meeting certain like-minded people &, for that, I was grateful. They seemed to like me, & christened me 'Satierik'. Most of these people were known as Dadaists by society & the press, who objected to their antics with a vehemence I scarcely understood. I would never wish to make a lobster blush, or even an egg; to me they were just fellow explorers.

From one of these fellows, named Man Ray, I received an invitation to attend an exhibition of his paintings at the Galerie Six. The invitation requested that visitors shouldn't bring 'flowers, wreaths or umbrellas'. Well, it took me several hours to decide whether or not to go without my umbrella &, in the end, I decided to risk a reproach & attend with my umbrella in hand.

When I arrived, the gallery was heaving & very cold. It turned out that the heating had just broken down. I sought Man Ray out, who looked very tired, & apologised immediately that I had brought my umbrella. In amongst the large crowd, he seemed confused. In English, he said he was cold, so I led him out of the gallery into a warm café opposite & ordered hot grogs for us both. I tipped my bowler at him & introduced myself, upon which he said that he was newly arrived from Amerika & couldn't speak a word of French. 'It doesn't matter,' I said in French & ordered more grogs. We got on famously.

On our way back to the gallery, we passed an iron-monger's & idly scanned the objects on display. Man Ray bought an iron &, together, we selected a box of tacks & a tube of glue. We proceeded to glue the tacks onto the iron, which pleased Man Ray enorm-ously, so much so that, when we got back to the gallery, he immediately placed it as one of the ex-hibits. He turned to me & said that I was the only musician 'with eyes'. How true.

Another good fellow I met at this time was Marcel Duchamp, who had a forehead as flat as a mirror, & a nose as straight as an arrow. Several years before,

Duchamp had given up painting for chess. I told him that was admirable, as I had considered giving up composition altogether many times, but had never managed to. 'I had 30 ideas. I painted 33 pictures,' he said. 'I don't want to copy myself like all the others.' We played several games of chess together, but I was always outfoxed by his crafty knight moves.

But the man I met at this time of whom I was most fond was another of my *vieux frères*: Constantin Brancusi. Of course, I had heard of this famous Romanian sculptor & was honoured to be invited to one of his legendary dinners. For this special occasion, I wore the first dinner suit I had ever owned. It was a gift from a very honourable tailor, a certain Monsieur Henriquet, who had heard that my suits became very dusty after my walks to & from Arcueil & therefore suggested I should have a good suit 'on standby'. I was very flattered & had my photograph taken with it on.

Brancusi's studio was in a ramshackle building at the end of a blind alley. Inside, everything was white: the floor, the walls, the ceiling; even the table on which we ate was a block of white stone. As soon as I stepped inside, I knew we would get along.

During a meal of goose, roasted in his sculptor's oven, & cabbage prepared Romanian-peasant style, I recounted to Brancusi the evening I played my *Pieces in the Form of a Pear* for the Queen of Romania. When I had finished, I crossed the drawing room, bowed deeply & kissed her hand. It was an utterly serious moment.

'What did she say?' Brancusi asked.

'She told me I had a fine old man's head.'

Brancusi laughed. He was no taller than me, but he was much more stocky & had a beard as square as a spade. He wore a floppy hat constantly & his hair was always falling out. He was the most hirsute man I ever met & he reminded me of a polite bear.

After an uproarious & delicious feast, Brancusi & I entertained the other guests by taking down the two violins hanging on his wall & duetting: the others voted our efforts pathetic. We then spent the rest of the evening teasing each other mercilessly. When everyone got tired of hearing our jokes, we'd pay no attention & carry on until well into the night. He was the only man who made me laugh. No failing, no absurdity, no folly escaped us. Whenever one became too big for his boots, the other had no hesitation at throwing down banana skins. I was never taken in by anything or anybody, & still less by myself. Brancusi understood all this. He was Socrates' brother.

There was a lot of infighting between all these newcomers. The worst offender was André Breton, who was jealous of Tristan Tzara's presiding influence over these fine fellows. When it all got too much for him, Breton publicly denounced Tzara & his Dadaist followers & proposed to found his own school, which he called Surrealism. In retaliation, Tzara called Breton to a public trial at the Closerie des Lilas, over which I was asked to preside as chairman.

This role was my pleasure to perform. Breton had openly admitted that he disliked music intensely. Moreover, Breton advocated a ridiculous process which he termed 'automatic writing', which was anathema to 'composition'. Tzara & the rest of our committee condemned Breton & I gleefully wrote the press release announcing our decision. Breton was an impostor.

A few months later, Tzara organised an evening of Dada works called *Soirée du Cœur à barbe*, for which I, somewhat reluctantly, agreed to play my *Pieces in the Form of a Pear*. Midway through my performance, Breton & his followers started some very inappropriate heckling. Tzara would have none of it & fighting broke out. Breton struck my good friend Pierre de Massot with his walking stick, & slapped another good soul in the face before being dragged out by the police, screaming, 'Murderer! Get out!' It was the end of Dadaism in Paris.

If people had asked me whether or not Dadaism was a success, I would have said that it was a success in its details & a failure in its essentials. At that time, there was something in the air, but the spirit of Dadaism was never supposed to be about Art. Dadaism might have produced a few charming pamphlets, but it was supposed to change the world, to revolutionise life itself. Well, I need hardly point out that, in that respect, it was a miserable failure.

I was saddened to see it run out of steam so quickly on account of a few boorish egos, but what saddened me much more was the death of Lenin. I'll never forget the day I discovered that Lenin had died. I saw the news on a news-stand in the *Métro*. I stood on the platform, speechless. For only the second time in my life, I cried.

Day Seven

This day is my last &, for the seventh time, I start it by walking around my room taking stock of the day ahead. I will visit the film studio to watch some of the filming in progress, which surely will be happening today. Yes. Perhaps it will help.

As I leave my room & walk along the attractive corridor, all is quiet. Downstairs, the foyer is empty. I pass Monsieur Takahashi's office and go into the passageway to the studio. Light pours down from its wells &, as I pass through them, the effect is rather like a stroboscope. I push open the swing doors & enter the film studio.

Where it was once so inanimate, it is now positively alive with activity. I amble around. People huddle in twos & threes, conferring with clipboards. Otherwise, men & women are hammering nails, lifting different-coloured pieces of cloth onto high poles, erecting false walls, shifting pieces of fake furniture. Two young women are painting what looks like the view of an Alpine valley from high up: pastures, little chalets; it must be Serif's view. Another set is the interior of a room. There is a bed, with an imposing crucifix on the wall at its head. The roof angles upwards so that the ridge of the roof is very high. Andreij is nearby, looking up into it. Very Gothic.

There are two enormous film cameras standing by. A young man is polishing the lens of one. The other is unattended, pointing downwards. It looks like it is asleep. Dotted around the place are huge lamps, set on precarious legs. Screens & coloured filters are stacked against a wall. It all reminds me of my own involvement with film, a glorious film, a revolutionary film.

After the failures of *Socrate* & my Furniture Music, I'd had enough of solo outings & sought collaborations once again. My wish came true with a commission offered to me by the Ballets Suédois. They left me to do whatever was my fancy & asked me to choose an artist to do the scenery. Well, the infernal Cocteau was angling to take part, but I was determined to have nothing more to do with him. I chose, instead, the artist of figures & fine ideas: Francis Picabia.

Once everything had been settled by contract, I received my part of the payment & immediately walked to a little shop on the boulevard Saint-Michel where I bought 12 dozen detachable collars. It was the only shop in Paris which still sold collars with little wings on them. I was delighted with my purchase & immediately returned to Arcueil to start work.

Picabia moved up to Paris from the Midi, where he spent his time, so that we could work together. Picabia was a Cuban Frenchman who had the physique of Humpty Dumpty & who wore kipper ties. His face was pasty & lumpy, like an overripe orange. He was a perfect puss.

Our work grew effortlessly, so in tune with each other's thoughts were we, & the product of our labours was a beautiful piece of nonsense. Picabia was most concerned about the title of our strange fruit, & eventually came up with *Relâche*, which means 'No Performance'. I approved wholeheartedly since we were certain to have the title upon at least one Paris theatre every evening &, some evenings, on all the theatres at the same time.

Picabia also came up with the idea of having a 'cinematic interlude' to be shown between the two acts of our 'instantaneist ballet'. To take care of this, Picabia enlisted the help of a young filmmaker called René Clair, who was taking Paris by storm with his frothy cinematic absurdities. Together, they came up with a scenario & filming began straight away.

My services as an actor were requested for one day only, which was to be filmed on the Paris rooftops. Picabia & I were instructed to jump up & down on the roof, on which also stood a menacing cannon. Picabia's hair & tie flew about as he jumped; I made much more considered leaps, umbrella in hand. We loaded the cannon with a pencil-shell & fired it.

Meanwhile, sitting on the edge of the precipitous roof were Marcel Duchamp & Man Ray, playing a game of chess. The pawns on the squares of the board dissolve into cars whirling around the place de la Concorde. The dancer, Jean Börlin, is shot & his coffin, pulled by a camel, is chased through the streets. It rolls off the hearse & lands in the grass, its lid opens & out pops Börlin.

When filming had finished, Clair, Picabia & I decided that the silent film would need an accompanying score, & I immediately offered to do it. I wanted to imbue my score with a revolutionary spirit, the same spirit with which Lenin had imbued Russian society. I had once seen a small film of a flower unfolding in speeded-up motion & thought it a sublime image of offering.

I consulted with Clair about the exact timing of

each sequence. I then broke up the score into a series of fragments to correspond with the sequences in the film & composed each of these fragments so that they could be repeated as many times as was necessary. In this way, my score matched perfectly sound with image. It was made to measure.

The finished film, called *Entr'acte*, was an elastic marvel. Its viewers had to keep up as it sprinted backwards & forwards in time & jumped through space. Cinema, it seemed to me, was truly an innovation. In my life, I heard great mention of a fellow named Albert Einstein & his theories of time & space. I understood little of such philosophies, but understood enough to know that they had something to do with apples & orbits. More than music, or painting, or writing, cinema was the embodiment of such new forms.

Time, that insidious force, is something that everyone understands, until you try to explain it. I'm certain of only one thing about it: that it travels at exactly one second per second, one year per year. I'm told that Time is the Fourth Dimension, after length, breadth & height. Well, for me, the first three are enough. I'm happy being immobile. Every artist needs immobility. To withdraw into a corner of a room is undoubtedly a meagre expression, but it has numerous images, some of great antiquity. It is there I had my greatest travels. I wonder if there is a Fifth Dimension? Memory? Dreams?

In any case, all was ready & we announced a public dress rehearsal of *Relâche*, but when the moment arrived, Börlin was too ill to dance. We hung a notice on the theatre entrance which said '*Relâche* – No Performance'. I poked my head outside the theatre doors expecting there to be no one, but saw instead quite a queue. I assured them that the performance had been cancelled, but they refused to believe me. They imagined it was all a Dadaist joke. Some young musicians introduced themselves to me & we passed a pleasant meal in celebration of the 'non-performance'.

The real première took place at the Théâtre des Champs-Élysées. The first act was greeted enthusiastically; the applause had hardly died down when the film screen descended. With the first images, rumblings & titters moved through the audience like waves. The bearded ballerina & the hearse-pulling camel were greeted with jeers & whistles, while the film's climax provoked an outcry & disorder among the packed rows of seats. A success.

When the ballet was over, there were cries of 'Author! Composer!' which we could hear all the way backstage. Despite my sincere protestations, Picabia bungled me into a little five-horsepower automobile & drove me onto the stage for the curtain call. I had never heard such loud applause. Despite my tiredness, I was moved. I bowed deeply & waved at them as I was driven offstage. It was my last public appearance; a few days later, I fell gravely ill.

There was a time when I was cheerful, & very lively. In those days, however, I was too alone for my own good. I came to look at myself in the mirror & it seemed to me that I had changed from a partridge into a cabbage. I was an old ruin living in a wretched place, which nobody visited. My eyes have always been bright, but it was my fate to have my previously robust Normandy frame become so ramshackle.

My walks to & from Arcueil were proving too much for me, & so I gladly accepted the many kind invitations to stay overnight at the residences of my cubist friends Derain & Braque. They would leave me alone with a little glass of something for company. But even the following morning, the walk home was too long to contemplate, so I patiently sat all day by the fireside in my hat & coat, clutching my umbrella, waiting for the moment I thought I had enough strength to start my journey back.

After a few weeks as their guest, my good friends told me they had organised a room for me at the Grand Hôtel. My room was too comfortable. I took the infernal telephone off its hook & devised a system of strings from the door handle to my chair so that I could open the door without getting up. I was too tired to get up. I spent all day sunk in a huge easy chair looking directly into a mirror. A mirror has no heart but plenty of ideas.

I once went to the Hall of Mirrors in that monstrosity they call Versailles. It was a system of facing mirrors which hung on the large walls of a room decorated in gilt & red velvet. If one positioned oneself correctly, one could see simultaneously one's left & right profiles, as well as a front view. It was a broken-up perspective worthy of my cubist friends. At another certain point, one could see oneself directly from the back. There I was, a long line of identical Saties receding endlessly into the wrong-way-round world. It was a very sobering experience to see oneself as others do. But the only thing that such thoughts & views proved was that mirrors are too laden with memories. I told my friends that I wanted to move.

The next thing I can recall is lying on a bed in a different room. My good friend Darius Milhaud was standing by the bed with his fiancée, Madeleine. They told me that I was in the Hôtel Istria & had been for two days. They said I had a fever. Apart from when I was a soldier, I had never been sick in my life. Milhaud took out a curious instrument which, when I asked him, he called a thermometer. He showed me the little strip of mercury. I had never seen one before & when he started shaking it, I said, 'You're going to break it.'

Apparently, I was too ill to stay there any longer; the doctor had ordered me to be moved to a hospital. Madeleine packed my things, which sent me into waves of panic. I mentioned that a bundle of laundry had to be collected in Arcueil & Madeleine offered to go. When she returned some hours later, I went through the bag of handkerchiefs but only counted 98 when I had sent 100 in to be cleaned. I blamed Madeleine & told her so.

I was moved to the Hôpital St-Joseph, to a private room that I later found out was owned by the Comte de Beaumont. There seemed to me to be an extraordinarily large number of nuns about the place until I was told that the hospital was run by the nuns. 'Ah,' I said. One of the nuns unpacked my things. I wanted my Hans Christian Andersen fairy tales to be kept by my bed. I told her to place my

horsehair brush & my pumice stone on the table.
'Have you no soap?' she asked. I told her that I never used the stuff. 'If you knew what it's made of:
sweat, human waste, it's revolting.' She seemed per-
plexed by this. By way of explanation, I said, 'It's
what the Chinese do. I rub & rub my skin with the
pumice stone until it's quite pink.' The nun wasn't
impressed & left the room with her lips pursed.

Despite all exertions of willpower, memories of
when I was bedridden as a soldier came flooding
back to me. I remembered only too well the sensation of lying flat in the expanse of white sheets, as I
was now. My pneumonia had nearly killed me but,
in another way, it was the making of me. I pulled
back the sheets & looked down my ancient skeleton.
I had been so young then. I imagined I looked like
Socrates on his deathbed now. No, I don't regret anything. I had a string quartet yet in my mind, but no
time. Apart from that, I don't regret anything.

I suddenly had many visitors; I didn't think I was
so popular. My publisher came to visit me with a
bunch of flowers. 'Already?' I said & put them to
one side. He presented me with a cheque for the
publishing contract for *Relâche*, which I stuffed in a
pile of old newspapers when he was gone. My *chère*
Valentine brought me *œufs de Villebon* & a set of

white handkerchiefs. My abdomen was very painful then & I would lay my hand on it while my visitors chattered away. I amassed quite a collection of presents & champagne, all of which I left unopened. The only food I ate was the occasional plate of cabbage.

Pleurisy set in. I could feel the bubbles in my lungs when I breathed. I slept mostly, woken only by flies crawling on my face. Once, I opened my eyes to see Picasso straightening the sheets of my bed. They were soaked. Brancusi brought me yoghurt & chicken soup, which he had made himself. He sat me up & fed me every day, like a child, but I tasted nothing. Until then, I hadn't understood how days could be both long & short at the same time. Francis Poulenc, with whom I'd fallen out, requested to see me. I was touched, but refused. One must stick to one's guns to the end.

One day, I recognised the voice that had been ringing in my ears for many months: it was my own. I realised that all the time I'd been talking to myself. Someone suggested that I should see the Abbé Saint. Perhaps it was me who did so? 'Fine,' I said, 'I'd like to see a saint before I die. Just give me time to put on a petticoat, & then I'm yours.' The priest came & a nun with a little bell. The priest looked like a Modigliani:

black on a blue background. I made my confession, but I had forgotten my prayers. I asked the nun to help me & we recited the Lord's Prayer together. All the while, I could see cows playing happily in a field. 'Ah, the cows,' I said & then a little bell rang.

The sound of a clapperboard snaps me out of my thoughts. They are filming Serif's memory. They have built a little rocky mound, on which Serif is standing. A wind machine recreates the mountain breezes. Someone shouts, 'Action!' & everyone goes quiet. Serif stands with his arms by his side, gazing at the painted view in front of him. A little smoke drifts past him. All is quiet; the staff & guests watch Serif. After a few minutes, someone shouts, 'Cut!' Serif turns around to face us; he is smiling. I suppose his task is complete now & he can give himself up to serenity & eternity.

I decide to make one final round of the lawns & gardens before I too must give myself up to oblivion. As I am approaching the hedge, I spy something white on the green grass. Feathers. I crouch down & count them: 17. I look up, expecting to feel the beat of white wings, but I can see nothing through the ceiling of clouds. Anyway, it is a good omen. Perhaps I should hand them out to my fellow travellers as a final gift of forgetfulness? I pick them up & put them carefully in my deep pockets.

At his office, Monsieur Takahashi's door is wide open. He is poring over some newspapers & looks up when I cough.

'Oh, Mister Satie, good. I was just going to look for you.' He gestures towards the papers. 'Your obituary has been printed. Would you like to see?'

I chuckle at the uniqueness of the enquiry. 'Of course I would,' I say.

The obituary is in *Le Figaro* & was written by André Cœuroy. It reads:

> This musician, whose influence on the evolution of contemporary French music has been considerable, has not always been fully understood; but at the same time he did everything he could to produce that situation.

'What absolute nonsense. I did everything I could to make my intentions as clear as day.'

'Sometimes we are grossly misunderstood, Monsieur Satie.'

'No doubt, no doubt. I wonder what became of my pianos?'

'Ah, I can tell you that, actually. There was an auction & Monsieur Georges Braque bought one. I don't know what happened to the other, I'm sorry.'

'It's an excellent home for it. Good old Georges.'

I clear my throat & brush down my jacket. 'Well, I have managed to do the impossible,' I say. 'I have chosen my memory . . .'

Monsieur Takahashi claps his hands.

'Excellent news,' he exclaims.

'. . . but I have one last request to ask of you.'

'Yes?'

'May I be permitted to compose my own film script?'

'Why, of course you can, it means less work for us.'

'*Bon*, it's settled then.'

I sit with Loulou on the wrought-iron bench in her little garden. For the first time, it strikes me that her garden is rather like how the Japanese cultivate theirs. I love Japanese gardens – the moss & the stones. I love them because all expression is pruned back, leaving only what is necessary. Gardens shouldn't be beautiful, they should be necessary.

The overcast sky has finally broken up to reveal a blue so deep it seems unreal. Cumulus clouds, shaped like anvils, mass above a mountain range, which stretches as far as the eye can see. There has been much talk of these peaks among the guests, but I am seeing them today for the first time. Clearly, there is the work of God's finger in them. An arrow of geese is soaring overhead between the mountain peaks. Perhaps the feathers are theirs. I point at them with my umbrella & Loulou smiles.

'At last,' she says.

In my room today, I made an origami boat for Loulou. I take it out of my pocket & present it to her. She takes it gravely, a little too gravely for my liking.

'Let's launch it, shall we?' I say.

She places it on the wobbly water. It bobs about for a bit. I have tried to remain inseparable from my music. I have tried to rid my works of all traces of subjectivity. Indeed, I have gone to great lengths to forbid myself from having any such thing. I did not want to change my life, ever, & so I simply ruled out all things material. Any change in my life was purely formal, not material. Yes, that's it.

For me, experience is a form of paralysis. My mind is always full of images, but to verify images kills them. It is always more enriching to imagine than to experience. The best of days are those of con-templation, unmarked by experience. Days like that are not connected to other days, but stand out in time. Perhaps that has been my mistake. The good Socrates said that an unexamined life is not worth living. Perhaps I should have paid more attention to how I lived my life as I was living it? Too late now. Though not quite, for my week here has been a kind of examination, albeit a very brief one.

I sometimes think that I did not have the time to walk through all the dramas that were assigned me. Great love affairs, fantastical receptions, euphoric vindication, all these came knocking at my door, but I was never at home. My poetic ecstasy has become, little by little, an eventless life. It is for this reason that I have decided on my memory. It has nothing to do with anyone else, & yet it was the start of everything for me. With it, I walked backwards through a mirror, & nothing was the same any more.

'You're going to go, aren't you?' Loulou says.

'Yes,' I reply. 'My task is accomplished, but I hope you will remember me. Our little conversations. Will you?'

'Yes, monsieur,' she says.

'I think they're ready for me. Here, take this.' I give Loulou my umbrella. 'It's a good one, so look after it.'

'Of course.'

'It's funny. I feel quite naked without it. Will you watch my little film with me?'

Loulou nods.

'Good. That would be very pleasant.'

My pieces are but little stones in the edifice, but stones of whiteness & brilliance.

I offer my arm to Loulou. 'Shall we go?'

PASSENGER No 609,981: ERIK ALFRED LESLIE SATIE

NATIONALITY: FRENCH/SCOTTISH

PROFESSION: COMPOSER OF MUSIC

BORN: 17 MAY 1866

DIED: 1 JULY 1925

HEIGHT: 1 m 67 cm

HAIR: GREY

FACE: OVAL

EYES: GREY

NOSE: LONG

MOUTH: AVERAGE

CHIN: BROAD

DISTINGUISHING FEATURES: NONE

The rice-paper moon is in place. It casts a glow over a night-time scene. There are cardboard trees that have been painted ink-black & white stars have been painted on the night-blue backdrop. Two men on ladders are holding long poles that are attached to a net full of duck down, which will fall gently like snow when they shake the poles.

Imagine if you will a young man, nearly 21 years old, lying one night in his cot in a military barracks. It is winter. There is 12 centimetres of snow on the ground outside. The night is cold, the dormitory is cold, he is cold.

The dark curtains billow with the draughts coming in through the cracks in the French doors. Behind the dark curtains, the young man can sense the whiteness of the snow. It is more blue than white. He lies there shivering with his arms folded. He is very unhappy.

His eyes dart to the dark corners of the room. The other men's breaths are deep & long. Satisfied they are really asleep, he throws back his blanket, takes off his vest & walks to the doors wearing only his baggy long johns.

He slips through the curtains & unlocks the door. There is a large stone slab that has been scraped clear of snow. He steps onto it. The cold shocks him immediately. For a moment he is lost, unsure of his bearings. He shifts his gangly frame & gazes around him at the flat white world & the moon casting an unearthly light on the snow.

There is a clearing from here to the perimeter fences with just two small trees separating him from them. The trees are silhouettes, standing as still as obedient children. He decides this is the correct direction &, with a rush, he starts to run.

He runs zigzag between the trees, kicking up the drifts of fake snow, like a child at play, & falling over & getting up & falling over again. He gathers up the snow into piles around him, covering himself in whiteness.

Lying down in the snow, he flaps his arms & legs to make an angel & breathes deeply to take in the cold air. After a little time has passed, he comes to rest & lies peacefully, looking up at the untwinkling stars, lying in the white world that is built on silence & stillness.

> THIS FILM SHOULD FADE TO WHITE, NOT BLACK.

Author's Note

While he appears in *The Velvet Gentleman* as a fictional character, my version of Erik Satie is based very closely on actual biographical detail. In particular, I am indebted to Ornella Volta for collecting and editing Satie's correspondence in *Satie Seen Through His Letters* and his writings in *A Mammal's Notebook*. Equally essential was *Satie Remembered*, edited by Robert Orledge. Finally, I owe a huge debt to Kore-eda Hirokazu's film *Afterlife*. As those who have seen it will quickly realise, I have stolen heavily from Hirokazu's film. For those who haven't seen it, I can't recommend it highly enough.

Also by Richard Skinner

ff

The Red Dancer

The Red Dancer opens in 1895 when, as a young woman in Amsterdam, Margaretha Zelle answers a lonely-hearts advertisement placed by a soldier twice her age in a local newspaper. But her marriage to Captain McLeod of the Dutch army ends in tragedy and acrimony and she leaves their posting in Indonesia. Heading for Paris, she adopts the stage name Mata Hari – 'Eye of the Morning' – and reinvents herself as an exotic dancer. Mata Hari's fame soon spreads throughout the cabarets and theatres of Europe and, as the major powers lurch towards inevitable conflict, she begins to attract the attention of numerous admirers – many of whom are officers, all too keen to share their secrets with a woman of notorious intrigue and allure.

Set against the dramatically imagined backdrop of pre-War Europe, Richard Skinner's novel weaves interlinking chapters of fiction and non-fiction to conjure up the life, loves and tragic end of a woman who continues to fascinate almost a century on from her death.

'An original and absorbing version of a cryptic life.' *Sunday Telegraph*

'A fictionalised life of Mata Hari that tentatively, delicately and poignantly fills in the person behind the myth.' *Observer*

'A short, riveting book that blends the known facts of Mata Hari's life with a large dose of fiction from Skinner's own fertile imagination . . . An assured debut.' *Sunday Express*

ff

Faber and Faber – a home for writers

Faber and Faber is one of the great independent publishing houses in London. We were established in 1929 by Geoffrey Faber and our first editor was T. S. Eliot. We are proud to publish prize-winning fiction and non-fiction, as well as an unrivalled list of modern poets and playwrights. Among our list of writers we have five Booker Prize winners and eleven Nobel Laureates, and we continue to seek out the most exciting and innovative writers at work today.

www.faber.co.uk – a home for readers

The Faber website is a place where you will find all the latest news on our writers and events. You can listen to podcasts, preview new books, read specially commissioned articles and access reading guides, as well as entering competitions and enjoying a whole range of offers and exclusives. You can also browse the list of Faber Finds, an exciting new project where reader recommendations are helping to bring a wealth of lost classics back into print using the latest on-demand technology.